Funeral Hotdish

Books by Jana Bommersbach

The Trunk Murderess: Winnie Ruth Judd
Cattle Kate
Bones in the Desert
A Squirrel's Story: A True Tale
Funeral Hotdish

Funeral Hotdish

Jana Bommersbach

Poisoned Pen Press

Poisoned Pen Press
6962 E. First Ave., Ste. 103
Scottsdale, AZ 85251
www.poisonedpenpress.com
info@poisonedpenpress.com

Printed in the United States of America

*This book is dedicated to my
North Dakota roots and my family lines:
Peterschick, Bommersbach, Schlener, Portner.*

Chapter One

Friday, October 15, 1999

"I AM SO, SO, SO, SO, SO, SO HAPPY!"

Amber Schlener never felt this fantastic in all her seventeen years. Even her terrible thirst didn't matter.

She wasn't just happy, she was ecstatic. Every pore in her body vibrated life. Every cell tingled with joy. She was thrilled and powerful. On her best days on the basketball court, she'd never had this much energy—this euphoria—that would keep her dancing forever and never get tired.

Her feet bounced like a marionette, on and off the floor of the old hayloft. She sprang up, the wood boards giving slightly under the pressure of all the dancers, but that was a good thing. Amber laughed out loud, surprised that she could dance with such abandon and such rhythm. Her arms flailed around her, doing their own interpretive dance. She watched them as if they belonged to someone else.

Suddenly, her nose demanded all her attention and she inhaled deeply the musty, moldy smell that would forever be embedded in these eighty-year-old walls. In its day, the scent had been the sweet smell of alfalfa bales that fed generations of Holsteins, but the odor changed as the hay dried out and sat stashed away. Amber couldn't think of a farm without the smell of alfalfa, and in a flash of brilliance, she decided that if North

Dakota ever added a state smell to its list of icons, it would be alfalfa. She had to remember to tell Johnny and he would agree.

Then she realized something incredible. The knee she'd wrenched in last week's game didn't hurt. "My knee doesn't hurt—IT DOESN'T HURT"—she kept yelling at Johnny, like it was the most miraculous truth in the world. Quickly she discovered her bad tooth—facing a dental appointment on Monday—didn't ache. "My tooth doesn't ache," she repeated to her boyfriend, louder with every telling.

"See, I told you it would be great," Johnny yelled into her ear. "Nothing to worry about." She grinned in agreement. Her hesitation had been foolish. Most of her classmates had agreed to try it. She was one of the last holdouts, but now she was so glad they'd convinced her.

Amber swirled and jumped and swayed and leaped to the ear-splitting music from Lonnie's turntable. He kept playing "The Devil Went Down to Georgia" by Charlie Daniels, interspersed with Bruce Springsteen's *Dancing in the Dark*. He'd tried to slip in Shania Twain's "That Don't Impress Me Much," but the ballad was too slow for the frantic dancers. Cher's "Believe" worked once, but these seventy-eight dancers wanted the hot fiddle or the driving guitar, so Charlie and Bruce were the headliners tonight.

Amber reveled in her pain-free, fantastically fabulous body. She loved the way her skirt swirled around her, twisting even more so it created its own unique dance. Oh, if Aunt Gertie could see her now. She'd admire how the dress they'd sewn together was flowing like a fancy dress in a television ad. Amber couldn't pull her eyes off her skirt. Who could guess that a piece of floral fabric, hemmed last night, could move so beautifully?

"Look Gertie, look," she screamed while she twirled, as though her elderly great-aunt, safe at home—probably already in her nightgown—could see this marvelous skirt now. When she held the skirt out like she was doing a curtsy, she couldn't believe how soft it was. She rubbed the fabric between her fingers and wondered why she'd never realized its luxurious feel in all the time it took to cut out the pattern and sew the pieces together.

This was the softest dress *ever.* She decided right then that she would wear this dress every day of her life.

"Feel it, Johnny, feel it," she hollered, but he was now in his own world, his arms wrapped around himself like he was discovering the strength of his massive shoulders.

Amber laughed again, more giggle than laugh, and now saw for the first time that she didn't only feel fantastic and happy and pain-free—better yet, she felt no fear. Of anything. She didn't fear her mother's scorn for Johnny. She didn't fear failing geometry. She didn't fear getting fat. She didn't fear what waited for her out there after graduation. She didn't even fear Johnny's creepy uncle, Leroy Roth and his Posse Comitatus rants.

"So this is how it feels not to be afraid of anything," she cried out loud, to nobody in particular, but to reaffirm to herself that this sensation was indeed possible. Until that moment, she wouldn't have believed it.

To think, she marveled, one little yellow pill could do all this!

The class valedictorian—not yet official, but everyone knew—bumped into her and started apologizing like he'd committed a crime.

"Roger, it's alright," Amber crooned, and reached out to hug him. He couldn't believe his luck. He never dreamed Amber Schlener would ever hug him. He hugged back like he was hanging onto a life raft. Then he watched her turn and hug Marilyn, and then Carolyn and then Jack. Some kid from another town came by and she hugged him, too. Roger didn't care that she was hugging everyone. He didn't care why she was being so generous with her affections. He just cared that she'd hugged him. He would remember the feeling even when he was an old man.

Johnny watched all this, not with jealousy and concern, but with glee. Amber was so happy, which made him happier than ever. He shed any concerns he had about talking her into this. He grew more powerful and sure and strong and joyful. He reached out and one-arm hugged his best friend around the neck, pointed his head at Amber, and shouted "Kenny, look at that!"

Kenny Franken threw back his head and bellowed—his own rapture so overwhelming, he thought he would burst. He shouted back, "They don't call it the Hug Drug for nothing!"

Steve stumbled into them as he missed a step in his version of dancing, and sang out the mantra he'd been repeating all night. "Wunnerful, wunnerful!" Johnny and Kenny found it a hoot that the ghost of Lawrence Welk should be visited on this dance—as far from "champagne music" as one could get—and egged Steve on. "Wunnerful, wunnerful," he screamed as he staggered away into a crowd that knew little about the state's favorite son except that famous phrase.

Amber was trying to tell someone something profound, but her voice was hoarse and raspy. She yelled at Johnny that she needed some water as she made a beeline to the orange Igloo against the barn wall. Used plastic glasses were scattered around the plank table. She picked up one and flung out the remains of the last drinker to fill it for herself. Even though it was warm, this was the best water she'd ever tasted. Amber thought she could drink this entire Igloo dry if they let her, and maybe if she did, she could get rid of this thirst. Johnny joined her and didn't even bother with a glass. He picked up the Igloo and tilted it to let it flow into his mouth in a steady stream. Amber roared and their classmates chanted, "Johnny, Johnny, Johnny," as he drank until he choked.

At that moment, Amber was as happy as any human being on the planet. She was the luckiest girl in all of North Dakota. What was the date? She wanted to remember because this was a date she'd put in her diary.

Friday, October 15, 1999.

She wasn't the only one who'd always want to remember when the Class of 2000 gathered to dance the night away in the Jacobsons' old hay loft.

It was supposed to be a party just for them, but word had gotten out—underclassmen from her school had come, so did kids from towns nearby, and if she'd have been paying attention, she would have realized it was almost impossible to squeeze any more up the narrow wooden steps that led to this loft. The more the merrier, Johnny said early in the evening. Amber adopted his invitation.

Someone offered her a bottle of Royal Crown, and a small sip burned so much she wished she hadn't. She handed the bottle back with a smile and yelled in the stranger's ear, "I'm not a drinker."

He smiled back at her and winked, "No baby, you're doin' alright all on your own." She saw Johnny swigging from someone else's bottle and it didn't even cross her mind that he might be getting too drunk to drive.

And then, like switching a channel, Amber thought of all the wonderful things ahead.

In seven months, she'd put on the rose-colored robe and miter hat with its gold tassel and walk down the aisle of the Northville Public High School. Her class of thirty-two would appear in alphabetical order, Amber marching in right behind Johnny. Everyone she loved would be in that high school gym—her mom, her surviving grandparents, her aunts and uncles, cousins, friends, and of course, Johnny.

"He's not only my first love, he's going to be my only love," she'd confided to Aunt Gertie, who she counted on to help sew her wedding dress someday.

Between now and graduation, there was nothing but excitement. Thanksgiving, Christmas, the Millennium—the world's not going to end, she knew now with certainty—the senior class trip, hopefully a basketball championship, the graduates' luncheon at that beautiful Victorian mansion on Lake Elsie, the senior play, finishing the yearbook, prom—oh, PROM, she and Maxine were already pattern shopping for their dresses—baccalaureate, the graduation ceremony, the family dinner after.

And then, with the scholarships that were sure to come through, off to UND and a teaching degree. Third grade, Amber thought. She wanted to teach third grade. She had little cousins that age and enjoyed them most—the younger ones were too whiny and the older ones too snotty, but a third-grader was a loving, wondrous child and she could already see coming home to Northville to teach third grade in the very school she'd attended all her life. She'd live on the farm with Johnny and drive the three miles into town each morning and eventually, they'd have their own children attending school right here in this safe little town that she loved.

Her best friend had the opposite dream and Amber couldn't imagine going off to the Twin Cities to live with strangers and not have family around. But that's what Maxine wanted, and so Amber had promised to visit her in Minneapolis whenever she could. With teaching third grade and raising a family and farming...Amber already worried their friendship wouldn't last and had doodled in her notebook, "Never lose Maxine." But now, as she danced atop this glorious night, she no longer had that worry.

Amber Schlener had no worries at all. Her dreams would all come true and the life ahead would be filled with love and delight. She was certain. More confident than she'd ever been. She laughed at herself that she'd been such a scaredy cat lately, fretting over every little thing and not having faith in herself. But that had disappeared. What a glorious feeling to put that behind her and face the world with this strength. If anyone had told her she was going to be president of the United States someday, she'd have believed it.

"Maxine, we'll be friends forever," she shouted to the blond cheerleader who was dancing a few feet away. Maxine couldn't hear her over the blaring music, but moved toward her, drawn by Amber's glorious smile. Whatever her precious friend was yelling had to be something good and Maxine wanted to hear.

The best friends were beaming at each other—laughing and kicking up their heels on the brink of their new lives—when things started to go black in Amber's head.

She blinked several times to clear her sight, but instead of seeing Maxine and her classmates all around her, she saw a slide show of images against a black background.

Johnny on his Dad's combine. Mom drying dishes. Aunt Gertie in her garden. A basketball net. Her father's gravestone. A

sewing machine. Her scuffed tennis shoes. Father Singer giving
out communion. The snowball bush at her grandma's old house.
"We Love Our Buccaneers" poster in the bakery window. The
Nun scarecrow. Her 4-H blue ribbon. The whirly balloon at the
Dairy Dell. Playing Dorothy in the children's summer theater.
Baskets of flowers on Main Street. The Wild Rice River sign
on the Interstate. Mom teaching her to dance. Mr. Carlblom
in geometry class. The Delaware State Quarter. Writing Mrs.
Johnny Roth, Mrs. Johnny Roth, Mrs. Johnny Roth. Buying
makeup with Maxine. The stained glass window in church. The
bride doll on her bed. Flinging a three-pointer. Washing her long
brown hair. Kissing Johnny.

And then the images came in so fast, she couldn't make them
out from the blur. Now and then, she'd think she recognized
something—"was that…was that…was that…?" But it shot by
so rapidly she wasn't sure and in the time it took to consider it,
a hundred other images had already raced past her eyes.

Amber didn't feel herself fall.

She couldn't hear Maxine screaming her name.

She never knew Johnny was already unconscious nearby.

The slide show stopped.

One ending frame.

The last thing Amber Schlener ever saw was the father she
knew only from his picture.

He was smiling at her.

Chapter Two

Friday, October 15, 1999

Like all journalists, Joya Bonner didn't want to admit her scoops were often due to dumb luck. Skill. Smarts. Intuition. Observation. Cleverness. She'd opt to all of these. But she preferred no one ever knew dumb luck led her list.

Still, plain old dumb luck got her the Sammy the Bull scoop. If she'd been honest with the audiences that asked, "How did you break the sensational story about Sammy's dirty Arizona connection?" she would have answered, "I was interviewing a student in the Goldbar Coffeehouse in Tempe when a character like actor Joe Pesci walked in."

Short, strutting, black leather jacket over a white tee-shirt, dark hair slicked back with a grease Joya didn't know was available these days, the guy looked like a Central Casting Mafia hitman. She wasn't the only one who saw the resemblance—the piano player pounded out the first few bars of the theme song from *The Godfather*. The strutting man beamed and waved at the tribute.

Joya chuckled to herself and wondered who he was, but decided that you see the strangest types on a university campus. Probably a history professor. Or poli sci.

She turned back to her interview with an earnest graduate assistant blowing the whistle on research fraud. Millions of dollars were at stake. The reputation of Arizona State University was on the line. This was a really big story.

The explanation was complicated and compelling. Joya riveted her attention on the young woman who promised she had documents to prove everything she was saying. Joya listened attentively—one of her best traits, one that came from years of listening to relatives visit back home in Northville, North Dakota. She'd learned there that if you listened, folks would tell you almost anything. It was a major secret of her success.

Her focus would have stayed on research fraud, except the girl left for the bathroom. While Joya waited, she scanned the room to catch the Pesci impersonator holding court in a corner, surrounded by students. She couldn't hear what he was saying, but she could tell he was pontificating. He's sure full of himself, she thought. A student handed him a paperback, and the guy signed it with a flourish. Then she heard the most astonishing thing. A pretty coed in a Sun Devils tee-shirt and jeans without knees interrupted, yelling, "Mr. Bull, Mr. Bull."

The other students tittered, the girl looked flummoxed, and "Mr. Bull" smiled like a streetwise bad-ass.

The girl was so excited she yelled her question so Joya could easily hear. "You didn't really kill nineteen people, did you?"

Joya Bonner stopped breathing as skill-smarts-intuition-observation-cleverness met dumb luck.

It couldn't be, she first thought. Nah. Impossible. Or is that why the guy looks familiar? Is that why he resembles a Mafia character? If that guy in the corner really is that guy, then what the hell is Sammy "the Bull" Gravano doing in Arizona?

Joya dismissed the grad student with an excuse, promising to resume the interview soon. Their next meeting would be months off, although she didn't know that then. What she did know was this—*nothing* trumps a university scandal like discovering you've found the most famous Mafia snitch in the nation right here in your own backyard.

She nursed a cup of coffee until he left, and followed him out of the coffeehouse. He got into a Lexus. Naturally, Joya nodded. She scribbled down the plate number: AZ476D.

Joya rushed back to her office at *Phoenix Rising* and rummaged through the library. Hadn't they just reviewed his book? Yes, they had.

Underboss: Sammy "the Bull" Gravano's Story of Life in the Mafia, by Peter Maas. A promo blurb promised, "Sammy 'the Bull' Gravano is the highest-ranking member of the Mafia in America ever to defect. In telling Gravano's story, Peter Maas brings us as never before into the innermost sanctums of the Cosa Nostra as if we were there ourselves—a secret underworld of power, lust, greed, betrayal, and deception, with the specter of violent death always waiting in the wings."

Next, Joya found their review by Peter Roman, whose lifeblood pumped Mafia red. Oh, he loved this book. There was even a hint of admiration for the man whose testimony sent thirty-six of his former associates to prison, including John "the Teflon Don" Gotti.

"To get the head of the Gambino crime family behind bars was so valuable," Roman had written, "that Sammy's own crimes were basically forgiven. He admitted to personally carrying out nineteen murders, but got less than five years in prison. Then he and his family entered the federal witness protection program."

The FBI program gave these witnesses a new name, a new home, and a new start. She'd heard that Arizona was the favorite dumping ground for people hiding out to stay alive.

So Arizona got Sammy too, she thought to herself. But isn't he supposed to be lying low? Isn't he supposed to be underground so the Gambinos can't find him and get their revenge? Why in the world is he holding court in a public ASU hangout where everyone knows his name?

Unless, she thought as her journalistic skepticism kicked in, this guy is an imposter and the real Sammy is safely socked away someplace else.

The possibilities swirled around in her head. What she should do is tell Peter Roman what she'd discovered and they'd work the story together. But she wasn't going to do that because she wasn't stupid—she'd already been burned enough times by that egomaniac who didn't play nice with others.

Last July still stung. Peter would steal this story as his own again. She wasn't going to let that happen. *Fool me once, shame on you; fool me twice, shame on me.* Plus, wouldn't it be tasty to break a big Mafia story smack under Peter's big nose? She could already see the headline: "Guess where the infamous Sammy 'the Bull' Gravano ended up? Arizona, of course."

It would kill Peter Roman to see her break a story like that. Which would be just fine with her, thank you very much.

She headed home, reminding herself to be careful.

Rob Stiller was already there, his Camaro parked on the street because the driveway was only long enough for one car, and since this was Joya's home, she got the honors.

She came in the front door, as she always did—the key to the kitchen door had been lost long ago—to see the dining table strewn with his badge, his holster, his black notebook, his car keys.

"I'm home," she yelled.

He answered from the backyard, where he was having a beer. "Hi. How was your day?"

"The same."

"Mine, too."

They always started that way—"dancing around the potato salad," one of her friends called it—cautious and noncommittal, as though he weren't a police detective nor she a reporter and their days were ever "the same." But they had rules in this house, because that's the only way it worked. He wasn't supposed to ask what shit she was stirring up and she wasn't supposed to ask what shit he was cleaning up.

They met a year ago, when Joya was probing problems at the city's morgue and Rob was getting autopsy results on a case he was working. He wore street clothes that day and didn't identify himself as a cop. Preoccupied with trying not to upchuck, she didn't ask, assuming he was one of the lab technicians.

Her struggle amused him as they sat in the viewing room, watching a murdered druggie get cut up. Rob had been here countless times, but this was Joya's first.

She'd later write, "The American Heritage Dictionary defines 'autopsy' as 'the examination of a dead body to determine the cause of death,' It sounds so civilized. It's anything but. 'Brutal' is a far more accurate word to describe what happens inside the Maricopa County Medical Examiner's Office several hundred times a year.

"It's not an unkind brutality nor an uncaring brutality, but there is no gentle way to get beyond the skin and fat and muscle that give us our worldly appearance."

On the other side of the viewing window, Dr. Janet Hans wore green scrubs under a pale-blue paper gown. Her face was covered with a green-and-white-striped mask with a plastic face plate.

"That's called a splash mask," Rob offered. Joya gulped as she wrote it down.

Dr. Hans adjusted her microphone so she could not only make the recording she needed for the record, but could keep Joya informed on each step. "This is the standard Y incision," the doctor said, and in three quick swipes of her scalpel, she cut the man's chest apart. Joya was surprised there wasn't much blood and what there was seeped out slowly.

"There's no beating heart to push blood through the body," Rob explained. Joya nodded like she should have been smart enough to figure that out herself, then added, "Oh God, dead skin cuts just like bread dough."

Rob had to admit she was right, although he'd never seen it that way before.

Joya held her breath as Dr. Hans peeled away the skin and fat of the man's chest to reveal his rib cage, then took a long-handled tree clipper to cut apart his ribs to get at his organs—the lungs and stomach and liver and spleen and guts. Each one was measured and a piece cut off for testing, then thrown into a plastic bag nestled between the man's legs.

Her eyes got big when Dr. Hans fired up the electric drill to cut apart the man's skull, then peeled away his scalp and face to get to the brain. Rob watched her closely now, but she didn't lose it. She gulped a couple times, fighting her gag reflexes, but she didn't vomit, she didn't faint, and she was really proud of herself. She took notes furiously, and Rob decided that was her way of coping.

She described it all in the story she'd write, ending, "When they're done, they put his scalp and face back in place, stuff the plastic bag that now contains his organs into his empty chest cavity and sew him up. Viewing one autopsy is enough to last anyone a lifetime."

Rob thought she was cute—not beautiful, but not hard on the eyes, either—and he was struck by how resolute she was. It was only later, when they were outside and she was gulping fresh air, that she admitted she'd been fighting off nausea all afternoon.

"But I knew the guys in homicide were just waiting for me to fold, and I wouldn't give them the satisfaction," she told him. When he laughed, she begged him, "Please don't be a homicide guy."

Everyone back at police headquarters loved that story. Her investigation forced changes they'd all been wanting at the morgue, so Rob gave her points for being a reporter who actually made a difference.

She had noticed him right away. Robert Stiller was a hard man to ignore, unless shoulders the width of a plow didn't impress and a dimple didn't entice. He might not be everyone's version of handsome, but he was hers. She liked how he smiled at her. He oozed cool sureness. She was thankful she was on the down side of her yo-yo dieting the day they met—and the putrid smells from the autopsy room assured she had no stomach for any food the rest of that day. Still, she never expected him to call.

When he did, she surprised herself by saying yes. She'd never before even considered dating a cop—a firefighter, sure, but a cop? Not a good fit with a journalist. Cops were conservative and militaristic and by-the-book kind of guys, and none of that was part of her DNA. How could she dress him up and take him to an ACLU dinner, or a gay rights fundraiser or a theater party? He'd never fit. Besides, getting him to rent a tux would be impossible. No, she was used to men who owned their own tuxes and fit in just fine with the formal dinners where she wore her fancy gowns and elaborate rhinestone jewelry.

He had to think twice before he made that first call, because she wasn't his idea of the perfect match, either. His buddies on the force wouldn't trust her, and she'd never fit in with the other wives and girlfriends. Besides, his ex was still a friend in this crowd and nobody was ready for him to bring someone new. But there was something about her, and he gave it a shot.

She said yes, thinking it would be a lark. What could it hurt to have a drink with him? But the drink went into dinner, and then a second date, and before long, well, he wasn't *so* conservative and militaristic. And he was *so* scrumptiously sexy. At least he didn't watch Fox News, with its fixation on destroying President Clinton and fueling every right-wing fantasy.

It wasn't long before he started staying over and then bringing over some clothes, and for the last four months, he'd spent most of every week here.

Social engagements weren't an issue because his weekends were spent with his kids. She was free to do her own thing, which gave great relief to both sides.

She told her mom and dad back in Northville that she was dating a cop, but left out the living together detail and didn't mention he was divorced. Ralph and Maggie Bonner thought thirty-eight was a good time for her to be settling down and her dad especially liked the cop part.

But Sheriff Joe Arpaio almost screwed it up, just as it was getting good.

Back in July—two weeks after Rob started staying over regularly—local stations led their evening news with an explosive story. "Sheriff's officers today foiled an attempt to blow up Sheriff Joe Arpaio with a car bomb. The sheriff was unavailable for comment, as he rushed home to comfort his terrified wife."

They showed "undercover" footage of a fresh-faced kid wearing a tee-shirt and Levis, arriving at the Roman Table restaurant on Seventh Avenue with a bearded man who slipped away as the kid walked toward the sheriff's car with a homemade bomb. Officers rushed in and nabbed him. Arpaio's chief deputy called a press conference in that parking lot, saying they'd caught the dangerous bomber through the help of an informant and good police work.

"Holy shit." Joya watched the footage of Jimmy Saville being caught red-handed in a city where the most famous crime of the last thirty years was a car bomb that killed *Arizona Republic* reporter Don Bolles. Saville's going to fry, she thought to herself.

Robbie came home that night like an uncaged tiger. He threw his things down and started pacing—swearing and mumbling and ranting. His phone would ring and he'd go off for privacy, but she could hear him yelling. She couldn't make out the subject and verb of his rant.

How was she supposed to act at a time like this? Their relationship was so new. Maybe she could get his mind off his troubles? So she said, "Hey, did you see they caught that kid that tried to bomb Sheriff Arpaio?"

That's when Rob exploded. "Don't be a fucking idiot. That kid was set up by the sheriff's office. It was a goddamned publicity stunt."

Rob thrashed his arms, looking like he wanted to throw something. Joya finally realized why he was so mad.

"That kid was just a patsy so the sheriff could get some prime-time coverage on television. Where did they get their 'undercover' footage? A goddamned pool reporter from Channel 3. The sheriff's office had a television crew hiding in the parking lot to catch all the action. And the idiots in the press fell for it."

Joya was so shocked, she grabbed the hot handle of a copper pot on the stove. When she ran to the sink to douse her burnt hand in cold water, Rob didn't even notice.

"And guess where the kid got the bomb material? The sheriff's office bought it for him. They showed him how to build it. They drove him to the restaurant. That bearded guy—that's a deputy! We're so goddamned mad about this we can hardly stand it."

Joya knew the "toughest sheriff in America" liked to prance and preen, but she never thought he'd go this far for a publicity stunt—entrap a kid into a bomb plot that wasn't real. She knew damn well that the kid would spend the rest of his life in prison—what jury wouldn't convict him? So the sheriff would steal a kid's life? This was too outlandish. Too mean. Too horrible.

"What is Phoenix PD going to do?" she finally asked. "You can't let him get away with this."

"Oh, that's rich," he sneered. "Your mighty media are convicting this kid on the evening news and you expect one law enforcement agency to rat out another? What planet do you live on?"

Rob was so angry, he begged off from dinner. "I gotta go. Think I'll stay at my place tonight. No telling when I'll be done." He didn't even bother with a peck goodbye.

Joya sat at her kitchen table, steaming and stewing and breathless with this secret knowledge.

Her first call was to Peter Roman. "Let's get to that kid in jail and let him tell us what happened," she ordered. Peter told her to hang on, he'd get with his contacts and call her back. But of course, he didn't. He stole the story for himself, and their editor backed him up. Jimmy Saville told Peter just what Robbie had told her. So did the lawyer who rushed in to help out the hapless kid.

Pete's story the next week said the only chance the poor kid had was for a jury to find that he'd been "entrapped" by the Maricopa County Sheriff's Office.

That had never happened in an Arizona court and no defense attorney in Phoenix would bet on it happening now.

Rob went nuts when he found out Joya had shared his information with Peter Roman. "You can't do that!" he spat at her. "I didn't tell you that as a reporter. I told you as my girlfriend. God, I'm an idiot."

He walked out that night, too, angry and disappointed. She fretted all night, worried that she'd screwed things up for good.

But she knew she'd do the same thing again if she had to. If Peter hadn't stolen the story, she would have pursued it on her own.

So if they were to have any chance, they had to make some rules. The Number One rule was No Shop Talk.

Of course, Peter Roman thought she was throwing away a great opportunity. "What good is it to bonk a detective if you aren't going to get anything?"

"You do it your way, Peter, and I'll do it mine. At least, I have some ethics."

"Ethics. Shit on ethics."

Peter Roman believed that. The SOB had once gotten his wife to cook a beautiful dinner for a politician "friend," and then blindsided him, sneaking into the kitchen to take notes on the table talk that made City Hall look bad. Peter couldn't see how that was an unethical betrayal of the first order.

Joya knew betrayal when she saw it. She also knew she'd never been happier than since she hooked up with Robbie. The no-tell rule was their best hope.

The exceptions were those things that neither saw as dangerous. If he had a cut-and-dried murder case, okay, but he didn't discuss the controversial ones at home. She could discuss her exposés, as long as they didn't touch the city or the police union.

But Sammy "the Bull" Gravano was a whole new category. Should she share her delicious discovery? What could it hurt? Phoenix PD had no reason to be interested in Sammy. Wouldn't it be fun to spring this news? Tell Rob how she happened on Sammy, and they'd both get a chuckle out of it? Show off for her detective boyfriend that she was a good detective, too! She'd swear him to secrecy, because she sure didn't want this getting out until she had her story in print.

Besides, maybe this one time she could ask him a favor. Could he run the plate and see who owned the Lexus? On the other hand—journalists are infamous for their on-other-hand thinking—maybe it was better to keep her mouth shut. She could always tell him the whole story later.

"I had that interview today about the ASU scandal." She counted this as one of the non-dangerous things they could discuss.

"How'd it go?" He had only a casual interest, but was polite enough to seem to care.

"Oh, great. I got some really good stuff. My source says they're scamming the Havasupai—you know, the tribe that lives in the bottom of the Grand Canyon. She calls it 'genetic rape.' How about you?"

Rob pretended there was nothing special about his day, even though they'd heard some tasty things on the wiretap, and he turned the conversation to the Kentucky Fried Chicken he'd picked up for dinner—original for him, baked for her.

"Great. Get me a side of green beans?" He assured her he had. "Say," she asked in her most casual voice, "what do you know about the witness protection program?"

It never occurred to her that this wasn't a safe question. Phoenix PD had nothing to do with the FBI's squirrel-away program. She was unpleasantly surprised when Robbie slowly lowered his beer and peered at her with those beautiful brown eyes.

"What does that have to do with ASU?" He was using his "bad cop" voice, and it was that, more than his question, that alerted her something was up.

"Just wondering. You know how my mind jumps around."

She quickly stood to mix herself a scotch and water, hoping she hadn't tipped anything. *Damn, I shouldn't have asked.*

Ding, ding, ding, ding—Rob knew exactly how her mind worked and he didn't like the neighborhood it was working right now. Six months ago, the question would have been received as innocently as it was asked, but that was six months ago, before they figured out the Lexus they were tailing was registered to a Jimmy Moran who was really Sammy the Bull.

She couldn't possibly… What are the odds? But he had a sinking feeling in his stomach. She'd gone to ASU for an interview and come back asking about the witness protection program. Damn, that's hitting too close.

Rob followed her into the butler's pantry off the kitchen where she kept her hootch, and leaned against the doorframe, blocking her way.

Oh, oh, she thought. *What door did I just open?*

"So tell me about your ASU interview." He used his "good cop" voice. She almost laughed at how transparent that was—you can't schmooze a schmoozer. She smiled up at him with her own beautiful brown eyes and punted.

"I think this girl is legit—I think she's got the goods on ASU. You won't believe how they've been exploiting the Indians. They're taking their blood, saying they're going to do research on diabetes—you know, the tribe has one of the highest rates in the nation—but they're not doing that. They're studying schizophrenia and in-breeding and something about the Bering Strait Theory that says Native Americans aren't natives at all, but immigrants from Asia. They're lying to the tribe. It breaks every rule of scientific research. It's going to tear ASU apart when this comes out. I bet it'll be a national story."

Rob wasn't really interested in this story, but Joya knew he was after something and for the life of her, she couldn't figure out what. So she carried on all through dinner, giving him excruciating details about the fraud story, stalling.

"How was the lab?" he asked her, as she forked into her coleslaw.

"What lab?"

"Isn't that where graduate students spilling the beans on research fraud hang out?"

Before she could stop herself she corrected him, "No, I interviewed her at the Goldbar Coffeehouse." The minute the words were out of her mouth, she knew she'd given herself away. Robbie's dismayed face confirmed it. Hell, she'd fallen for one of the oldest tricks in the book.

They looked at each other and you could see the wheels turning.

Shit, his eyes said. *She knows.*

Damn, her eyes said. *He knows I know, but how does he know?*

She put down the plastic container of coleslaw and they ate in silence. He felt like an elephant was sitting on his chest. She felt like a python was strangling her.

Her reporter's mind ran through the possibilities—her homicide detective boyfriend knew about Sammy the Bull because he'd done yet another murder while hiding out here under the witness protection program, and Rob was trying to solve it. Okay, that could be it. Or he knew about Sammy because he was getting information from him about some other bad-ass who was murdering people in Phoenix. That could be it.

Rob had an easier job of it, since he knew all about the Goldbar and the "court" Sammy liked to hold there. Shit, she could ruin everything!

He took a deep breath. "So how is Sammy the Bull these days?"

"Just fine," she sang as she got up to clear the table. Turning away from him, her heart raced and her face stretched into an "oh-my-God." This was going to be interesting! She returned to the table with coffee for him and tea for her.

They regarded each other like matador and bull. This could get just that ugly if they weren't careful.

God, I love this man, Joya thought.

I don't want to lose this woman, Rob thought.

For certain, neither one could walk away from this.

"So tell me," she said.

"You tell me."

"No, you're the one who knew about Sammy the Bull— remember, I'm the one who just now discovered he was in town—so I think it's your turn."

"Come on," he coaxed. "I've gotta hear how you stumbled on him. What, he walked in the coffeehouse and the piano player did the Mafia song?"

"Exactly," she yelped and fessed up, sharing the whole story. He laughed appropriately at the "Mr. Bull" line.

"Your turn." She pointed when she was done. "How did you know he was here? He's being a bad boy? Don't tell me his count is up to twenty or twenty-one?"

Maybe she was giddy because of her startling discovery, or maybe she was pleased as punch for uncovering something that impressed her boyfriend, but she truly expected Rob to share his story on finding out that Sammy the Bull was at home in the Grand Canyon State.

The fall was crushing. She listened with disbelief.

"Joya, I've never asked you this in the entire time we've been together.…" Rob started in his by-the-book police voice. Her mind's eye saw him packing his clothes and walking out the door. "…but I'm asking you now. Forget this. I'm not kidding. You've got to. Please."

Joya envisioned packing up his clothes and pushing him out the door.

Her strike back was immediate. "That's not going to happen, and you know better than to ask." She felt sick.

He looked into his coffee cup and wondered if he dared push—or if he was pushing himself out of her life—and knew the stakes were so high he *had* to push.

"Joya. This isn't a story about a Mafia guy ending up in Arizona in the witness protection program. This is a story that will get people killed. Sammy at the top of that list. Do you know how many goons out there want to make their mark by whacking Sammy the Bull? His family is here now and they'll go after them, too. He's got a wife and a daughter and a son and every one of them are marked. You write a story telling the world Sammy the Bull is in Phoenix and what do you get—an award? An interview on Pat McMahon's TV show? And what does Sammy and his family get? Gravestones. Do you want to get these people killed?"

Rob felt dirty, spreading it on so thick. He hoped she didn't know enough about the Mafia to realize the family being marked was a lie. He hoped he'd touch the decency inside her. Six months of hard work depended on it. Six months of stakeouts and undercover surveillance and weeding through mountains of wiretaps.

He put his hand on her arm and she pulled away.

"I'm sorry. You're nuts if you think I'd sit on this. Robbie, the goddamned piano player at the coffeehouse knows he's Sammy the Bull. Those college students know he's Sammy the Bull. Apparently, he's important enough that the Phoenix PD knows he's here. So why is it me that's going to get him killed? It's not, and you know it. That's bullshit. This guy is strutting around ASU like he's a rock star and all of a sudden, it's ME who has to keep his secret to keep him alive? Don't treat me like a fool. Now you can either help me with this story or you can get out of my way. It's up to you."

Joya had never spoken to Robbie like that before. Had she gone too far? Not that it wasn't where she needed to go, but she knew this couldn't be good for them.

Rob was taking his own measure. He'd failed to ward her off—hell, he hadn't expected it to work in the first place—and now he had to decide how deceitful he could be and still keep her.

If he told her the whole story now—if he shared information she couldn't even guess—he'd jeopardize the entire investigation. It wasn't only the Phoenix PD with a stake in his next words. How about the Drug Enforcement Administration? How about Customs? Try telling them their sting was upset because your reporter girlfriend happened to be in a Tempe coffeehouse when Sammy waltzed through.

But when she found out the truth—when she discovered why it was so goddamned important not to announce that Sammy the Bull was in Phoenix until after they had him back in handcuffs—she'd leave him in anger.

He didn't want that. But he wouldn't blow all this hard work, either. Jesus, they'd pulled him off homicide to work this case because he was such a good investigator—that reputation would be shot to hell if she spilled the beans. The only way he'd save the case was to save his relationship, because if he walked out, she'd work night and day to get that story into the paper.

Shit, he consoled himself, she'd probably figure it out by herself anyway. She's such a bulldog—and she's got this streak of dumb luck—she'd probably stumble onto the rest of it, too.

If he were to save one of the biggest cases he'd ever worked and save the best relationship he'd ever had, Rob Stiller had to own up. The best he could hope for was a deal with his girlfriend that would give him and the DEA time to finish their work.

Joya's mind was jumping through hoops, too—thinking on your feet was a must for an investigative reporter—and it was very clear that the real story here wasn't that Sammy the Bull was in Arizona. The real story had something to do with the Phoenix Police Department and its homicide detective sitting across from her. She was seeing only the tip of this iceberg. What was everything below? She didn't know, but she knew who did, and now she had to get it out of him.

Rob took a deep breath and started his plea. "Right now, this has to be under a cone of silence," he demanded. "I'm not kidding, Joya. I'm going to tell you something that would ruin my career. You've got to promise me, you won't fuck me over on this."

Joya felt a twinge of guilt as she reached over and touched his arm. "Of course I wouldn't fuck you over." She used her most reassuring voice and told herself she really meant it. Then, using the same silence-is-golden rule that police themselves often used, she sat there staring at him, not saying a word, waiting for him to continue.

"If I tell you what's going on, you've got to promise not to write anything until the right time," he declared. "I mean it. Promise me. I'll help you. You'll be the only one with the inside story. But for that, I need your promise that this story doesn't break too soon and screw things up."

Joya Bonner had a long-standing policy that she didn't negotiate for stories. Nobody got to dictate terms or times. You make a deal and you're dealing with a devil, is how she always thought of it.

But on the other hand, without revealing a detail, her boyfriend had revealed there was a much, much bigger story here than simply a Mafia guy ending up in Arizona. She'd only see the rest of this iceberg if she cut a deal with a guy who already knew how wide it was and how deep it went.

She laid down some tough, non-negotiable terms: She had exclusive access to the investigation. She would see everything. She could interview anyone she wanted. She'd eventually get access to Sammy. He agreed to every one.

Rob was so relieved that she was pulling back, he'd have promised her anything. Both of them thought they'd won.

Over the next hour, Detective Rob Stiller laid out an incredible story that would one day knock Arizona on its ear. "A new Arizona Mafia," he'd said. Those words kept bouncing around Joya's mind.

She clearly saw why this story had to wait. Revealing that Sammy "the Bull" Gravano was in town was nothing. What he was doing would blow the doors off. But they'd never stop him if the story came out too soon.

"I have the exclusive," she emphasized to Rob when he was done. It wasn't a question, but a declaration of their agreement.

"Absolutely."

"Robbie, this is like a bad movie."

"Yeah, a bad movie where a lot of people can get hurt."

What a day, Joya mused, as she and Robbie went off to bed and fantastic sex.

It was Friday, October 15, 1999.

Chapter Three

Monday, October 18, 1999

K.C. Franken had never been more aware of his responsibilities as the town's funeral director than when he waited for his son to bring Amber's body from the Breckenridge Hospital.

He'd had the biggest fight of his marriage over this, his wife spitting at him that it was inhuman to send Kenny to fetch the body of his classmate—the girl he'd watched die on that loft floor—while his best friend still lay in a coma.

"Your own son could have died," Margaret yelled at him. "He's grieving. He's been through enough. I'm already afraid he'll do something to avenge this. Don't push him. Let him alone!"

But that was the point, K.C. told her. It could have been Kenny. It could have been any of them. It could have been all of them. It was the luck of the draw that it wasn't. Their firstborn had to learn that when you take dangerous risks, sometimes you pick the short straw. Margaret didn't understand that sending Kenny in the funeral coach to pick up Amber's body was his way of teaching their son that lesson.

Her only words that worried him were the "pushing-the-boy" part. It wouldn't take much, and there were thirteen other boys in that Class of 2000 he had to worry about, too.

He could still hear Ralph Bonner's words after mass yesterday. "You guys keep an eye on your boys, because no telling what they'll do to him. And there's no sense this gets any worse. Let the law handle it."

Heads had bobbed in agreement because Bonner was a town leader known for his level-headedness.

"I'm worried about her uncles," Bernard Stine said. Everyone considered his words, since the former grocery-store owner was a man whose words were always sparse.

"I'm worried about LeRoy," someone else offered, but then, everybody always worried about crazy LeRoy Roth and his right-wing conspiracy theories.

"If I were you, I'd worry about me because I want to take care of that piece of trash myself." That was Earl Krump, and everyone knew this retired farmer wasn't kidding.

"Take it easy. Take it easy." Ralph Bonner wanted to quiet things down.

"Do you think they'll send someone from Fargo to investigate?" The men looked to one another, waiting for reassurance that professional lawmen would be in town soon.

Instead, they got the answer they dreaded. "Naw, I hear Sheriff Potter has already been to the hospital and declared the body a 'crime scene.' That son of a bitch."

"Sure, *now* he comes, like he didn't know what was going on. We told him we had a drug dealer in town. The bastard wouldn't listen." That was Earl Krump again.

"The sheriff's as worthless as a tit on a hog." K.C. couldn't remember who made that salient point, but the words could have come out of his own mouth.

He hadn't said much, but his own fury matched Earl's. Sure, he was worried that Kenny and the boys would go after the pusher, but he worried about himself, too. If he were given the chance to make this right, K.C. Franken knew he could beat that kid within an inch of his life.

But he couldn't think about that now. He had too much ahead of him. Too many responsibilities. Too many memories.

It wasn't just his boy he thought about as he waited in the Franken Funeral Home on Main Street. He remembered his own classmate from years ago, the man who'd never known the beautiful daughter born after a drunk driver took his life.

K.C. hung out with Richard Schlener when they were going to Northville High School, Class of 1979. Richard was dating Nettie Hastreiter then. K.C. had yet to meet Margaret. Richard was the basketball captain, K.C., the football captain. When K.C.'s dad sent him to fetch a body in another town, sometimes he took Richard with him—it was a legitimate reason to ditch classes, and teachers didn't ask many questions when you said you needed help for this particular errand. Richard had drawn the line, though, on K.C.'s regular job for the family business. So K.C. dug graves by himself and would eventually joke that he worked his way from the ground up.

K.C. was one of six groomsmen who stood up when Richard and Nettie got married, and a couple years later, all those guys gathered at the Corner Bar to toast the father-to-be. That's the same bar where they got wasted the night after Richard was killed.

When they released Richard's body after the accident—or the mangled mess of a body left when a drunk plowed into him at eighty miles an hour—K.C.'s dad stepped aside. "Son, I want you to handle this funeral." He walked out the door.

K.C. stood there, shocked and dismayed, for the longest time, hating his dad for half of it, thanking him for the other half. Then he went to work. That was the day he knew he was meant to be a funeral director, because if you can embalm your best friend; if you can guide his grieving family through the painful decisions; if you can manage the details for his funeral, then you can handle anything. His dad was sure, too—this was the test that told Mr. Franken he could safely pass down the family business to K.C.

But now, thinking about preparing Richard's daughter, Amber—and knowing it could have been his own son—K.C. shuddered for the first time in years.

He set the thermostat to sixty-two degrees in the Preparation Room. "Physicians and Licensed Personnel Only" said the antique sign painted on the door fifty years ago when his dad built this place. Even when he remodeled, K.C. painted around that sign.

Kenny drove into the garage and K.C. couldn't tell if his red eyes were from crying or from rage. But those eyes also held a defiance. He shrugged off his dad's hand on his arm as they opened the back of the limousine.

For a second, K.C. thought the body bag contained Richard all over again. But only a second. They wheeled Amber into the preparation room, where Kenny put his foot down.

"I'm not staying for this," he screamed at his dad. K.C. knew this wasn't the son who'd carry on the family business.

Pretty Amber wasn't pretty anymore. Her chest wore the "Y" incision of the autopsy. Her hair was a mess. Her skin was gray and blotchy. Although he'd never admit it to Margaret, K.C. was glad Kenny hadn't seen her like this.

Her hysterical friends had picked her up off the loft floor and rushed for help. The boys half-carried, half-dragged Johnny to a second car, jamming his right leg in the stairway and breaking it below the knee. They angrily debated if they should speed to Fargo and the best hospitals in the state, or stop closer to home in Breck. The we-have-no-time-to-waste argument won, and the caravan blared their horns as they screeched into the emergency entrance. It made no difference. The girl was dead on arrival, regardless of where they'd taken her. She was dead before they got down the hayloft steps. Her friends just wouldn't believe it.

But their decision to go to the nearest hospital saved Johnny's life. At least so far. The medical care he got there made the difference. He was still in a coma, and his folks had him transferred to Fargo, but it was the hospital in Breckenridge, Minnesota—the twin city to Wahpeton, North Dakota—that saved him.

K.C. carefully draped a white sheet over the body on the embalming table—that's how he had to think of this for the next couple hours—not Amber, not the daughter of his friend, not his son's classmate, not one of the town's favorite basketball players—he had to think of this as "the body," and that was all.

He took a couple deep breaths, all professional now. He started the process to replace the blood in the body with a formaldehyde mixture. He opened the carotid artery and the jugular vein in the neck so he could pump the embalming fluid in the artery and the displaced blood would flow out the vein. It took over two hours for the body to be preserved and disinfected. Now it could be made presentable for the last viewing.

K.C. would do that later. Over the years, he'd perfected his skills so the person looked natural—asleep but peaceful. That's what his dad had promised when he ran the home, and that's what K.C. promised now.

He looked silly in the drugstore, inspecting the makeup jars and tubes, but he needed foundation makeup in every hue to match any skin. He was even more self-conscious when he bought up tubes of lipstick on sale that ran from pink to red. His nail polish selections all went to the pale side—clear, pink, beige. No one ever wanted red polish on the nails of their loved one.

He'd do the makeup tomorrow. Normally his mom would style the hair, but because this one was so young, K.C. hoped he could get the new beautician in town to do it. Just out of beauty school, she knew the latest styles. He'd never asked her before—some beauticians couldn't handle doing the hair of a corpse—but he was going to ask now.

He finished cleaning up the Preparation Room. Its green linoleum floors shined and the white porcelain sink was spotless. He changed his shirt. Time to meet the family to plan out the final details.

As he walked out of the Preparation Room, "the body" became Amber again. The technical part of his job was done. Now the important part was starting—the part that made K.C. so trusted and respected. In the next couple days, his entire focus was to make this final journey as easy as possible on the family. Anyone could be trained to do what he'd just done in the Preparation Room. The real test of a mortician was how he could do this next part.

Nettie Schlener fell into K.C.'s arms as she walked through the front door of his funeral home. He held his longtime friend and classmate, whispering, "I'm so sorry." Behind her came one of her brothers, her three sisters, and two of Amber's cousins. While the family resemblance was strong in each face, even stronger were the red eyes and solemn, sunken cheeks of grief. K.C. noted the fury of revenge in the face of Dennis Hastreiter. The men were right to worry about Amber's uncles.

K.C. led them into the office/conference room with its large wooden table and chairs for ten. He knew this family as well as his own, which helped him anticipate what they'd want and need at this terrible moment.

Father Singer was running a few minutes late—the priest always sat in on these sessions for the Catholics—and so K.C. began at the top of his checklist.

Date of birth: August 1, 1982.

Place of birth: Fargo, North Dakota

Social Security number: 502-67-3730

"Does someone want to write Amber's biography for the obituary and the mass card?" K.C. asked. He knew it wouldn't be Nettie, but probably one of her sisters would take charge.

"I could," one of her cousins offered, looking to the other for support and help. But when the second cousin frantically shook her head "no," K.C. jumped in. "Or I could take care of it with your help. I'd be honored to do it." Nettie nodded to him and the cousins both looked relieved.

"What were Amber's activities and accomplishments that you want everyone to know?" he gently asked so he could fill in the "life history."

"Her basketball," Nettie said. "She was captain of the team." And then she dissolved into tears as her sisters rushed to comfort her.

Dennis cleared his throat to overtake his own emotions. "She's on the poster that the booster club put up all over town. It's a picture of her laying up for a shot."

"We Love our Buccaneers," one of the cousins said, as though K.C. didn't know the poster that graced almost every business window—not his, of course, because that wouldn't have been proper.

"Her 4-H work," her Aunt Arlene offered. "She was doing a history project on the Bagg Bonanza Farm over by Mooreton. Getting old pictures, telling the story."

Everyone turned their attention to Arlene, like this was the most important story she'd ever tell, and she got the hint to continue: "You know, hardly anybody knows about the Bonanza Farms—they were the largest farms in the world, right here in Dakota Territory in the late eighteen hundreds and early nineteen hundreds. Some were two hundred thousand acres. They were the nation's first corporate farms. The Bagg Farm is one of the few left. Amber told me she thought that's why North Dakota outlawed corporate farms and said every farm has to be family owned. She thought the bonanza farms taught us that corporate farming isn't the way to go."

Everyone in the room hung on Arlene's words. K.C. had seen this happen countless times before. Give a family something to think about, anything besides the fact that their hearts were broken and they could barely breathe.

One of the cousins—the one a year behind Amber—asked timidly, "Do you think it would be okay, Aunt Nettie, if I took that on as my own 4-H project and finished it in Amber's honor?"

"That would be wonderful, darling. Amber would have loved that. Thank you."

Another aunt suggested they mention that Amber was on the Honor Roll.

"What about her acting?" the youngest cousin asked, remembering when she had played a munchkin to Amber's Dorothy in the children's play last summer. Amber had been in every play since she was in the third grade. She was one of the crabs in *Blackbeard the Pirate*, a mouse in *The Pied Piper*, the genie in *Aladdin,* and ended her acting career as the lead in *The Wizard of Oz.*

"That summer program is the best thing that happens to this town," Aunt Mary Ann said, and everyone knew she was right. Northville wasn't the kind of town that had money for arts programs. Its public library had such a tiny budget it barely held on, and if it weren't for donated books, there wouldn't be a library at all. So the Missoula Children's Theater program was a godsend. For one week every summer, two actors in a red truck full of costumes, makeup, lights, sets and scripts drove into town to put on a play with local kids. The town provided their lodging and food, the talent, a stage, and an accompanist. Local businesses coughed up donations.

"She loved those plays," Nettie said. "Be sure to mention that."

Father Singer finally arrived, carrying his black leather appointment book as though he couldn't remember the only thing on his plate for the next couple days. He'd already been out to Nettie's house to pray with the family, so it was the business of the funeral he was here to schedule.

"The mass will be at ten a.m. on Wednesday," he announced, as though this were news. He'd moved these masses back an hour when he came to the parish ten years ago, and everyone was grateful. By ten a.m., chores are long done and there was a chance to get in some serious field work. Any earlier cut into the heart of the farm day. A lot more men had been able to make funerals since Father Singer instituted the civilized hour.

"Have you settled on the pallbearers?" K.C. offered that the Class of 2000 all wanted to walk Amber's casket down the long, central aisle of St. Vincent's. Nettie closed her eyes as she nodded yes.

Nettie named an old friend she wanted to be the soloist and Father assured her the church choir would be on hand and reminded her that the Judith Circle was in charge of the funeral dinner.

"That's Aunt Gertie's circle," Nettie said, and everyone assumed their elderly aunt would pass on this one so she could sit in the front rows with the rest of the family. Not a soul in town would expect Gertie Bach to do her circle duties for the funeral of her great-niece. But Nettie knew there were others who would step up.

"Visitation." Father had only to say that one word to bring new tears around the table. The first thing they'd face in the ritual of saying goodbye was the visitation the night before the funeral. Visitation. Such a friendly, caring word of courtesy. Yet one that brought with it so much pain. This would be the first time any of them would see Amber—the family's private "viewing" was scheduled for two hours before the doors opened to everyone else. Then they'd sit there, as their friends and neighbors filed pass the casket, and take the words of solace that were offered. Again and again, they'd say the same "thank you" to the same words of sorrow, because how many words are there to express this kind of grief?

"We could do it here, but K.C. can only seat two hundred twenty in his chapel," Father continued. "I would expect far more." He paused, to let everyone think a second. Father started to say, "We could do it at the church, of course…" when the youngest cousin offered, "Amber would want it at the school. In the gym. Where she played. She'd want her friends to see what can happen."

You could hear Nettie's breath suck in. Everyone looked at the girl—Dennis at his oldest daughter—as she lowered her eyes like she'd just said something awful.

"Yes. Yes. Yes," Nettie repeated, her head thrown back to look beyond the ceiling. "Let them see what happens when they do stupid things. Let them see! You agree, Richard, don't you? It's a wonderful idea. These children think they're going to live forever and they can do anything and it will be okay, and they've got to learn. This will help teach them, Richard, won't it?"

Dennis, K.C., and Father Singer stared at Nettie like she was a loon, speaking out loud to her late husband. The women and girls in the room looked at the floor.

"I failed her," Nettie proclaimed, as sure as a revival tent preacher. "I failed our daughter. Please forgive me, oh Richard, please forgive me. I should have never let her go out with that goddamned Johnny Roth. I tried to stop her but I should have forbidden it. I should have put my foot down. You would have. You must hate me for failing our girl. I'm sorry, Richard. I'm so sorry. I failed you so badly. And now I won't join you. We won't get our everlasting life together in heaven. I'll burn in hell when my time comes."

Arlene jumped up and enveloped her sister in her arms and soothed, "Don't Nettie, don't."

Mary Ann put her hand in front of her mouth and whispered to her brother, "She does this all the time. She's always talking to him—her dead husband. Sometimes she acts like he's talking back."

Dennis was bug-eyed, his face a mixture of fear and embarrassment.

Father Singer saw a woman outside her mind—the kind the church purged—but he knew it wasn't the devil that had hold of his parishioner. It was grief. Unbearable, intolerable grief.

In all his years, K.C. had never witnessed anything this creepy.

Then it was over. Nettie lowered her gaze and hugged her sister back and calmly said, "Where were we?" Around the room people cleared their throats and resettled themselves in their chairs and pretended nothing had happened.

"Do I smell cinnamon? I swear I smell cinnamon."

Mary Ann gave Dennis a look of, "Yeah, that too."

K.C. got his composure back and moved on. He laid on the table a variety of memorial cards that would be custom-ordered for Amber and handed out at the visitation and the funeral. Nettie turned to her nieces, looking for their guidance, and they chose one with the picture of a pink rose entwined in a rosary over the words "In Loving Memory."

"Amber loved pink roses," the cousins said, as Nettie ran her hand over the picture.

"Yes, she did. They were her favorite." Nettie already knew the funeral spray with "Beloved Daughter" on the white sash would be pink roses.

Nettie chose a consoling poem entitled "Safely Home" to go with a picture of Amber. She read it out loud. "I am home in heaven, dear ones; Oh, so happy and so bright! There is perfect joy and beauty in this everlasting light."

Nettie wanted the obituary to appear in the local paper, the Wahpeton paper, and the *Fargo Forum*. K.C. said he'd take care of that.

Father had all he needed and got up to leave. He didn't have to ask the touchy question about cremation—the church was finally allowing it—because he knew Nettie didn't approve of it. He was grateful for that, because he didn't either. But he allowed funeral masses for the cremated, even if his predecessor hadn't. He gave everyone a blessing.

K.C. knew the hardest part was about to begin. He softly said, "Nettie, let me show you the caskets." She looked at him like he had two heads, as though she wasn't here planning a funeral at all, but maybe just stopped in, and then the reality of the day came back to her and the tears poured out of her eyes again.

It took a few moments for her to compose herself. Her brother even suggested that he and their sisters could do this part, but Nettie said she was going to pick it out herself. The cousins decided they'd already seen enough, heard enough, and they begged off going back into the casket showroom.

"I think I have the perfect thing," K.C. offered, as he led Nettie past his top-of-the-line solid bronze casket—$7,425—and stopped at the lavender casket with silver hardware from Batesville that went for $1,860. It was lined with a light-pink crepe velvet.

Nettie almost collapsed as she looked at the casket that would hold her daughter. Dennis rushed forward to hold her up, as she covered her eyes with her hands and sobbed. Her sisters weren't doing any better, and if he wasn't using both hands to hold up his sister, Dennis would have been wiping away his own tears.

Sister Arlene had a strange thought as she stood there, looking at the steel box gussied up to look elegant. She and her sisters loved to go shopping and would look at every single thing before making their selection—money was always dear and not to be squandered on the wrong choice. But here they were, about to spend more than they'd ever spent on anything except a refrigerator, and comparison shopping was the farthest thing from their minds.

"It's perfect," Nettie finally said. "The pink lining..." And she could say no more.

"Yes, perfect," Mary Ann said. Arlene repeated, "Perfect."

"Don't worry. I'll take care of everything." Everyone was so grateful for K.C. Nettie and her sisters rushed to leave, anxious to get out of the showroom.

Dennis lingered, whispering to himself, "This shouldn't be happening. This isn't right."

K.C. was the only one who noticed Dennis' face, his eyes glued to the lavender casket.

They weren't the eyes of a man who agreed with his sisters that this was the perfect casket.

They weren't the eyes of a man who was relieved this day was finally coming to an end.

They weren't the eyes of an uncle grieving his niece.

They were the eyes of a man who wanted to kill somebody.

K.C. recognized those eyes. They were the eyes he saw when he looked in a mirror.

Chapter Four

Joya Bonner always loved Saturday mornings.

Unhurried, wake-up snuggles—sometimes sex—and intimate conversation possible only between a couple lying together. She loved these moments with Rob. They'd tell each other stories and share embarrassing moments. They'd laugh at themselves. They'd brag a little. They'd coo at one another. She was sure these mornings were the mortar of their relationship.

Today was different.

Rehashing last night's revelations, they talked of strategies. How she'd tell her hard-nosed editor and keep him in check. How he'd tell his whip-cracking chief and make him agree. Both knew they were walking a thin line with their bosses, but there was no turning back.

Rob's arm around her shoulders got tighter and he pulled her closer.

"You've got to be very careful, Joya." Rob sounded so serious—his cop/cop voice, like when he announced "you have the right to remain silent..." It was a voice of power and certainty, like a cloak of safety for her to wear around her shoulders.

"Really. Because it's not a game when you mess with the Mafia. They're dangerous. Those boys have their own rules—you've already had one reporter blown up in this town. What does that tell you about how they look at you guys? Sometimes I think they'd rather go after you than us. So promise me you'll be careful."

Joya wrapped herself in her boyfriend's concern and promised to be careful. Not wanting to sound too girly, she added for the sake of her ego, "But don't worry, honey. I've faced bad guys before."

"Not like this, Joya. Not like this."

He hugged her tight and kissed her hairline and whispered, "Please, please take this seriously and be careful." That wasn't a cop's voice at all. That was the voice of a man truly worried that a woman he loved was in danger.

"I will, darling, I will." She wasn't fooling.

It was time for them both to get on with the day. He was taking his kids to breakfast and then the zoo, where an elephant painted pictures holding a brush in her trunk. Joya never asked about the rest of the weekend, knowing there would be times when Rob and his ex would be doing something with the kids and she didn't want to know about that.

She got ready for her morning walk, pulling on her University of Michigan sweatshirt this time of year—a tee-shirt with the same logo in warmer months—and was out the door with her homemade cassette tapes. Her walk took her through the historic neighborhoods of downtown Phoenix, the only part of this sprawling metropolis that resembled old Arizona.

Today she was listening to the driving blues of her friend, Hans Olson, a legend in these parts and a superstar in Europe, even if he hadn't gotten the kind of nationwide success he deserved.

His guitar and harmonica and infectious lyrics kept her moving, which was the whole point. Besides Tina Turner and Michael Jackson, nobody could get her ass down the sidewalk like Hans Olson.

She didn't hear Hans' words so much now as the words Rob had whispered in their bed. How she was supposed to "be careful?" Besides the obvious fact of not walking up to the guy and saying, "Hi, Sammy."

The words kept swirling. "Be careful...Dangerous....Please."

She was approaching the Burton Barr Public Library on Central Avenue, named in honor of the late Republican lawmaker even Democrats loved, when she heard the gunshot. Joya hit the sidewalk so hard, she bounced. The palms of both hands stung from the impact. Her left knee was gashed and bleeding. Her right knee wore a long scrape, like someone had tried to sandpaper off the skin. Joya realized she was crying, but didn't know if it was from pain or panic.

A twenty-something on a bike came to a quick stop, letting his bike drop as he ran to her.

"Ma'am, are you okay?"

Did she really look old enough to be called ma'am?

"I think they're shooting at me," Joya hysterically blurted out before she had time to think. It startled not only her, but her Samaritan. His eyes darted around to see if he was in the wrong place at the wrong time.

"Didn't you hear that shot?" She regained at least some composure.

The young man shook his head like he was clearing cobwebs. "No. That wasn't a shot. It was a car backfiring. I saw it. Black smoke pouring out the tailpipe. Cars like that shouldn't be allowed on our streets. Here, let me help you up."

Joya, coming back to her senses, felt foolish—a car backfired! Not an assassination attempt! Jeez, drama queen, let a little helpful suggestion from your boyfriend set you off.

A security guard from the library rushed up the sidewalk— he'd seen her hit the ground and unlocked the twenty-foot glass door to come to her aid.

"Are you okay? Oh, my, that's some nasty bruises. Oh, aren't you Joya Bonner? Miss Bonner, here, let me help you."

The twenty-something looked at her with new respect—she was *somebody*, but he had no idea who. Somebody who had reason to believe she was a target. He didn't want to know who she was. He wanted very much to be on his way.

He gratefully turned the somebody woman over to the library guard, picked up his bike, and rode off. Later, much later, when he realized who she was, he'd understand why she was worried.

The guard held Joya's arm as she steadied herself. "Come in—let's get that blood washed off. You've got dirt in that gash."

The guard served as a human crutch while she limped into the library that wouldn't be open to the public for hours. She eased down on a bench in the entryway. The wall was etched with private donors' names—hers among them. She waited for the guard to return from the restroom with wet paper towels.

She felt so stupid. So embarrassed. She better buck up like this was nothing. She took the paper towel and swabbed her knee, thanking the guard profusely.

"I'm such a clumsy cluck," she told him, hoping he'd been out of earshot for her hysteria. "Trip over my own feet! You're so kind to help me."

"Of course, Miss Bonner. Of course."

"You know, I'm coming back here tonight for Dinner in the Stacks." She tried to sound normal. "I've got a new dress. Sure glad it's long so nobody will see this mess." She laughed out loud and he chuckled with her.

Her right knee was already turning blue. The gash stopped bleeding. Her palms still stung.

The guard could feel her unease and tried to help: "I hear they're expecting six hundred people tonight. Best ever!"

"I know. We should raise a lot of money. Lord knows the library needs it."

They chatted a couple minutes. Joya stood up and tried out her legs, testing if she could make it home on her own.

"I could get someone to drive you home in a little while—I can't leave, I'm the only one here, but someone else is scheduled to work in about a half hour."

"I don't live far. I'm going to be okay. See, I can walk just fine. You've been so helpful. I thank you so much."

She walked as straight as she could while she knew he was still watching, then limped the rest of the way home—wiping away angry tears at her overreaction, her idiocy, and the realization that she was more scared than she knew.

She wouldn't mention any of this to Rob—or anyone else. This wasn't what "be careful" meant.

Normally after her walk she'd shower, mix up a banana-orange smoothie, drink a pot of French-pressed coffee, do the Saturday Sudoku puzzle in the *Republic* and then grab her African shopping basket for the Phoenix Farmer's Market downtown. Today she skipped the market to rest her legs, and steadied her nerves with a shot of Patron tequila. Cactus liquor was medicinal and she needed it today.

In her recliner, she pushed the remote control to bring up her taped shows: *The Young and the Restless, Sex and the City, The Sopranos.* Today she'd skip *The Sopranos.* But if she'd been quizzed on the shows before her eyes, she couldn't have recited a single plot line. She was busy thinking about Sammy, and Rob's revelations, and her need to get under control. She felt both thrilled and disturbed.

Here she was on the verge of a mega story. But to get to it, she had to trust a cop. Personal feelings or not, it was still tough to overcome her natural aversion to trusting a cop.

For most of America, the police were always the good guys. It was bred as respect for authority, twined with the belief that being on the side of the law was the only place to be. Of course, a steady diet of cop shows on TV showed they were always right, always catching bad guys and always forgiven any transgression because they were the good guys.

Joya knew there were lots of good cops—Rob was one of them—but she also knew the other side of that story, and it wasn't pretty.

Deceit, disrespect for the law, the ends justifying any means, protecting their own no matter what, destroying evidence, choking prisoners, inventing evidence, lying on the stand—these were not the sins most saw when they looked at a cop, but Joya could cite chapter and verse to prove that they were also part of some cops' DNA.

Sheriff Arpaio's publicity stunt over the fake bomb was just the latest evidence. She'd known for a long time that you couldn't always trust a cop—since she studied what really happened inside the Phoenix Police Department when the *Republic* crack investigative reporter Don Bolles was assassinated at noon on June 2, 1976.

Joya was still in high school when he was murdered, but when she moved to Arizona, she attended journalism workshops on his techniques and reporting tips. He'd loved taking new reporters under his wing, and telling his war stories about covering the Mafia and public corruption. He'd once written a series of articles detailing how the mob was moving into Arizona, taking over legitimate businesses, laundering money, killing people who got in their way. He was particularly distrustful of Emprise, the company that ran the dog tracks in Arizona.

He knew his investigations were dangerous, but that never stopped him. Couldn't have stopped him. He seemed to revel in the peril—it was the mark of a fearless reporter. But he also felt confident that the unwritten code would keep him out of harm's way—the mob code that said you never killed a cop or a reporter, because the repercussions were too severe. Scare them, beat them up, okay, but never kill them. At least that's what everyone thought until they killed Bolles.

Joya always wished she'd known Bolles, that she could have been one of his students. He was one of her idols—right up there with the first "muckraker," Ida Tarbell. As she nursed her bruised knee and bruised ego this Saturday morning, she thought of how he'd have handled this Sammy story. She smiled, thinking he'd be jumping with glee, much like she was.

Then she remembered something else they'd taught at those workshops. Don Bolles knew what "be careful" meant, and he took precautions so nobody could ambush him. Joya so clearly remembered that he stuck scotch tape on the hood of his car, always checking to be sure it wasn't broken by someone tampering with the engine. The tape was still on his white Datsun when it blew up at a hotel in downtown Phoenix. The precaution had been worthless because nobody tampered with his engine. They put the bomb under his car—right under his legs.

Joya let her mind page through that horrible day, which had been chronicled in newspapers across the nation. Bolles got a call from a dog breeder and small-time hood named John Adamson—he claimed to have information on a new Mafia scheme in Arizona. Bolles should have ignored it. He'd walked away from investigative work when he found his own newspaper wouldn't push for the reforms that were needed.

Instead, he was covering the Arizona Legislature—he joked that he'd gone from the sublime to the ridiculous—and, by all rights, should have told this Adamson guy he wasn't interested.

But even old dogs still like to hunt, and seasoned investigative reporters are like old dogs. He couldn't help himself. If there were something new he didn't know about, he wanted to know. Bolles agreed to the meet, demanding—yet another of his precautions—that it be in a public place. Adamson suggested a downtown hotel, and that sounded fine to Bolles. They'd meet at 11:30. Bolles hung around the hotel for a half hour before he gave up and left to find himself some lunch. That night—his wedding anniversary—he was going to a nice dinner with his wife before they took in the hottest new movie, *All the President's Men*. He got into his car and turned the key.

Bolles lived for eleven days after the bombing, as they amputated one limb after another. By the time he died on June 13, they'd taken both legs and an arm. The entire nation was reeling in disbelief. All the time, the police chief of Phoenix was swearing his men and women officers would find the killers and bring them to justice. The chief had personally made that pledge to the packed *Republic* newsroom.

Every story Joya ever read about Don Bolles included the awe that he named his killers as he lay dying.

"They finally got me. The Mafia. Emprise. Find John [Adamson]."

It was years before anyone knew that while Bolles lay dying, the police department's Organized Crime Bureau was purging files on some of these very people, as well as the leading politicians of Arizona. They shredded some files; threw others away; renumbered their file system trying to cover up the deletions. Nobody ever explained why they were protecting the very people Bolles had named in his last cogent breath, but protecting them they were.

Joya always regretted that she hadn't discovered the deceit. Her paper's competition, the *Phoenix New Times*, broke that story. Besides her own alternative weekly, nobody much cared why there was a purge or what was lost or why the investigative unit had gone to such trouble to cover it all up. The *Republic* ignored the story—their own guy had been murdered, and they ignored the story! Television stations took their cues on what was news from the *Republic*, so they were mute, too. Besides, TV reporters in those days were hired for their good looks and stay-in-place hair, not their investigative skills.

What should have been a permanent stain on the Phoenix Police Department—should have opened up new investigations and maybe solved the question of who ordered Bolles' assassination—went away because the media didn't push. Whoever or whatever convinced the *Republic* to stonewall the shredding assured that Bolles' murderer went free. Bolles himself would have laughed. "Business as usual," he'd have said.

For Joya, it was the straw that broke the camel's back. Kill a reporter. Get away with it. She had never trusted a cop since. Her disdain for the *Arizona Republic* was irreversible.

Now she was in a horrible position. Could she trust the cop she was dating? Could she trust his higher-ups, who would have to sign off on the deal? Could she trust a law enforcement agency that had betrayed Don Bolles? Sure, those guys were retired now, but did they leave a lingering taint? Could the same kind of corruptions happen today? She had trouble thinking of anything else.

She was relieved when her heavy eyes led into a long Saturday nap. She dreamed of celebrations, not murder.

She awoke and scolded herself. "Shake it off, Joya. Shake it off." She watered plants in the backyard and filled the bird feeders and grabbed a banana before she got herself ready for the library dinner. She dressed in her beaded black gown; she acted like everything was fine.

Joya's usual Sunday had its own rituals, even if they didn't resemble the way she'd been raised. For the first seventeen years of her life in Northville, North Dakota, Sundays meant St. Vincent's Catholic Church, a magnificent cathedral with two-story stained-glass windows and elaborate statues of the saints. The Stations of the Cross weren't pictures on the wall, like in many Phoenix churches, but carved statutes depicting the agony of the crucifixion. As a little girl, she'd loved going into the church alone and kneeling at the communion rail that separated the congregation from the altar and the priest. She'd wanted to be on that altar, to help serve the mass, but girls weren't allowed. Only altar boys. That had changed, but too late for her.

Now the railing was gone and the priest faced the congregation—but none of those changes had been enough to keep Joya Bonner a "capital C" Catholic. Still, she had a soft spot in her heart for the church where she made her First Communion, walking down the aisle in a white dress with a white veil, like a bride. There were a dozen pictures of her from that day, and an ornate certificate that her mother framed. St. Vincent's was the church where she made her confirmation, and where, as a teenager, she dreamed she'd be married.

But life had taken a different turn. Sundays weren't spent in church, but with a group of friends over brunch. Little Northville couldn't hold her like big Phoenix could. For the last decade, she'd worked for an irascible weekly where she had made a name for herself as a journalist no one messed with.

Still every Sunday, Joya dutifully called home to her folks. Most of the time, she was the one doing the sharing—telling them about her week and what was going on in Phoenix. Their news was usually pretty skimpy—what Grandma was up to and anything new with the aunts and uncles, how Dad's garden was progressing or if the leaves had turned. It was normally the conversation of people whose lives were going along quite nicely with no traumas to report. But that wasn't the visit they had this Sunday.

"You aren't going to believe the tragedy here," her mother began and Joya held her breath, praying it wasn't someone in the family. It wasn't, but it came close enough.

"It's Amber Schlener—Nettie's daughter? You went to her basketball game last Christmas. Remember?"

Of course Joya remembered. The Schleners weren't close relatives, but Gertie Bach was a cousin to her grandma, and Gertie was like a second mother to Amber. The girl had visited the folks' house many times, and there was no debate that she could net a basketball. Joya expected to hear she'd broken her leg and couldn't play on this year's team.

"What happened?" She shifted the phone from one hand to the other.

"She's dead."

The words hung like a sinker weight on a fishing line. Joya wasn't sure she'd heard right.

"Dead? What do you mean, dead?"

"She overdosed on dope," her father said—the man who always cut to the bottom line.

"Amber was on dope?" Joya yelled into the phone.

"She wasn't ON dope, Ralph. She only took it once they said and she died. Friday night at a dance out on the Jacobson place. Her boyfriend's still in a coma."

"WHAT?" None of this made sense. Kids don't overdose on dope in Northville, North Dakota. They don't die from taking something once; they don't even take anything. They get drunk, maybe—okay, they probably get drunk—but that was as far as it would go. Besides, where would somebody in that little town get any dope? There certainly wasn't a market there, and she'd never heard of a drug dealer who hung around where there wasn't a profit.

Dope in Northville? A hometown of garden trinkets, statutes of the Virgin Mary, wooden flower baskets, fiberglass deer,

bowling balls covered with glass beads to make a "gazing ball."
A town filled with backyard gardens—tomatoes, beans, beets,
cucumbers, cabbages the size of basketballs, zucchini as big as
softball bats. She never, ever, thought of that town and saw a
dirty drug dealer.

"This doesn't make any sense." Her voice faltered.

"The town is just devastated," Maggie Bonner agreed. "The
funeral's Wednesday at St. Vincent's. Our circle has the funeral
dinner."

"I've got to call Gertie." Joya knew the old woman would
be shattered.

"Oh, please do, but wait till after the funeral."

"Okay, I'll call her next week. Give her a hug for me." They
were all so far away.

"They're doing the visitation at the high school. In the gym.
Where she played basketball. I hope that wakes those kids up."
Ralph thought kicks to the gut were a good lesson for the teens
of Northville.

"Start at the beginning," Joya begged. Maggie and Ralph,
talking over one another, filled her in as best they could, but
they really didn't know much. They didn't remember what kind
of dope it had been.

"What difference does it make? Dope is dope," Ralph pronounced.

"Where did it come from?" Joya wanted to know.

Now Ralph was full of information. "It's that Crabapple
kid—he's the pusher. You know, we went to the sheriff about
him last year when we first heard he was pushing dope, but the
sheriff didn't do nothing. We're waiting to see if he does anything
now. He better."

"This is so sad," Joya said. They all commiserated together
about what a shame, what a loss.

"Boy, I never thought I'd hear something like this out of
Northville," Joya declared.

"Neither did I," her father said.

"What is this world coming to?" her mother wanted to know.

"I hope they put that punk away," Joya offered.

"They better," her dad said again.

"I'm sure they'll get him this time," her mother declared.

"Yeah, sure," her father scoffed.

As Joya hung up, she cringed at how ominous her father's voice sounded. He had good reason to hate the sheriff before this, and now—oh, for Ralph Bonner to say "I told you so" when a pretty little girl was dead. That had to be killing him. He wasn't the kind of man to let this lie. His lifelong buddies weren't, either. The sheriff better take care of this because who knows what they'd do to him. Make him pay one way or another. See this crime was punished.

But Joya's heart wasn't on revenge, it was on sadness for the loss of a sweet young girl who shouldn't have died. It astonished her that this could have happened. In Northville, of all places.

The hearts that were broken belonged to people she knew and loved. Nettie, who'd already lost so much and now this. Poor old Gertie, whose grief had to be unbearable. Her mom and dad. Neighbors. Cousins. Her mind swept the few streets of Northville, and Joya couldn't imagine a single citizen who wasn't heartbroken.

Even if there'd been time—even if she could have gotten off work on the spur of the moment and could afford a last-minute flight to Fargo, Joya wouldn't have gone home for the funeral. Not now. Not with the biggest story of her life staring her in the face.

She'd send a condolence card and next week she'd call Gertie, and for now, she'd say a prayer for Amber.

Chapter Five

Wednesday, October 20, 1999

Gertie Bach was always the first to arrive at the church basement the days the Judith Circle handled the funeral dinner.

As Circle president, she was in charge and took her responsibilities seriously. By the time everyone else arrived two hours before the funeral mass, she'd have everything set out for the makings of the casserole they always served.

But nobody was expecting Gertie today—not when it was Amber they were cooking for. That hadn't stopped Gertie from coming even earlier than usual. At seven a.m. she pulled up to the side of St. Vincent's Catholic Church—the tallest building in Northville, next to the water tower.

She'd driven the eight blocks from her two-bedroom home without the usual anxiety she felt lately whenever she was behind the wheel. She'd have to give up the car soon, but really, she'd never had an accident and the few close calls weren't her fault, anyway. Losing her independence, losing her mobility, becoming one of those old people who has to be hauled around everywhere, always bothering someone…Gertie dreaded that day. Whenever she put the key in the ignition, she said a special prayer to St. Christopher to get her wherever she was going without hurting anyone. Today there wasn't a single soul on Main Street during her trip to the church, which was a blessing, since Gertie was operating only on autopilot.

She had gotten into the car in her driveway without bemoaning, as she did every single day, that Leo Marx hadn't put in his garden this year, which was a sure sign he was ready to die. She'd started the car without her prayer and if St. Christopher—who wasn't even officially a saint anymore, but Gertie didn't care—were indeed watching over her, he was disappointed he wasn't called on to help today.

Gertie pulled out of the driveway without seeing the Johnson boy's car parked at Linda Myers house again, and her not even divorced yet. She'd made the first turn without noting the White Church was almost through the regular painting that gave it its name. She was halfway down Main Street without noticing the drug store remodeling she'd been monitoring all summer. She never saw the two pickups she could have hit in front of Harley's Hardware that always opened early for the farmers. Her friend Rose had a prize-winning garden across from the church that was in full bloom—the Peggy Lee roses were particularly wonderful this year—but Gertie didn't see a single petal. She hadn't even looked in the car's mirror to realize she'd forgotten to comb out her roller curls. She looked like she was on her way to the beauty parlor.

Gertie entered through the church basement door and made her way immediately to the back steps, climbing slowly to the sanctuary. This was automatic, too, since her memory banks knew these steps like a pair of old shoes. Once her cane hit the marble floor of the main church, its echo brought her back to the present moment.

She found herself at the back of the massive, ornate church where she'd been baptized eighty-two years ago, a church she'd cleaned and tended and fussed over all these years, from which she'd buried her parents and would herself be buried, not too many months from now.

Her eyes widened and she made a pitiful sound from the back of her throat, because she didn't know how she'd gotten here. For a second or two— a blissful, lovely, comforting second or two—she couldn't remember why she'd come this morning.

She wouldn't get any more gifts like that today, when all the pain came flooding back. She slowly, noisily, thumbed her way down the center aisle and over to the side altar where the Virgin Mary balanced on a pedestal. Gertie could never look at that statue without seeing the carved marble altar that used to surround Mary, an altar torn away in a modernization from Vatican II that she neither understood nor favored. The Virgin's shrine looked so bare to her now.

Nine candles were already burning beneath Mary's statue when Gertie put her three dollars into the metal box and lit hers. Even at this moment, she knew she couldn't properly kneel, so she half-sat, half-kneeled in the first pew. She closed her eyes and got no farther than "Hail Mary, full of grace," before the tears came again.

Gertie Bach said her own private rosary through sobs and sighs before she opened her eyes. She took her time, because she never said the rosary in the rote way many did, the sing-song way that comes naturally when you're saying the same prayer fifty times. She said each word as an individual prayer to be certain the Blessed Mother was pleased with her efforts.

The Catholic Church has some lovely prayers, but the one that speaks to its core—the one that is only Catholic and is the first prayer a member of the faithful utters in a time of need—is the Hail Mary. Gertie had never once worried that her Protestant friends thought Catholics were a little nutty over Mary. She knew the truth. The Mother of God didn't create this church. She didn't name it or give it its rules. No member of her gender had any real decision-making rights in its hierarchy. But the Mother of God was the one who got things done and every Catholic knew it.

So Gertie prayed from her heart to the Blessed Mother for the soul of Amber Schlener.

It was getting on eight a.m. when she made her way down the back stairs to the church basement's kitchen.

Maggie Bonner arrived promptly at eight, astonished to see Gertie in her bib apron. "Oh God, Gertie, we don't expect you to be here today. You have to be with the family."

Gertie waved her off and kept organizing the ingredients like a general getting her troops in order. Maggie deposited the plastic sacks full of fresh buns from the bakery on the service counter, and walked over to her old friend.

"Gertie, I'm so sorry." She took the woman in her arms. "Joya sends her love. She'd be here if she could." She kindly stretched the truth.

Gertie tried to hide her face, hoping her eyes weren't too red and the tears would hold back. But the crying she'd already done this day—done last night at the wake, done the day before when she sat with Nettie, done since she first heard and collapsed on her living room floor—that kind of crying leaves an unmistakable swelling around the eyes.

"I know," Maggie cooed, as she rubbed her friend's back. "It's so hard. I just can't believe it. It's such a shame. She was such a special girl." They were the identical words Maggie had whispered to Nettie the night before at the visitation in the high school gym. Oh, that had been terrible—all those teenagers wailing in grief. All those townsfolk crying in agony. Maggie had never been to a visitation where emotions were so raw, so wrenching.

Gertie kept nodding against Maggie's shoulder. And then, as though her breath came from the pit of her lungs, she straightened up to her full five-feet-five-inches, wiped her nose with the handkerchief from her apron pocket, and gave a closed-mouth smile. "Come on, we have a lot of hungry people to feed today. We need to buck up."

"You're sure you want to be here?" Maggie probed again.

Gertie gave a definitive nod. "It's the last thing I can do for her." Her voice caught.

"Of course. Of course." Maggie smiled and wiped her own tears with her fingers.

There was another reason. Being here in the basement preparing dinner meant Gertie couldn't go out to the cemetery to bury

Amber. Circle members always shed their aprons and climbed the back stairs for the funeral, but the minute the casket was out the front door, they came back down to finish the meal that would be ready when mourners returned to the church.

Maggie herself was glad she wouldn't have to witness that unbearably sad moment when Amber was put into the ground, so she could imagine how much Gertie wanted to avoid it. Better to visit the grave later, when it was all filled in and grass was growing over the mound of dirt and the headstone was in place—it was hard enough then. Maggie had no doubt Gertie would visit Amber in the cemetery a mile out of town. Just like Maggie visited her own people, who'd been buried there since 1897.

Maggie blanched as she noticed Gertie's roller-curler hair. The old woman was so distracted, she'd never realize the mistake, so Maggie stepped in to fix the problem: "The least I can do for you today is comb out your hair, dear friend."

Gertie looked puzzled, but one touch of her head and she realized. Maggie grabbed a comb from her purse and quickly turned the roller shapes into a nice hairstyle.

"Are those all the buns?" Gertie covered her embarrassment and got back on track.

"No, I've got more in the car, but I couldn't carry them all in one load. We ordered five hundred. Do you think that will be enough?" Gertie thought it would.

"I've also got my Jello-O salad and my cake." Maggie started for the door.

"Did you bring your pickles?" Gertie did a mental inventory of Maggie's contribution.

"Oh damn, I forgot my pickles. I better run home and get them."

"No need. If the others come through, we'll have enough. Besides, there's a couple jars left over from the Esther Circle, but I'm sure those girls won't mind if we used them today." Maggie agreed.

Over the next half-hour, the other eight women of the Judith Circle straggled in, each bringing her own cake or pan of bars and

Jello-O salad. Every woman arrived with a jar of her homemade pickles, much to Maggie's relief. All blinked in surprise when they saw Gertie with her apron over her black dress, but Maggie signaled them not to make a fuss.

Even though the entire circle understood the usual hotdish recipe was being tripled for the first time in memory, they were astonished by the mound of ingredients Gertie set out on the counter. Each woman walked through the kitchen, marveling at how gigantic sixty pounds of hamburger looked, or how twenty-seven cans of tomato paste all set in a row resembled a battalion.

Each and every one said a few words about the shame of it all and the pain of it all and those things you say when you don't know what to say but need to say something.

Gertie shook the dime jar to get everyone's attention. "This is no time to lollygag, ladies. We have a lot of work to do." Everyone hopped to and took on a job.

"What is that?" the newest member asked, pointing to the mason jar half full of dimes.

"Gertie, tell her the story," Maggie yelled, hoping the distraction would help the old woman.

"You watch today. An old woman in a flat straw hat will come in and sit at the back table. She'll eat three plates of food and stuff rolls in her purse. Don't you pay any mind. That's Cissy German. She comes to every funeral. She always leaves us a dime. The dimes go in that jar. It's our 'tip jar.'" Gertie almost giggled as she finished.

Maggie started cutting the nine pounds of bacon into small pieces. Angie Krump grabbed the eight bunches of celery for dicing. Norma Stine started opening, by hand, the twenty-four tall cans of tomato juice because Wanda Bach was already using the electric opener on eighty-four cans of soup. That left the onions for Mary Entangle, who complained she always got this job, and nobody bothered to tell her that if she wasn't always late, she'd get a better task.

The rest of the circle took over the dining room, setting out paper placemats with napkins, forks, knives, and glasses. Salt and pepper shakers were scattered on the tables, and nobody was too happy to see most of them needed refilling—another item to raise at the combined circle meeting next month. The silk flowers K.C.'s dad had donated years ago went out, each sitting on a paper doily. So did the mismatched collection of toothpick holders—one a tiny beer barrel, another a wee lantern, one a shot glass with the words "Las Vegas." Gertie, for one, hated them. They looked tawdry on a funeral lunch table, but nobody dared leave them off and nobody had bothered finding the pretty collectible ones that were classier.

General Motors could learn a thing or two about assembly-line precision from watching the Judith Circle get ready for a five hundred-plate funeral dinner.

As busy as they were—as solemn the occasion—any notion that these women did their assigned tasks in silence is nonsense. Except when she's actually measuring an ingredient or double-checking the recipe, silence isn't a normal part of a woman's cooking routine. If she's alone, she's likely to be talking to herself, reciting the steps she's taking or counting out the measure and scolding herself when she spills the flour—"Oh, you sloppi-goose." But when she's with a group, this is the time to "visit," to be polite about it, or gossip if not.

Their first choice was not to talk about why they were here or how awful the next few hours were going to be or how could poor Nettie ever pull through this, so they talked about the things that gave them a reason to keep going.

"Did you know I'm going to be a grandmother again?" Mary offered the news that always brought joyful congratulations. "My third!"

Angie said that was nothing, she already had seven, which set everyone to counting. By the time they were done, they figured the grandmothers in the crowd—excluding Gertie and her sister, Wanda, of course—could claim a total of sixteen. The younger women, who had a total of twenty-one children yet to raise, were silently praying for the relief of grandmotherhood.

Maggie reported she expected Joya home for Christmas. Norma said they weren't going to Arizona this winter because Bernard's dad wasn't doing well. Angie said her family planned a winter reunion and she expected seventy-five. One of the town girls reminded everyone there was a wedding dance this weekend at the Legion Hall and knowing it was the Schultz clan, everyone expected a good time and a plentiful bar.

A farm wife said her husband was beside himself because corn prices had fallen again. "He says what good is it to spend four dollars a bushel growing corn when it's selling for three dollars?" Everyone voiced their agreement.

Gertie used to have her own contributions to these brag-fests, even though she'd never had children of her own. But she could tell about "my Amber," the girl who fulfilled all her mothering fantasies. She'd cared for Amber since she was born, as Nettie fought off the depression of her husband's death and then searched for jobs to support them. Gertie had been there through the knee scrapes and the first bike ride; she read her books and then collected books for the voracious reader Amber became. She'd taught the girl to sew and crochet, stood up for Johnny when no one else would, supervised Amber's homework, and never missed a basketball game. "You should see the dress my Amber is making," she bragged while making one funeral dinner. "My Amber is learning to make pierogies, and she's pretty good," she bragged at another. Everyone knew Amber wanted to teach third grade because Gertie had told them. Again and again. She and Amber had started collecting the new state quarters— they already had Delaware, New Jersey, and Connecticut—and Amber vowed to collect all fifty over the next ten years and use them to teach her third graders history. North Dakota's State Quarter wasn't scheduled to be released until 2006, and Gertie hoped she'd still be here to see that happen.

But that didn't make any difference anymore. Now, those stories were done. Now she had nothing—and nobody. If she let herself dwell on that, she knew her heart would stop.

Gertie knew it was coming, and she vowed she wouldn't listen when the women got around to talking about what everyone in town was talking about. *I'll just close my ears*, she said to herself, as she turned red meat into browned hamburger.

The women in the dining room—women out of earshot of Gertie—started it. But eventually, everyone joined in. And of course, Gertie listened.

"I don't even know what Ecstasy is," one of them said, and neither did anyone else, but somebody heard it was supposed to make you "feel good."

"I hear the entire class took it."

"Not everyone, but most of them."

"What were they doing?"

"Somebody said it was just a goof. Their senior prank. They thought all the kids in the cities were doing it, so they'd try it too."

"It's supposed to be safe."

"You're not supposed to die from it."

"Who got it for them?"

"Where did it come from?"

"Can you believe there's stuff like that *here?*"

Someone—doing a quick survey to be sure there were no Roths in this circle—offered, "That Johnny Roth was the one behind it, I'm told. He got it from some kid in town who's selling drugs. Can you believe that? We've got a drug dealer in town!"

"It's the kid they call Crabapple." That was Maggie Bonner, who'd come into the dining room to share some of her knowledge. "He's one of those Harding boys—the one Huntsie hired at the body shop."

"Oh, my God. I know him. He worked on my car!" Angie spit out the words like she was guilty of something for having the boy fix her transmission.

"It's Darryl. I think he was the youngest—they farmed the old Hermann place north of town." Norma could always be counted on to know the location of any family in these parts. "But they lost it in the eighties—remember, his dad shot himself in the barn the day of the auction?"

"That's *him?*"

"Yeah. They had four boys in that family—three girls—they all left after the foreclosure. Except this one. He was just a little boy then. Stayed on with his grandma, but she's gone now. He lives north of town on the old Johnson place."

"How old is he?" Nobody knew for sure, but Norma guessed in his early twenties.

"You know, they suspected him for a long time but Sheriff Potter just sat on his hands." That was Maggie again, offering only a thimble of what she knew.

"They did? Who?"

Maggie stayed quiet, thinking it best not to tell too much just now. But she did offer the latest news. "Oh, he skipped right away, that's what I heard."

"He left town?" Angie wondered if her Earl knew.

"Yeah, they say he was at the dance and he ran as soon as he saw what was happening. He's not only a pusher, he's a coward."

"If he's smart, he'll never come back here."

"I hate to think what would happen to him if he did."

"I hope they catch him and put him away forever."

"Better that than letting someone get their hands on him." That caused a pause, as each woman of the Judith Circle imagined a town full of someones.

In the kitchen, Gertie had big pots of water boiling as she finished browning the meat. "Bacon," she yelled, and Maggie rushed back to deliver the bits. They spit as they hit the hot cast-iron pan. Gertie wielded her wooden spoon like a baton, letting the bacon cook, but not crisp. When it was just right, it joined the hamburger in one of the three electric roasters that would be brimming before Mass.

"I wonder how Huntsie's feeling," Angie continued. "He couldn't have known or he'd never have hired that kid."

"I feel sorry for him. You know Huntsie. He'll take some blame."

"Celery," Gertie ordered, still pretending she wasn't listening in. She got her wish, adding the pieces to the film of bacon grease she'd left in the pan.

Maggie helped finish up the onions—Mary never could get them done in time—and was ready when they were announced.

"Anyone know how Johnny's doing?"

"He's still in a coma. They're not sure he'll come out of it."

"You know, he loved Amber. This will kill him."

"Nettie was right to try and keep her daughter away from that boy."

"Oh, I don't think he's a bad kid. Maybe a little wild. But he's really not a bad kid."

"Well, how about that uncle of his? Always yelling about the government and refusing to pay his taxes. I think he's nuts."

"Yes. LeRoy Roth is nuts. That, I know for sure."

The celery was soft and the onions were barely transparent when they went into a roaster. From one of her big pots, Gertie used a king-sized strainer to capture the macaroni that had started to cook. This moment was crucial, because if the macaroni went even a minute too long, it would be too mushy by the time it finished baking. Nobody liked mushy hotdish.

"That poor girl. She had so much to live for. And to die like that…"

"What a shame."

"What a waste."

Gertie made certain all her roasters had equal ingredients before she dumped the bags of frozen mixed vegetables into the pots of boiling water. They needed three minutes in their bath. "Are the soups mixed?" she asked over her shoulder and Wanda assured her they were, although there were two cans of celery soup yet to open.

Somewhere in this kitchen there was a written recipe for the dish that was consuming so much attention. If anyone bothered to consult it, it wasn't Gertie.

But for the curious, there was a piece of lined tablet paper with handwritten instructions on how to feed a funeral crowd. Probably any church anywhere in North Dakota had a recipe like this. The one in Northville was smeared with grease and tomato sauce, but then, few favorite recipes anywhere in town didn't wear the evidence of their popularity.

At the top of the page, printed in neat capital letters, was the unappetizing title of the casserole served at every St. Vincent's funeral:

FUNERAL HOTDISH

Chapter Six

Wednesday, October 20, 1999

The St. Vincent's funeral bell started ringing at nine forty-five a.m.

Most churches don't even have such a bell anymore. If they ring any at all, it's their regular bell with tuned chimes. But St. Vincent's still has a twelve-hundred-pound A-flat bell that's been devoted to funerals since 1909, when they shipped it all the way from the Menelly Co. of Troy, New York.

It's so loud you can hear it all over town. It's such an awful sound that anybody who hears it feels its sadness—and relives the moment it rang for one of theirs. If the Catholic Church wants to transform death into a joyous celebration of life in heaven, somebody better tell the people of St. Vincent's they have to get a new bell first.

There's no joy in the single stroke it makes. One long note. Eerie reverberation. That sound alone can bring tears to your eyes. And in this town, you always know whose casket is being carried up the front steps as the sad bell sings its final song.

Amber's family arrived behind the funeral coach—K.C. never let anyone call it a hearse—in a white limousine. K.C. had ordered it special from the funeral home in Wahpeton. He thought it more appropriate than the black limo he owned.

The lavender casket gleamed as it was carried up the steps, the boys and girls of the Class of 2000 gathered around it—the boys in suits, the girls in their best Sunday dresses. The boys took hold of the casket handles, while some girls walked in front of it and the rest behind. One boy had to guide Maxine because she was so broken up, she couldn't walk on her own.

Nettie walked immediately after them, on Dennis' arm. As the procession moved down the main aisle, Nettie's family was overcome to see every single seat filled by their friends and neighbors. All except the first five rows on each side, which were reserved for the immediate family. Nettie was too blinded by grief to see any of it.

When the casket reached the altar, K.C. opened the lid and repositioned the spray of pink roses with "Beloved Daughter" on the sash. To the right was a standing bouquet of pink roses with "Cherished Granddaughter." On the left, another arrangement—this one of mixed flowers—with "Wonderful Niece." A basket of daisies sat on the floor with "Beautiful Cousin." Then it became impossible to distinguish one from the next in the wall of flowers that filled the front of the church.

Amber looked pretty again. Everyone remarked at the visitation that K.C had done a wonderful job. She was wearing a white silk dress she'd been making from a Vogue pattern. It wasn't hemmed and the zipper was still pinned in place, but K.C. had assured Nettie that didn't matter. On her right shoulder was a corsage of pink roses. Johnny Roth's mother had sent them to the girl she always hoped would tame her son. Everyone thought it was damn nice of Nettie to let her daughter wear it.

The funeral bell kept tolling until the entire family was in its seats. For the next hour, Father John tried to bring comfort and words of salvation to a gathering that drowned him out with their sobs. His voice even broke once.

Anyone peeking into St. Vincent's on this day, would have seen tears in the eyes of men you'd never imagine knew how to cry. Would have seen teenage girls shuddering in grief as they clung to one another, while macho teenage boys hid wet Kleenexes. Would have seen women biting their lips trying not to let their sorrow add to the grief of others. Would have seen an entire town weep—a safe little place in safe North Dakota with its lowest-crime-rate-in-the-nation and its fixation on family values.

But that wasn't strange under the circumstances. Youth plucked from its glory is always sad, in any setting. Why should one so young be cheated out of life when so many already old were willing to leave this all behind? Who wouldn't cry losing a pretty girl who'd never have children and make a beautiful home or even dance at her senior prom?

So the curious spying on St. Vincent's that day would have been touched, but not surprised, at the public show of grief.

Yet that's not all that would have been noticed.

Anyone paying attention—anyone who's own eyes didn't cloud up or weren't distracted searching for a hankie—anyone really looking would have been frightened by the fury behind so many wet eyes.

Our Father, who art in heaven.

"What a goddamned shame."

"I don't think they'll ever get over this."

"Oh, Amber, the prom won't be the same without you."

"Geez, Spud made it. I thought he was on a long haul."

"Leona will make a profit this month. I've never seen so many flowers."

Hallowed be thy name.

"This shit has got to stop."

"Did I turn off the iron?"

"Richard, our daughter is in heaven with you. Wish I was there, too."

"What's left for Nettie now? Oh, that poor woman."

"I never want to be buried. I'm going to be cremated."

What is this world turning into?

Thy kingdom come, thy will be done, on earth as it is in heaven.

"What's she going to do with Amber's clothes? Please, not Goodwill."

"I've got to stop and get a part for the tractor."

"This is going to kill Grandma and Grandpa. They doted on that girl."

"We bought all that nail polish. Maybe her mother will give it to me."

"I didn't put my life on the line in Korea for a punk to ruin our town."

Give us this day our daily bread and forgive us our trespasses.

"This isn't going to happen to me. I'll never take that stuff again."

"Shirley brought her whole brood. One, two, three, four, five, six now."

"Everybody's here. Lutherans, Protestants. Methodists."

"It isn't right that an old man buries his granddaughter."

"You should have seen our daughter play basketball. She was good!"

"Amber loved wearing her dad's old school jacket."

"That fucking sheriff."

As we forgive those who trespass against us.

"She always was a good-looking girl. Even when she was chubby."

"What do the kids say? This sucks."

"I fought her over Johnny. But she wouldn't listen."

"They're hauling the trailer away tomorrow. Finally. Thank God."

"I used my egg money to buy Amber's First Communion veil."

And lead us not into temptation, but deliver us from evil.

"I'm going to get that guy. I'm gonna get him."

"Damn, the Catholics have a big church."

"I don't want people looking at me when I'm dead."

"Do they have to burn incense? I hate that smell."

"I'm glad Johnny is still in a coma. He couldn't live through this."

"Oh, God, why? Why did you take my husband and my daughter?"

"That could be my girl. You try to protect them, but you can't, really."

Amen.

What words best describe a cemetery?

Neat. Orderly. Eerie. Dreary. Places you go only when you have to—and even sometimes when you should, you don't.

Never portrayed as welcoming. Or pretty. Not unless you've been to the one the Catholics have outside Northville. Nothing dreary about this place, or scary, either.

They still tell the story about the little girl who lived on the farm across the road years ago who liked to play here. One of her games was to decorate every grave with the lilacs that separate the cemetery from the wheat field. She'd always put the first flowers on her grandfather's grave—a man killed by drunk drivers as he walked to work years before this child was born. It would take her four days of picking and hauling to put a flower on every single grave. The groundskeeper had a fit the first time it happened. But when he figured out what was going on, he thought it was so dear he let it go, even though it meant extra work every time he had to pick up all the dead blooms.

St. Vincent's Calvary Cemetery is that kind of resting place.

It covers a small hill—a geographic feature pretty unusual in this tabletop-flat part of the Red River Valley. For some reason, there's a little hill out here and that's where the first Catholics decided to put their cemetery. The Protestant version lies on a flat piece of real estate on the way and it suffers as much from comparison as from its plainness.

The Catholics put a low rock wall all the way around their cemetery and fancy iron gates at the entrance. Nobody remembers the gates ever being closed and they're rusted in place by now. The cemetery rises in front of you as you drive up the long entrance, the road splitting around a giant marble altar flanked by two towering alabaster angels. Christ on the cross dominates the altar. You could say Mass out here, but nobody remembers anyone doing that. Mostly, people just wander around it, admiring the beautiful angels that were imported from Germany decades ago. It's such a charming spot that young girls in town have been known to fantasize about getting married under the alabaster angels. Adults just laugh, never admitting those aren't new thoughts.

A straight line of evergreens marches down the right border of the cemetery, giving a crisp demarcation. Someone decades ago thought a place like this should have a stately look. Whoever he was won only half the battle. You can bet it was a good woman who demanded the left border be soft and fluffy, where purple and white lilacs bloom their heads off every spring.

Scattered here and there all over the hill are large ash and black walnut trees. The best spots are at the top of the hill. The oldest families have them. As you enter, you can't tell that the hill slopes down the back, with just one narrow road giving you access to the separate part where the suicides are buried. That isn't hallowed ground.

Amber Schlener was laid to rest beside her father near the top of the hill. Even without a tree, it was a lovely spot anyway. Her great-grandparents were two plots down, under the large family stone. There was space for grandma and grandpa someday. Her mother's people were across the way. Nettie didn't notice, but her sisters did, that the Schlener plots were now filled up, Amber taking the spot that was supposed to be Nettie's someday. Her sisters wondered where she'd find a final resting place.

Peter Wavers dug the grave the day before, and set up a white tent over the open hole. It was surrounded by a metal frame with a hydraulic lift, waiting to hold the casket. Green indoor-outdoor carpeting camouflaged the mound of dirt on the other side of the hole—now covered with bouquets from the church, which had been rushed out here in the back of K.C.'s station wagon by his younger sons. White plastic chairs had been set up on one side of the grave for the immediate family.

A lot of the men stayed back, some having a smoke, all keeping their voices down, as Father said the final prayers that mercifully ended this ritual.

"I want that son of a bitch to pay." Nobody would remember who spoke the words first, but it didn't matter because they were thick on every man's lips.

"He ran. I don't even know where he is."

"We could find him."

"Maybe he'll never come back."

"But then he's just some other town's problem? That doesn't seem right."

"If Crabapple ever comes back to this town…"

But everyone suspected he would—back to the town where he was reared and where his constant thievery of Mrs. Stein's apples earned him a nickname that would forever stick.

"That family never did count for much. And he's been a bad apple since he was a kid." Nobody caught the irony of that statement.

"We've got to nail him this time. Last time, Sheriff Potter

turned a blind eye because he said there wasn't any evidence. We've got to get the evidence."

"What kind of evidence does that shithead need?" This was Earl Krump, whose temper was never far below his skin. "The son of a bitch has been dealing drugs for two years and everybody knows it. Why can't they do a stakeout or something and catch him pushing shit to our kids? He's too damn lazy, that's why. He'd rather arrest the kids for speeding than get the bastard who's selling them speed."

There wasn't a man in that cluster that didn't share Earl's rising blood pressure.

"And if that still doesn't do it, we've got to do something."

"We can't let him get away with it again."

It wasn't an idle threat, but it wasn't a lethal one, either. As every one of these men would eventually swear to their wives, "We just wanted justice. That's all."

Chapter Seven

Wednesday, October 20—Sunday, December 12, 1999

The longer he stayed stoned, the more Darryl "Crabapple" Harding convinced himself everything would be alright.

He'd been scared enough to run that Friday night, when he first watched Johnny stiffen and fall to the floor, hitting hard on the wooden planks of the hayloft. Seconds later, he'd seen Amber crumple like a rag doll whose stuffing had been sucked out. Shit. What went wrong? Whatever it was, it wasn't good. Crabapple never liked to be around when things weren't good.

He was the first one down the wooden stairs, running to his pickup and stopping only briefly at his house to pick up a few clothes and his stash before hightailing it to his cousin's apartment in Minneapolis. During the four-hour drive, he kept telling himself, "There's nothing really wrong. There's nothing really wrong. They just had a bad reaction. Everything's going to be okay. Just hang low a couple days. That's all."

But there was this gnawing pain in his gut, because this felt too much like all the other bad breaks he'd had his whole life. If Crabapple's life were a poker game, he never got a full house. Even in the rummy games he used to play with his grandma, he never got a wild card. He was a boy who didn't know the softness of love—Grandma had tried, but she was so old and so tired when she got saddled with him. He never had a lot of friends. He never had idle time because he'd supported himself since he was a kid.

Girls weren't drawn to him, although if you looked closely, he had a cute crooked smile. But his eyes were too watery blue and his hands too dirty. He smelled of motor oil and didn't own a decent suit. Except for the attention he got selling drugs, he wasn't a kid most paid any mind to. He'd gotten used to the loneliness. Wasn't so bad. He had his Schlitz and drugs, his hunting and fishing. He got a real high when he pulled a big walleye out of the Baker slough or bagged a deer. Those were the kinds of things a man had to do on his own anyway.

Crabapple arrived at Ben's apartment in the wee hours of Saturday, finding the Friday night party wasn't yet over. A half-dozen folks were sprawled around the one-bedroom apartment littered with beer cans, empty whiskey bottles, ashtrays overflowing. A few warbled while a guy tried to play a guitar. Others were making-out. Ben was sitting on the kitchen counter, trying not to fall off. One couple was having sex in the corner.

Man, Crabapple thought, they don't party like this in North Dakota!

His cousin welcomed him. "Sure," he could stay for awhile. Nobody bothered asking why he was here or what was wrong because it made no difference. What counted was Crabapple came with a fresh stash, which ignited the party all over again. If he'd been sober, he'd have been dismayed at his profits going up in smoke or in a quick swallow, but he'd been popping Ecstasy all the way here to keep himself awake, so sharing seemed like the right thing to do.

It wasn't until two days later that anything resembling sobriety showed up.

Crabapple found himself on Monday in a filthy, seedy apartment that smelled of weed and dirt.

Minneapolis is a beautiful community that lives up to its name—a combination of the Dakota word for "water" and the Greek word for "city." As it grew out and up from the Mississippi River, its boundaries filled with parks and lakes and neat neighborhoods that could have starred in "Father Knows Best." It attracted exquisite high-rises and acclaimed architecture and a state fair that is legendary. It was a place where a girl could "turn the world on with her smile," and when actress Mary Tyler Moore threw her hat into the air in the heart of the city's business district, she wasn't the only girl who dreamed this city held her future. Maxine back in Northville had that same mental image.

But all that had nothing to do with the ugly neighborhood around the Greyhound bus depot in downtown Minneapolis, where Ben Harding rented a one-bedroom apartment.

This is the part of town most people never see, the people raising families and doting over grandchildren and proud of their sports teams. Most in Minneapolis spend the summer going to the Minnesota Twins games, the fall with the Minnesota Vikings and the winter with the Minnesota Timberwolves—Okay, more time in playoff games than championships, but fans are loyal anyway. Summers are spent between home and a lake somewhere—the state boasts ten thousand to chose from—and churches of every denomination are full on Sunday mornings.

Nobody goes to church in the bowels of the city where down-and-outers hang out and where even the city's street sweepers are tardy.

Ben normally slept in the only bedroom, but not always, depending on who else was around and if there was money to be made by passing on the female who shared his bed at the moment. Right now it was a girl who called herself "Poodle," and with her shaggy white hair and skinny legs, fit the name.

There was a couch in the only other room of the apartment, the second-best place, usually snatched by whoever was spending the most money. That left space on the floor and whatever bedroll or blanket could be found to soften the linoleum. There was a galley kitchen under the windows that overlooked the street below, barely visible through the grease and grime that clung to the glass. It was supposed to be a kitchen, but cooking was hit and miss. No one did any dishes or picked up the mounds of takeout food wrappers that cluttered the floor.

Crabapple knew he didn't have much of a palace at home, but it was a palace compared to this. He hadn't been here in a year or so, and he didn't remember it being this bad. Phone conversations with his cousin gave him the impression things were going well, with drug sales up and Ben enjoying the "good life" of a low-level drug dealer. Now the real truth was obvious: sure, Ben dealt a lot, but he used up all his profits on himself or his friends. From what Crabapple could tell, the only "good life" Ben had was a Nokia cell phone.

Crabapple borrowed the phone early Monday morning to leave a message for Huntsie, calling when he knew the old man wouldn't be in the shop yet. In his mind, he left a coherent, believable message that he was called out of town for a family emergency and would be back when he could. In reality, his message went like this: "Huntsie. Um, this is Crab…Darryl… um, I'm here in…I'm away…had to go…my family, yeah, my family…emergency…somebody died…I…um…will be back after things cool…I'll be back later. Don't give my job away, okay? (He laughs.) See ya, buddy. Oh yeah, this is Darryl."

Once that was over, he relaxed again. Poodle looked tasty and she traded him for three Ecstasy pills. Things had to be getting better back home, and things here were just fine, as he swam in a fog of sex and pills.

Crabapple had been there a whole week when he used the phone again to call a buddy back home. "So, how's everything going?" he asked in a breezy tone.

The shocked, angry voice on the other end arrested that attitude in a second. "How's it going? Are you fuckin' nuts? They buried Amber last week. Johnny's still in a coma. How do you suppose it's going? Everybody wants your head."

Crabapple demanded a repeat because none of those words made any sense. Amber was dead? DEAD? Johnny was STILL in a coma? What coma? "How'd she die?" He was astonished. "Why is Johnny in a coma?"

The friend on the other end of the line snorted into the phone, as if Crabapple was being obtuse on purpose. "Oh, come on, it was those pills you sold him. She died of an overdose."

"You don't overdose on Ex," Crabapple chided, as though the friend were a dunce. "It had to be something else. Besides, who says I sold him anything? This ain't my fault. How the hell is this my fault?" By now, he was screaming into the phone.

"Man, everybody's blaming you," the friend insisted. "They know you sold them the drugs. People are pretty hot here. I'd stay away, man." And then, in a quick exit that told Crabapple this one couldn't be counted as a friend anymore, his buddy signed off. "Gotta go. Take care of yourself."

Crabapple had never heard of anyone dying from a pill of Ecstasy. This stuff was supposed to be safe and cheap and a real moneymaker. Crabapple was buying up pills for ten dollars apiece and selling them for twenty to thirty dollars, depending on what the traffic would bear. Ben had turned him onto the new drug, and one fabulous hit—the euphoria, the heightened senses, the unlimited energy, the profound sense of fearlessness, the desire to hug everyone—made it a sure thing.

He couldn't remember how many pills Johnny had bought, but not that many. Crabapple figured the guy had pooled money from his friends and bought enough for one each—so, what... ten, twenty? Hell, Crabapple had taken half that amount himself and here he was, living and breathing like always. Everyone else had come through, too, with no problems. Sure, Crabapple had a hangover, but he wasn't sure that was from the Ecstasy or all the junk he'd been adding to his drug stew. How in the hell did somebody die? DIE? How did Johnny end up in a coma?

Shit, oh shit, oh goddamn shit. This was a mess.

Then his brain started doing some fancy editing. "They know you sold them," the pal had said, but how did they know that if Johnny was still in a coma? Sure, they suspected it was Crabapple, but he'd only sold to Johnny, so the rest was speculation. They couldn't prove anything unless Johnny talked. And maybe Johnny would never talk. Damn, he didn't want Johnny to die, but he didn't want anyone hanging a drug charge around his neck, either. Maybe Johnny wouldn't admit anything because he'd be in trouble, too. Maybe there'd never be anything to tie Crabapple's little side business with this mess.

He sat there for a moment, trying to sort all this out, still befuddled that there was even a chance that the harmless pill had hurt someone. Fuck, it wasn't like he was selling heroin or even meth. No, Crabapple stayed away from that junk. What he sold was a momentary high—like drinking a six-pack—and nobody thought it was wrong that you could buy all the six-packs you wanted and that was legal. But buy a little baggie of pot, or buy a couple Ex pills, and that was illegal. Crabapple wasn't the only one who thought that hypocrisy was ridiculous and unfair.

He shared the awful news from home with Cousin Ben.

"Man, that's a bummer," he said, in what Crabapple thought was a totally inadequate response.

"It couldn't have been the Ex, could it?" Crabapple asked, begging to get an answer to exonerate him from this situation.

"Not really," Ben came back. "Think I heard of a kid in Europe that died, but you don't hear about it around here. That shit is safe, man. How many times you done it? I've been doing it for a couple years. We're still here! It probably wasn't the Ex. They probably had some other problem and who knows what went wrong. Don't worry about it, man. It's not your fault."

But just when he began feeling consoled, Ben looked at him with suspicious eyes. "Where'd you get those pills, anyway?"

"From you!" Crabapple spit back. "It was that batch out of Arizona. What, were they bad or something?"

Ben slowly shook his head like he wasn't getting caught in this trap. "Now come on, cuz, you know better than that. There was nothing wrong with those pills. They're righteous. Come from a big outfit that runs pills all across the country. No way they'd be passing off a bad batch."

Ben now started asking the kind of questions that assure a cover-your-ass moment. How many pills did he sell? How many guys bought them? Ben started a long, slow, self-assured smile when Crabapple told him about the single buy by the high school bigshot.

"Man, you've got nothing to worry about," Ben said. "You say the kid is still in a coma? And when he comes out, what's the chance his memory will be good enough? Or he'll fess up to buying drugs? Man, don't worry about it. Circumstantial evidence." Ben was sounding like he had a law degree.

"But I tell you one thing, cuz, none of this can get back to me and my contacts in Phoenix. You hear? We'd both have a lot bigger problem if that ever happened, because I hear the ring out there is run by a big Mafia guy. Those boys don't fuck around, you know. Are you hearing me?"

Crabapple nodded, but Ben demanded a verbal promise and Crabapple promised he'd never tell where he got the pills. That's all he'd need—those hotheads at home and then some Mafia guy out of Arizona. Holy crap, what a mess.

Ben crooked his finger at Poodle and she sauntered over. "I think our boy here needs a little mind-bending recreation, so why not be good to him?" Poodle took Crabapple by the hand into the bedroom, shutting the door behind them.

Crabapple stayed as stoned as he could, using up the stash he hadn't shared, taking some from others who came to party. Things were pretty loose here, and it wasn't hard to stay lit up, especially if you were Ben's cousin. Sometimes he'd realize he'd gone a whole day without eating. Sometimes he'd flounder himself on McDonald's hamburgers. He lost track of when he slept and who he slept with, and one day melted into another.

But a good high also makes a man bold. Makes him think he's king of the hill. Makes him smart and clever. The stoned world is a world of fabulous self-delusion. That's one reason it's so hard to kick—you feel ten feet tall, like you're the center of the universe. When you feel wonderful, you believe you're wonderful.

Crabapple didn't dare call Huntsie again and he could no longer remember anyone else's phone number, and besides, he didn't really want to know what was going on. Things were going to be okay. This was fun. Why not have fun now and then?

If anyone had told Crabapple Harding that he would hide out at his cousin's for two months, that he'd spend almost sixty days in a stoned haze and lose ten pounds, he'd have sworn it couldn't be true. Naturally, it was a great surprise when he finally sobered up enough to realize what had happened.

"Damn it, I missed deer season," he said on December 12, when someone mentioned the date. At first he was sure that wasn't right—they had to be joshing him—but someone brought in a newspaper and yes, indeed, deer season in North Dakota was already closed. Crabapple felt real regret and loss. His deer rifle was waiting, he had a new daylight fluorescent orange vest, he knew the fields he wanted to walk. None of that mattered now, because he'd been living in a stoned haze for so long that his most favorite time of the year had passed. No deer sausage for him this year. No feeling like a rich man with a freezer full of fresh-killed meat.

Hell, he'd have to hurry to make the pheasant season that closed in early January. He couldn't miss that, too. He loved pheasant the way his grandma made it, baked with cream of mushroom soup. Give him baked pheasant or deer sausage and he was a happy man. Those thoughts bounced around his head as it cleared from the drug haze.

He decided it was time to go home.

Ben spotted him twenty dollars for gas and wished him luck. Crabapple headed off, sure that whatever waited for him wouldn't be so bad. He'd faced bad scrapes all his life. This was simply the latest one.

"I'm just not lucky," he said, and everyone agreed he was right.

But he had gotten lucky when he found that the clean-cut kids in Northville liked to break out now and then, and he could make extra money selling weed. When the casino went in, the Indian kids had money to join the party and his business had boomed. Then along came these wonderful little pills, and for once in his life, he was sure he was holding a full house. Until, shit, that went south, too.

He stopped at Burger King on his way out of town, treating himself to a malt along with burger and fries, and talked to himself all the way home—promising he was done with the drug trade and vowing he'd deny everything and it would go away. He'd convince Huntsie to take him back and he'd work his ass off at the shop. Someday he'd own his own place. Be his own boss. That would be great. He'd find himself a girl—not like Poodle, but a real nice girl—and he'd get married and have kids and he wouldn't run out on them or treat them bad.

Life didn't have to be a toilet. He could change that. He could clean up. He could sober up. He could leave the bad hand he'd been dealt behind him and chose from a clean deck.

As Darryl "Crabapple" Harding pulled onto Interstate 94, he was full of piss and vinegar and sure that everything would be okay.

Chapter Eight

Wednesday, October 20—Sunday, November 21, 1999

The fifth floor of the Phoenix Police Department's headquarters is a hallowed place. The floor houses the homicide division. The floor where all important police briefings are given. The place where the medical examiner meets every Wednesday morning with officers to go over the priority of forensic tests. The room where wiretaps are monitored. In short, this is the heart of fighting crime in the nation's sixth-largest city.

Joya had never been allowed up here before, not even when she was investigating the morgue. Stepping off the elevator today, she expected to see more than gray metal desks overflowing with file folders, battered chairs in the conference room, and a coffee-stained carpet. Even so, she felt glad to finally reach this inner sanctum. She almost didn't make it.

There had been hell to pay when Rob revealed what had happened to his superiors. Officers could hear the police chief screaming behind the closed door and more than one thought it might cost Rob his job. Joya was summoned—she smiled to herself, imagining how she'd tell the chief she was too busy that day to come over for a visit. Maybe she would have tried it, except she knew it would hurt Rob.

When she walked into Chief Tomayer's office, two things struck her. The room itself looked like a country club smoking lounge, big leather chairs around a massive oak table, a desk in the back that was clean as a whistle. This was a man who ruled by meetings, not paperwork. Photos of the chief with every important person in Arizona covered the walls—all smiling, all puffed up. Joya couldn't read the award plaques from a distance, but she fully expected one declared that Chief Tomayer walked on water. The chief himself looked regal—all he needed was his hat—and pranced like he was ready to take her to the woodshed. Only his jaw muscles gave him away as he ground his teeth continually.

Lawrence Tomayer had a Hollywood-handsome face. Standing six-foot-five, maybe two hundred pounds, black hair specked with gray, cool blue eyes, a chin dimple that Kirk Douglas would envy, he was a fine specimen of a man. Joya guessed, correctly, that he'd tasted success early in life and never lost his appetite. She'd seen him triumph at City Council meetings, milking money for his department from a dry cow. Other city departments envied the pull he had at City Hall. He was not only Phoenix' top cop, he was Phoenix' top dog.

Joya was both pleased and anxious to see him now grinding his teeth. Venting. Threatening. "No possible way, young lady. You cannot be inside this investigation. That's absurd. When it's all over, then I'll give you access to my men. But not before then."

"That sure doesn't work for me," she told him, pretending to be calm and collected when she was praying he couldn't hear her heart pounding. Even for an experienced, tough reporter with awards and a fierce reputation, when it came to facing off against that uniform, that badge, that gun and all those medals, it was as intimidating as hell is hot.

She knew she held all the cards, and now she had to be careful. Like the song says, *Know when to hold 'em, know when to fold 'em, know when to walk away, know when to run.*

"I know Sammy the Bull is in town. I've seen him. I know he's supposed to be hiding out under the witness protection program. I know your department thinks he's running an Ecstasy drug ring. I know you've got other federal agencies working with you—not the FBI, but everybody else. I know all that right now, and the only way I don't write that story is if we work together."

The chief glared like he wanted to find some reason to arrest her. She recognized the look. But she had an ace in the hole. Here was a police chief whose department intended to humiliate the FBI by arresting their all-time favorite snitch before they knew what hit them.

In public, no law enforcement agency will speak badly about another. But in private, other peace officers hate the FBI. They're renamed "Fucking Bumbling Idiots," notorious for being selfish and never sharing information back. As one rap goes, "We're the FBI—we'll give you the sleeves off our vests."

So what the Phoenix PD was planning to do took balls. And balls are connected to the ego.

Joya played her ace. "If anyone can pull this off under the noses of the FBI, Chief Tomayer, it's your guys. Now, if the Scottsdale police were trying to do this, I wouldn't even bother working with them, because those buffoons couldn't find their way down a lighted runway. But Phoenix PD is a different story. You're probably the only police force in this state experienced enough to do this. I can't think of anyone else that's got the balls—excuse me, sir, I mean the skills." She paused for effect. "Now, *that's* the story I want to tell. We're not just talking about an arrest—we're talking about an incredible undercover effort to stop a major crime. The public needs to see that. They need to see the Phoenix Police Department at its best. The bragging rights you guys will earn with this are incredible. The public's going to eat it up. You're gonna look great. It's one helluva story."

She watched the slow smile warm his eyes as her flattery took the edge off. She had him.

"If you think you don't like this, you should have heard my editor," she confided, rolling her eyes at the mighty battle she'd already fought back at the paper. "I've convinced him that this is a fabulous story that we can't break until Sammy is behind bars. But my editor only buys that if he knows I'm inside, getting the scoop on this case. If he thinks you're trying to stiff me, he won't let me hold off. Now, neither of us wants that. You have my word. You have his word. You just have to keep up your end of the bargain."

Sensing agreement, she spoke slowly, laying out her plan. "Let me hang out and watch what happens. I promise I'll stay out of the way. You won't even know I'm around. I won't bother your guys if they don't want to talk to me. But someday, Chief, the public will eat up the story of how dogged you guys were to catch Sammy. They're going to lap up every morsel about how smart you guys were. And I personally can't wait to see those FBI guys with egg all over their faces."

She was convincing and she was right. There weren't many other options. She and the chief shook hands. When they walked out of his office, a half-dozen officers busied themselves, as if they hadn't been eavesdropping. Rob looked like he'd put down a five hundred-pound weight.

"You son of a bitch, this might actually work to your advantage," one of the detectives whispered to Rob as they took the elevator up to the fifth floor.

Joya quickly learned the first lesson of detective work: it amounts to hours and hours of tedium. Worthless tedium. She thought they'd catch him red-handed—tipped off by wiretaps that told when a drop was coming and where. Of course, it wasn't anywhere near that easy.

The first couple weeks, not much happened. Nobody was making any drug deals, nobody was talking about Sammy. The word "bull" was never uttered.

She was given a gray metal chair at the back of a small, windowless room and told to stay quiet. There was usually one guy at the large monitoring desk filled with recorders. Sometimes the officer wore a headphone so only he could hear what was being said over the tapped line, but normally, it was turned on for the room to hear. Detectives popped in now and then to see what was going on.

The captain in charge clearly didn't like having her there. When she brought in a cup of coffee, he barked, "Don't spill that." When she had a coughing jag, he snarked, "If you're going to make noise, get out of here." She learned the first day that when they brought in sandwiches for lunch, there wasn't one for her. So she packed her own lunch and acted like she wasn't a stranger in a strange land.

Then came the second lesson of detective work. Sitting for hours, getting nothing of value, inspires war stories about days when something actually happens. And in this case, the guys doing the telling were sometimes the guys who had stumbled onto Sammy with all innocence, just as she had.

She'd eventually write:

> The first time Phoenix undercover agent Jim Cope was told the drug ring he was trying to bust was headed by Sammy "the Bull" Gravano, he thought it was just puffery.
>
> Having grown up in New Jersey, Cope certainly knew the reputation of the Mafia underboss who'd become famous turning on John Gotti and sending the "Teflon Don" up the river.
>
> But come on, this is Phoenix, Arizona. This is a drug ring catering to the Rave and Scottsdale club scene. Cope has no reason to believe Sammy can be anywhere near the state. Besides, the guy is in his fifties now—far too old to be clubbing it.
>
> "I thought, if I went back and told the guys that Sammy the Bull was involved, they'd laugh me out of the station house," Cope remembers. "They'd think I was nuts."
>
> So the police sergeant asks around, quietly, cautiously. More names keep coming up and the questions keep mounting. Is Sammy in Arizona? Why is he here? What's he doing? Does he have a

son named Gerard? Is that the Gerard
Gravano who's making the club scene
with a druggie named Mike Papa?

Joya knew exactly how the cops felt. She'd sold this story to her editor on the basis that Sammy *was* heading up this drug ring. Now she was discovering the police still weren't sure. Jesus, she thought, maybe this drug stuff is all a wild goose chase and the only story here is simply that Sammy's in town. But she didn't let on to anyone back at the paper that she had any doubt about this story. Her gut told her the pompous guy in the coffeehouse wasn't a solid citizen—he loved his bad-ass reputation. And Rob assured her that all his senses told him Sammy was involved in drug activity.

Others weren't so sure.

"No, we don't know Sammy's involved at all." Joya felt her stomach fall when the hostile captain shared his thoughts. They were sitting in the monitoring room one day when nobody was saying anything important on the taped phones. The captain—tall, skinny, cold—had told her he never wanted his name in any story, and she agreed. She could quote him, but not name him. So far he hadn't said anything worth quoting, but he clearly had been in on this stakeout from the start. She had to find a way to soften him up, so she started small talk.

"You'd think for something this important, they'd give you guys a better room to work in," she joshed. "Look at this place. It could be a cave. No windows. Egg-carton walls. Uncomfortable chairs. Bet they haven't painted for years. They should give you guys big, plush chairs and decent coffee. Now, that would make monitoring wiretaps more pleasant."

The guy actually smiled. Small win. Then she posed a simple question. "Were you surprised to find Sammy had gotten into drugs?"

That's when he unloaded, and Joya prayed her big "scoop" wouldn't come back to bite her.

He said, "We know guys are bragging in the clubs that they've got a 'New York guy' as their backer, but really? You know how guys will say almost anything to get laid. So are these guys hinting about Sammy to up their odds of scoring? Or are they really working for Sammy? It's easy for a twenty-year-old kid to say 'I'm backed by Sammy' and poor Sammy doesn't know a thing. I know these kids are dirty, but is there new dirt on Sammy? I still don't know."

She saw him watching her face and he seemed to enjoy the dismay she couldn't hide.

"But we had to look into it," he added.

"When's the first time you thought it might be true?"

"When we found his whole family was here."

"His family's here? I heard they refused to go into the witness protection program with him."

"Well, they did come. His ex-wife, Debra, has a restaurant in Scottsdale. Get this, it's called Uncle Sal's Italian Ristorante, and guess what the slogan is? 'The best kept secret in Scottsdale.'" They both roared.

Tracking the fifty-ish Debra, with her big hair and New Jersey nails, took one trip to the Corporation Commission that keeps records on Arizona businesses. Hanging around at Uncle Sal's soon revealed the pretty thirty-ish woman with an endowed chest and low-cut blouses was daughter Karen. And nobody could miss the twenty-four-year-old tintype of his father, Gerard.

To top it off, Detective Cope thought the Marathon Construction Company in Tempe sounded familiar. Wasn't that the name of Sammy's construction company back in New Jersey? Another trip to the Corporation Commission found the firm had opened in 1995 and was owned by "Jimmy Moran."

"We staked out Marathon," Cope told Joya, "and one morning this forty-thousand-dollar Lexus drives up and out pops Sammy, wearing a white tee-shirt and black leather jacket. He looked just like his picture in the book. You'd have to be blind not to see it was him." She knew the look.

"We sent someone in to price a remodel job, and sure enough, Sammy introduces himself as Jimmy Moran."

Discovering Sammy was indeed in town was enough to launch a full-press investigation.

"Wouldn't it have been a lot easier just to go to the FBI and ask them if they'd stashed Sammy here in their witness protection program?" she asked the captain one day, pretending to be clueless.

"Go to the FBI? Are you nuts? The first thing they'd do is run to Sammy and tell him Phoenix PD was looking at him. Or they'd move him out of town. Talk about queering the whole thing. No, of course we wouldn't go to the FBI."

Joya already knew that, but the quote was worth her guise of innocence. The more she got this guy to talk, the softer he got on her being around.

She also knew Phoenix PD had gone to the Arizona Department of Public Safety, the Drug Enforcement Administration and Customs. All were in on the hunt. "This is *our* case," another officer stressed, pounding his middle finger on the table.

She knew something was up the first time she heard the name "Shorty Whip Wop."

"Are they talking about who I think they're talking about?" she gingerly asked.

"Who do you think it is?" the captain quizzed.

"Sammy."

He cocked his finger at her like she'd hit the target.

"Boy, if he knew that was their name for him, he wouldn't like it," she declared, and the captain laughed. Another small win.

Joya left the fifth floor at night and hit the computer in her home office, writing up scenes like how Sergeant Cope stumbled on Sammy—this wasn't a story she'd compose in the usual way. The way Joya normally worked, she'd do all her interviews and gather all her documents and then sit down and map out the story. She wasn't a journalist who made up her mind and then went looking for the evidence to support that—she worked the opposite way, wherever the evidence led, that's where she went.

But this story was different. This story had a plausible premise that was yet to be proved, but if it were, would be a blockbuster. When this story broke, she wouldn't have the luxury of days or weeks to write a story, she'd have only hours to get it in print. This wasn't a comfortable way to work and she prayed she wasn't skating on thin ice. She hoped that by writing as she went— writing while the words were still fresh in her ears and her notes made total sense—eventually she could string the scenes together.

One of the ways Joya passed the time on the fifth floor was reading Sammy's book. She knew he hadn't really written it, but Peter Maas had taped him for hours and then transcribed his thoughts. The stories were riveting. She created this scene for her story:

If you ever read Sammy's book, you came away realizing there really are people whose value systems are out of whack.

Nobody dares get too haughty here about how ruthless and revolting that subculture of crime is; after all, much of America wallows in it most Sunday nights when HBO runs *The Sopranos*.

So it's not surprising the book sold well. *Time*'s review probably summed it up best: "*Underboss* is fascinating for its anthropologically detailed portrait of a subculture some of us can't get enough of."

In the book, Sammy talks about killing nineteen people without emotion— even supplying the detail that his first kill was to the radio playing a Beatles song. He talks about his indescribable joy at becoming a "made man." He talks about feeling justified in betraying Gotti because Gotti had betrayed him.

But nowhere is he more animated than when he talks about how his family reacted to his decision to turn on his friends.

To quote from the book: "I called them to come see me [in prison], my wife and daughter, not my son, who was only fourteen. I told them I was going to cooperate.

"Debbie says, 'No!' She's shocked, she's scared, she's everything. My daughter is hysterical. Completely and totally. Her idol, her father, is about to join forces with the enemy. And I'm thinking, Jesus, how did I fuck up my whole life so badly? She's crying, 'No, Dad, *please!*' and she runs right out of the visiting room.

"My wife's eyes are full of tears. She says, 'I have to tell you, Sammy, I'm not going into any witness protection program. I'm not going to be part of this. I was never part of that part of your life, and I'm not going to be part of this. I'm not going to be part of anything.'

"I said, 'Deb, I understand your position and I respect it. You're a mother, not a gangster. You do what you got to do as a mother and I'll understand it one hundred percent.'

"She gives me a hug and she leaves. My heart is breaking. I've never been through anything like this, never thought it could happen. But I know in my gut that for the first time in my life, I'm finally doing the right thing. I was going the route I chose. I wasn't turning back.

"I was thinking of my son. I was worried about him. I had all kinds of thoughts about him. His father, the underboss, is going to jail. His father is a big hero in the neighborhood. And my son might try to follow in my footsteps and I can't stop it because I'd be in jail. He's going to be running around, his father is this big underboss, and people are going to cater to him and he's going to wind up in the fucking life. He's a tough kid, but a good kid. He's not for the life. I had

```
always sheltered him from it. And if
he winds up in the life, he's sure to
end up either being whacked or going
to jail himself."
```

It surprised Joya that she felt sick to her stomach when she learned Sammy was right to worry about his only son.

It was the day she heard on the wiretap, "Do you have the money for Shorty Whip Wop?"

The captain was tilted back on his chair, twirling a pen between his fingers, when he plunged his feet to the floor and started scribbling. He snapped his fingers at her and pointed to the door. She ran out and yelled to the other detectives, "He wants you in here now."

They rushed in, listened, looked at the notes, and started slapping each other on the back.

"Yes, yes, yes," someone chanted, under his breath so they wouldn't miss any phone chatter. These were the words they were waiting to hear. It was the day Joya started breathing easier. Because the known drug dealer named Mike Papa, who hung around with Sammy's son, was asking Gerard if he had the drug money for Sammy.

Drug deals are done in code. Nobody's so dense they'll say something stupid like, "Do you have the money that's owed to Sammy the Bull who's heading this drug ring?"

So the sentence didn't mean anything by itself. Hardly anything meant anything by itself. It was like building a wall brick by brick and some of the bricks were a little wonky. But this brick was solid. This coded message was important. Drug dealers were talking about Sammy.

By Thanksgiving, Phoenix Police had monitored hundreds of conversations, but they still hadn't built the wall. The slow pace was wearing on Joya.

She had begun this story like she always did, thrilled and excited and convinced it was going to be such fun. At first blush, it was. But that wore off quickly when the real work to get the story set in. She'd overlooked this part of investigative work—the fatiguing, uninteresting, stupid, dull, humdrum part. Surviving this is what separated regular reporters from those who earned the title of investigative journalist. Regular reporters spent a day to a week on one story, then moved on to the next topic. They never spent enough time on one thing to get bored. Investigative journalists spent months, sometimes years, developing the information that blew the lid off something. Joya had been through this before, but always forgot about it when the next story came around. It was like women who forget the pain of childbirth and get pregnant again.

She wondered how cops did it, day after day, week after week, always dealing with the ugliness of crime. Not all her stories were about this underbelly of the law. She wrote about wonderful, beautiful things, too.

She'd spent a week at a burn camp in northern Arizona with children with hideous outer appearances but whose inner souls were beautiful. This camp was a haven where others resembled their wounds and nobody cared. Joya had never been more touched.

She knew what it was like to write about good things that made people feel better. Here she was writing about a murdering criminal who'd gotten a ridiculous second chance and turned back to crime all over again and what was the point? You can't change the stripes on a tiger—who didn't know that?

She wanted this story so much because it was so explosive, it had a guaranteed readership; it would give her great street creds; her "inside" status would be the envy of every other reporter; her paper would show up every other news outlet in town; and she'd show up Peter. That a criminal would be put away wasn't the end all for her, it was the delivery system of her ego dope.

But over the last month, only a few bricks were in place, and Joya knew her editor wouldn't let her hang on here forever. She'd fudged a little in her reports to him, making little things sound bigger than they were. Making tiny steps appear as Size

12s. She was in deep now and could never justify throwing away a month of her time—this story had to pan out. They had to catch Sammy selling drugs. And as the days passed and the clues got harder to see, she got more and more anxious.

The first one to suffer was Rob.

"Why is everything taking so long?" she asked him one night in bed, and he didn't like the question.

"Oh, maybe because we're not doing our job and are just playing around for the fun of it."

"Okay, Mr. Sarcastic. That's not what I meant. I mean, if there's really a big drug ring out there that Sammy's running, shouldn't you be catching them selling drugs? So far I've sat through hours of wiretaps and heard only hints. I haven't heard one drug deal set up. I haven't heard Sammy utter a word. Maybe the captain is right and this is all smoke and mirrors."

Rob threw back the chenille bedspread and sat on the edge of the four-poster bed.

"I tried to tell you that stakeout work is tedious. You want the version you see on television. You want action and you want it delivered on a silver plate. Sorry, babe, that's not how it works. If you think we've got nothing, then maybe you shouldn't be wasting your time hanging around the fifth floor."

He got up and she could hear him getting a drink of water in the bathroom.

She knew she'd gone too far. Damn it. She'd fooled herself into the fantasy that she and Rob would come home at night and talk about the case and salivate over the evidence, and laugh about the FBI. None of that happened. It couldn't be farther from the reality of fighting about this case every time they opened their mouths.

She'd vowed she wouldn't talk about it anymore with Rob, but that was ridiculous, too. What else was there to talk about? She spent her days and nights studying Sammy the Bull, and Rob was out scouring the hillsides, trying to find the links, and when you're that consumed with one subject, not talking about it reduces you to silence.

She felt him slipping away. He felt her slipping away. She feared she was pushing him away. He was pushing back. None of this was good. A sex life that had taken up three out of five nights was down to—maybe—one night a week. Weekends when Rob went off with his kids were a giant relief from the strain both endured.

She turned the volume up to ten. That's the way she thought of her manic attempts at normalcy. If she walked farther on Saturday mornings and shopped more intently at the Farmer's Market, and gardened until her hands were chapped, she could set things right. When that didn't work, she started baking.

"I always cut out those delicious recipes from magazines, but I never bake them," she told a friend. "Well, I'm going to bake them now."

She bought exotic ingredients that were useful for one dish and stocked up on spices she couldn't always pronounce, and she baked her heart out.

Cakes. Pies. Lemon bars. Date-filled cookies. Brownies. Muffins. Madelines. Popovers. Strudels. Bars.

She'd carry her latest creation to a neighbor because, Godforbid, she'd eat this fattening stuff herself. On a stroke of genius, she started taking her sweets to the police station with her. It's almost comical how the way to a man's good graces is through a piece of chocolate cake.

"Hey, Joya, what am I, chopped liver?" Chief Tomayer asked her one day when he came up to the monitoring room. "I hear my detectives are getting fat on the goodies you're bringing in, but I never see any."

"I won't make that mistake again, Chief," she cooed, and started preparing special plates for him.

None of this relieved the anxious feeling that this would blow up in her face. What if they never caught Sammy? What if she'd wasted all this time? How could she justify her salary if she wasn't producing anything? How long would her editor be patient?

Even the Sunday calls home to her folks were strained. She couldn't tell them about the story she was working on and some weeks it took too much energy to make up a story they'd believe. She'd ask about one relative after another and they'd give the latest. Sometimes it was rote.

"Oh, they're okay."

"Just the same."

"Nothing new."

In her turmoil, she yearned for the same, nothing new, okay kind of life.

"If I went back to Northville, I'd have my folks. Church on Sundays. The casino on Mondays. Coffee every morning at Cousin Alice's bakery. I'd join the women gossiping and watch the men shooting dice. I'd have a garden with real vegetables. I'd never have to take another blood pressure pill."

That wasn't going to happen. So she usually fed off the Sunday calls that reminded her what life could be like. But something was off.

"Everybody here just feels shitty," her mother announced one Sunday. Then she launched into another sad story about how Nettie wasn't getting past Amber's death.

"And Gertie has gotten so old, so fast, since Amber died."

Joya understood grief and lost. What she didn't understand was why these calls included an ugly undertone.

"So what's really up?" Joya finally asked, coming out of her own fog to ask about her parents'.

"The town's still reeling over Amber," her mother announced, and Joya was surprised. Amber had died in mid-October. It was almost Thanksgiving. Shouldn't things have calmed down by now?

"Still?" she asked, before she could catch herself.

"Joya Ann Bonner, you may live in a world where good girls die needlessly every day, but we don't." Her dad spit out the words.

"No, of course not. I'm so sorry, that's not what I meant. I meant it's been a month or so since she died, and I would have thought the town would be healing by now."

"Healing? How the hell are we supposed to heal?" She could

see her dad's contorted face in her mind and knew it was bright red in anger.

"Johnny's still in a coma," her mother said, as though that were all of it.

"Oh boy, that's gotta be tough." Joya felt ashamed she'd forgotten all about him. "That poor kid. Do they think he'll be alright?"

"They don't know. His mother says she thinks he will, but who knows? There probably will be brain damage."

"He better wake up because the sheriff's not going to do anything unless Johnny fesses up," her dad declared.

"Fesses up about what?" How did she have so little information about a very big deal in her hometown?

"About the drugs. About how Crabapple sold him the drugs." Her dad's tone was now one of a man who thought his daughter was a dolt for not understanding the simplest thing.

"You've got a *drug dealer* in Northville and they haven't caught him yet? It can't be that hard to find a drug dealer in Northville. And what'd you call him? Crabapple? What kind of name is that?"

"He left town," her mother noted, while her father bitterly talked over her, "No, they haven't caught him. It's that kid who works for Huntsie. It's his nickname."

"Where'd he go?"

"Nobody knows. He left the same night Amber died."

"Oh, God. That's terrible. He'll probably never come back. If he sold drugs that killed somebody, I bet he just keeps running."

"I hope so." Her mother mumbled under her breath.

"That bastard better come home and face the music," her father bellowed.

"We need to let the law take care of this," her mother loudly interjected.

"Bullshit," her dad said back. Joya knew she'd tapped into a continuing fight between her parents. But her law and order, NRA-member dad was objecting to the law taking care of a drug dealer? That didn't make sense.

"I'm a little lost here, Dad. Of course the police—or it's the sheriff there, isn't it?—the sheriff should take care of this."

Her dad yelled into the phone. "If we had a sheriff that got off his ass and did his job, yeah, but we don't have that kind of sheriff. How can I expect he'll do a better job this year?"

"Ralph, calm down. I'm sure he'll do his job now that poor Amber is dead." Her mother didn't sound convinced, and her dad certainly wasn't buying it.

Lights were flashing and bells were clanging as last year's fiasco came back to Joya. Her dad and his pals were furious when the sheriff wouldn't stop a kid they thought was pushing drugs. She could still hear her dad mimicking the sheriff. "No proof. You got no proof. All you got is what the little bird shot at." Well, Amber was now dead, and wasn't that proof? And if it were proof, then this Crabapple kid was in real trouble, which made him dangerous.

"Dad, I've done some stories about drug deals. These people are nasty. They don't let anything get in their way. They're dangerous. I agree with Mom that this is a job for the sheriff. Even a lazy sheriff isn't going to let a death go unpunished—he'd never get reelected if he did. And in this case, he's after….what is he after? Cocaine? Heroin?"

Even as she said the words, Joya thought it was absurd to think the Amber she knew had snorted cocaine or shot up horse. All she knew about Amber's demise was her dad's original pronouncement that "dope is dope."

"One of those pills," he told her now. "Those party pills. What do they call them? Estatic? Something like that."

Joya stopped breathing. Now she was the one screaming into the phone. "Ecstasy? You mean Ecstasy?"

Startled, her parents in unison acknowledged that was it.

"Whoa, honey…" began her mother.

"Where'd it come from?" Joya pressed on, with horrible possibilities dancing in her head.

"Who knows?" her dad said. "I suppose Fargo or Minneapolis. They don't make that stuff around here."

"You know, kids don't normally die from Ecstasy," Joya informed them, thinking it was news they didn't know.

"That's what they say," her Dad came back. "But Amber's dead. And Johnny might as well be."

"Don't say that," her mother admonished. "He could still come out of it."

Joya missed the next couple of sentences as her mind chased the absurd possibility that the Ecstasy ring they thought Sammy headed in the Southwest had reached all the way to North Dakota. Was that even possible? But in her distraction, she almost missed her mother's complaint: "The last thing we need is for somebody to take the law into his own hands."

"What? What'd you say?"

Maggie Bonner said the words again. Joya's father snorted in rebuttal.

"Oh, God, no! That would be terrible," Joya declared, waiting for her father to agree that law enforcement must be in charge here. He didn't say that. He didn't say anything. His silence sent a chill down her back.

She could feel her hands sting from hitting the pavement. The shot-backfire was fresh in her ears. She needed to scare her dad like she'd been scared.

"Dad, the Mafia is behind a lot of drug rings in this country. And the last people in the world you want to mess with is the Mafia. They don't think twice about killing anybody who gets in their way. They go after families, too. You mess with the Mafia and everybody you know is in danger. Let the sheriff take care of this. They're trained to deal with criminals like that."

Her dad stayed silent. No wonder her mother was worried.

Ralph Bonner changed the subject, putting an ending the discussion. Joya's nervousness hit on high alert. By the time she hung up, she walked out of the fog of her depression to a roiling stomach.

Ecstasy had found its way to Northville.

Her mom and dad were fighting over a drug dealer—*a drug dealer*—named Crabapple.

Her dad was ready to take the law into his own hands.
Maybe Sammy…?
All that was stone cold bad.

Joya immediately dialed Cousin Alice's number in Northville.
Sunday afternoon. The bakery was closed. She should be home.
But she wasn't. Joya left a worried message: "Hey, Alice, just had
an unbelievable call with my folks. What's this about Ecstasy and
some guy named Crabapple? Is my dad turning into a vigilante?
Call me. What the hell's going on back there?"

Monday, when she got home from work, there was a voice
mail from Alice.

"Things are a mess here, but there's nothing you can do.
Don't worry. This is a bad time for us. You know what they say,
'It takes a village to bury a child.'"

Joya felt chills up and down her spine.

Chapter Nine

Tuesday, November 23, 1999

Nettie Schlener had to learn to live a life she no longer wanted to live.

From the moment she heard the horrible words that her daughter was dead, everything had been sucked out of her. Joy. Hope. Happiness. Wonderment. Contentment. Delight. Cheer. Gladness. Enjoyment.

In its place were intolerable burdens. Grief. Sorrow. Anger. Worry. Distress. Misery. Heartache. Wretchedness. Gloom. Hatred. Despair.

Her sister Arlene told her she'd predictably go through seven stages of loss—from shock and denial to pain and guilt to anger and bargaining to depression to an upward turn and then reconstruction until she reached acceptance and hope.

But Nettie never got beyond the anger. She never emerged from the depression. She never moved close to hope.

Her daughter's death was even worse than her husband's seventeen years ago. Although if anyone had told her that then, she would have screamed in disbelief.

"I had the perfect life," she'd tell anyone who'd listen. When no one was around these days, she'd tell herself. "I married my high school sweetheart in an elaborate wedding with six bridesmaids in blue. I wore a lace gown with a long veil that trailed me as Dad walked me down the aisle of St. Vincent's. Richard was so handsome, and everyone said I was beautiful. It was one of the best weddings Northville has ever had!"

If she had her druthers, she'd still be wearing that gown and dancing with her groom. And some days now, she thought she was.

"We had a good marriage," Nettie announced, greeting family that rushed to her home at the news of Amber's death. They looked aghast at her, knowing she wasn't in this moment, but unclear what moment she was in. "Richard farmed and worked at Heartland Candies in Hankinson in the winter. You know, he made lollipops. That's why they call Hankinson 'the sucker capital of America.' Isn't that funny?"

Something was funny here alright, but it wasn't a seventeen-year lapse in reality.

"It was the life we'd always imagined living. It was just perfect. And then, praise the Lord, I got pregnant."

Her family let her talk because what else could they do?

"We announced the happy news at the two Thanksgiving dinners we ate that year, one with his folks, the other with mine. You were all there. Remember how thrilled you were? We didn't even have a spare bedroom in the trailer, but we fixed up a nice spot we called the 'nursery.' Richard built a rocking crib in the barn—he started it the first day he learned we were pregnant."

Nettie was almost dancing across her living room as she entertained her horrified family.

"My sisters gave me the most adorable baby shower! I bet half the town came to the Senior Citizen Center they rented. You know, the Center always has a fake Christmas tree in the corner that they decorate for each holiday. They have hearts for Valentine's Day and pumpkins for fall, and of course, orna-ments for Christmas. Well, my darling sisters got permission to remove the summer flowers and replace them with baby toys and trinkets. It was just adorable."

And then Nettie stopped talking and started crying and everyone guessed she'd come back to the present. But they were wrong. Nettie had gone to the spot in her heart that had been the darkest until now—the spot she'd never reveal to anyone. The spot she would deny was even there.

Two nights after the shower, Nettie and Richard had a fight, a stupid quarrel about the baby's name.

She and Richard normally saw eye to eye on everything. They had since they'd started dating in their sophomore year. She was strong-willed, like him (and he loved her for it) and normally they worked everything out by talking it through. But Nettie's hormones were playing havoc with her emotions and *she* would decide the name of their first child.

If a boy, she wanted him named after her father. If a girl, after her mother. That meant Amos or Eunice.

Richard laughed out loud, convinced his wife was joking. She started to cry when she realized he thought the names were ridiculous.

"Those are fine names, fine names," he cooed to quiet her down. "But not for our child. Those are old people names. You want to honor your parents, but do you really want our boy called Amos? Or our girl called Eunice? Think of the horrible nicknames they'll get. Ammo. Mousey. Unnie. Ewie. God, we can't saddle the kid with that!"

He was sure she'd see his wisdom, and offered his own personal selections, Joshua if a boy, Amber if a girl.

"What's so special about those names?" she spat back at him. "What, is Amber an old girlfriend's name? It sure isn't your mom's. And Joshua. When did you get cozy with biblical names?"

If Richard Schlener had had more experience with hormonal pregnant women, he'd have realized this was a momentary fixation that would pass, like her taste for sour pickles. But he was as new to this as she was, and she wouldn't stop crying and wouldn't stop insisting *her* child was going to carry *her* parent's name and if *he* didn't like it, *he* could go to hell.

"Oh, so if we're thinking of parents' names, it's only *your* parents? What about mine?" he asked in anger. "Ben and Magdalena. Yup, I could get to liking those for our kid."

"Don't be absurd," she snapped. That did it.

"You know, I think I will just go to hell and hit Jerry's Bar for a drink. Because you're driving me to drink, lady. But I'll tell you one thing. No child of *mine* is going to wear an old person's name!"

He stormed out of the trailer on his dad's farm and headed into town on a gravel road he'd driven a thousand times. He came to a rolling stop where the road met the paved highway and whipped a right. He went a little wide, straddling the white lane marker when a kid from Gwinner came barreling down the road and hit him at eighty miles an hour.

Nettie never told anyone that the last words she said to her husband were in anger during an idiotic fight. She never admitted to anyone, not even her sisters, that if she hadn't been so ridiculous that night in picking a fight, her Richard would never have been on that road and wouldn't have ended up in a casket. She never admitted anything was wrong that night because to tell would admit that she had caused her husband's death. She couldn't bear for people to know that.

That stain was Nettie's life secret. Her baby girl was born two months later, drawing her out of grief enough to be present and function. She named the baby Amber Magdalena. She told everyone that was the name they'd decided together.

But there was no such reprieve now. Now that she'd lost both her husband and the baby they'd made. Now that there was nothing left for her. Nothing.

Her family worried she'd never come back from that ledge of agony. They'd have been sick to know Nettie didn't want to.

As she looked at Amber in that pretty lavender casket, Nettie wished there were an embalming fluid for the living. Something to make everything look like it was alright. But there wasn't. She was resolved that nothing would ever be alright again.

The "acceptance" stage of grief is often called "a gift not afforded to everyone." Nettie was one of those left empty-handed.

Harley gave her a week off with pay from the hardware store after Amber's death. Nettie wasn't sure if she should be grateful or if she should despise him for thinking a week was enough.

But she needed the paycheck and staying at home alone was unbearable, so she went back to work and pretended she was "recovering."

She gained twenty pounds in the first month, because the only thing—the ONLY THING—that gave her any comfort was sugar. She'd stop at Alice's Bakery on her way to work and buy a half-dozen donuts, claiming she was sharing with Harley and customers, but she'd secretly eat them all herself during the morning. At noon, she'd go to the corner bar for one of their hamburgers with fries and drink a couple Cokes. After she got off work at three p.m., she'd hit Alice's again, hanging in the kitchen with a cup of coffee and cookies or a cupcake—Alice never kept track—and spend the only minutes of her day in anything resembling normalcy.

Nettie was two years behind Alice in high school and they'd had a casual friendship all these years. Nettie had always been most likely to hang with her sisters, but since Amber's death, it was more painful to be with a blood relative than with a girl you'd known most of your life who had other interests beyond your loss and grief.

To her sisters, Nettie explained, "I like Alice because she knows all the town gossip—she's like her own newspaper, radio, and TV all in one!"

Alice Peters knew everything about everybody, because so many people passed through her delicious bakery every day. When you're a willing listener in a bakery that always smells of sweet treats, and you have an endless coffeepot at the ready, people naturally hang out and talk.

Gossip in a small town is like currency. Alice not only had a full till, she loved to spend it.

"You know my secret?" Alice asked Nettie one day, stretching to entertain the sad woman. "I understand the difference in how men and women gossip."

Nettie had never considered such a thing, but welcomed the relief of listening to a secret.

"Women gossip like a doubles game of ping-pong, everybody talking at once and throwing an idea back and forth. They'll chew on a thing until it's shredded, and then they move on. But men parcel out their thoughts slowly—two, three trains of thought hanging there with everyone naturally keeping track. Like multiple lanes of bowling where everyone knows each score. And in the middle of one train, somebody will tell a joke, and when they pick up again, nobody has to be reminded where they left off. So if you want gossip from women, they hand it over neat and tidy. But if you want it from men, you've got to hang in there for hours to get the whole story. I can eavesdrop with the best of them."

Nettie laughed and Alice congratulated herself that she'd gotten the grieving woman to laugh for the first time in a long time.

It was no surprise that Nettie hung out at the bakery—everyone assumed it was for the sugar, and that's where it started, but she really was after the ever-growing gossip garden. Some days the harvest was abundant. Some days it was just weeds. But it was always something and when you're hopeless and bereft, you hang on to anything.

Besides, Alice often needed help decorating cookies or frosting cupcakes, and Nettie offered her services. It was a few more dollars and she had nothing else to do, anyway. Alice always tried to get out of the bakery by six p.m.—she had to be back at four-thirty a.m. to get the bread in her Reed Oven—and sometimes she and Nettie would run out to Dakota Magic Casino for supper. Other nights, Nettie would go home alone. The trailer was long gone and she'd inherited the farmhouse when Richard's folks died. She'd either defrost a pizza or grab a bag of chips and pour some Black Velvet over ice.

The next mindless, meaningless day would start at six a.m. and she'd go through the motions all over again.

Except on Wednesdays. Wednesdays she only worked half days and she never stopped at Alice's. On Wednesdays, she picked up her standing order at Leona's flower shop and took the two pink roses to Amber's grave.

Nettie would lie on the ground next to her daughter's headstone, even when there was snow, and talk to the girl who could never talk back.

This was the only place she ever felt any comfort. "Strange," she once said to herself, "you'd think this was the last place I'd want to be. But this is where Amber is. And I have so much to tell her. All those things I never said. All those things she needs to know."

Anyone overhearing her conversation would have been able to walk into a courtroom, put a hand on the Bible, and swear Nettie Schlener was nuts.

Nettie spoke to the grave as though she and Amber were sitting around the kitchen table having supper. She told the headstone the news in town and how the girls' basketball team was doing. She told about beloved Aunt Gertie and the reports weren't very good; the lady was failing fast. She'd hit a parked car last week and the family took away her keys. Poor thing cried all day. Nettie told about strange customers at the hardware and how Alice's new cake recipe tasted. She even gave updates on Johnny.

"He's still in a coma," she'd report. "His mother is always with him. His father....well, you know his father. They don't know if he'll ever come out of it."

There were regular news flashes on her cousins, aunts and uncles. "Your Uncle Dennis was so angry when you died," Nettie told her. "I worried he might do something that would get him in trouble. But he's calmed down. You know, they always do. Those men get so riled up and they're like red hot pokers, but it doesn't last. They say a woman holds a grudge a lot deeper than a man, and I think they're right. Besides, Dennis has his kids to raise and they're all active in sports and 4-H and his wife is into scrapbooking big-time, so she's always going off to scrapbook conventions and leaving him to take care of everything at home. I'm betting sometimes he wishes he'd listened to Dad that Susie wasn't the right woman for him."

Nettie told her dead daughter that Maxine refused any of her clothes—even though Nettie was sure she and the other girls would want them. She ended up carting them to the Dakota Boy's Ranch Thrift Shop in Fargo. "Remember how we liked shopping there?" After questions like that she'd pause, as though she expected an answer.

And then, in a voice just above a whisper, she'd tell Amber about Crabapple.

She'd end with her arms around the tombstone, kissing its cold surface.

Chapter Ten

Thanksgiving Day, 1999

Ralph Bonner's World War II Marine picture hung in the hallway of his home in Northville, and Alice Peters never went down that hall without admiring her handsome uncle.

She smiled up at the picture and vowed that this was going to be a great Thanksgiving Day. And damned, if it wasn't!

It was like recess. It was like half-time. It was a time-out.

It was a day when not one person mentioned Amber Schlener or Johnny Roth or Nettie Schlener. And certainly, nobody mentioned Crabapple.

"This is a day of thanksgiving, to be grateful for all we have," Maggie Bonner announced as she sat her family around the dining room table, the kitchen table and the two card tables set up in the living room. Maggie and Ralph had a large home, but nobody had a home big enough to seat all the immediate relatives around one table.

Ralph had a brother and sister and their families—seven there.

Maggie had two sisters and a favorite niece with a large brood—eleven there.

Maggie and Ralph's two boys and their families brought the total to twenty-six.

Thanksgiving was the only yearly holiday this blended clan shared together. All the others, the individual families had to juggle in-laws and out-laws. But Thanksgiving had been special since Ma and Pa Bonner demanded their kids come home for Thanksgiving, even after they got married.

This was the day that carried on the unofficial pastime of North Dakota—telling family stories. Joya Bonner always said she became a good reporter because she grew up listening to her elders and knew she was expected to accurately pass these stories on.

"How old were you, Ralph, when you first went to work?" Alice asked, knowing her mother would love to tell about the family's regard for its firstborn.

"He was ten," her mother jumped in. "He shoveled coal down at the railroad, and came home all dirty. He put every penny in Ma's hands. And she needed it—Pa's paycheck was never enough. When he was twelve, he bought me a new pair of shoes for school. I cried, I was so happy because all the other girls had new shoes and mine were patched. He was always showing up with sticks of peppermint candy, and you know, except for the peanut brittle Ma made, we never got candy. He was fifteen when he stood up to the old man who came home drunk and angry and we all were afraid of him. Ralph quit school at sixteen when Dad got him a job on the Great Northern. He gave half his pay to Ma. He'd give me a quarter every payday. And of course, he had to have some for himself. Man, he was a handsome kid. The girls just loved him. Didn't they, Maggie?"

Everyone laughed and Ralph acted embarrassed by the attention. If his sister told that story once, she'd told it a hundred times, but she loved telling it and he secretly loved hearing it.

"I can't believe you guys were afraid of Grandpa Bonner," Alice offered, standing up for the man she and Joya had always adored, even if he did smell of snuff.

"Just a little," Ralph jumped in, giving his siblings the eye that this was enough information.

"How come you never farmed?" Alice asked, and that led to the stories of how Great-Grandpa Bonner immigrated from Bruckenthal, Austria, and since he was a cobbler, they settled in town, and then Grandpa got a job on the railroad when he was just a boy...

Alice smiled to herself midway through the afternoon, as pumpkin, apple, and mince pie were offered. This is what life is supposed to be. Families carrying on traditions and telling stories and caring about one another in a town so safe, trikes are left on the driveway overnight and Harley's Hardware keeps its Miracle Grow potting soil on the sidewalk.

Alice couldn't imagine living anywhere else, especially not a big city with its awful, dirty problems that were broadcast every night on the evening news. What normally passed for crime in Northville were the few things Mrs. Jersey slipped into her purse at the drugstore. But every month, Mr. Jersey got a bill that he paid without a word, so that really didn't count. You'd never see trash on the street or a traffic jam, even though there wasn't a single traffic light.

Alice felt blessed to live in a town where nobody knew your address, but everyone knew where you lived.

"Tell me a story, Uncle Alph," Danny demanded, as he climbed into his uncle's lap and put his finger in Ralph's pumpkin pie.

"It's okay, it's okay," Ralph told the table as Danny's father and mother both tried to shush him. Ralph had a special spot in his heart for his brother's "slow" son, and they were in the storytelling mood anyway.

"Tell him the one about the poor John Wendle family," Alice suggested, assuming her role as the town's messenger.

"Danny wouldn't like that one," Ralph cautioned, and Alice saw the wisdom. You don't tell a slow fourth-grader the story about a man who stands facing a blizzard and freezes to death saving his family. It would send the kid into hysterics.

Ralph had a better idea.

"Okay, Danny, want to hear how we deal with bad guys in Northville?"

Around the table, several sucked in their breath, fearing what was coming, but relieved when they heard it was the "Yegg" story.

"You weren't even born yet—neither was your dad—when these bad men tried to rob the Northville State Bank back in '29," Ralph began. "You know what they called burglars back then—they called them 'yeggs.'"

"Like eggs?" Danny interrupted. Everyone laughed.

"Yes, like eggs. They got in through a back window and were trying to steal everything the bank had. You know, your grandpa had his money in that bank, and so did a lot of other people in town, and it would have been just terrible if they'd gotten away with it. But thankfully, one of the Barton boys was on his way home from his railroad job and he saw them. He ran home and woke up his four brothers and everyone grabbed a shotgun. Two of them watched the bank while the others ran to tell the bank president what was up. Well, while they waited—I'm not sure this was the smartest thing—the men watching the bank decided to shoot their shotguns to scare the robbers and alert the town. Those robbers came rushing out of that bank and shot back and the Barton boys reloaded and wounded two of them. They followed the blood and held those men until the sheriff arrived. The Fargo Forum even wrote a story about the whole thing. They said, 'Local Boys Give Bandits Plenty of Number 6 Shot.'

"See Danny, in Northville, we take care of our families and we take care of business. We don't let people rob us."

The whole table was silent because they knew Ralph wasn't talking about the yeggs anymore.

Chapter Eleven

Sunday, December 12, 1999

Johnny Roth came out of his coma on December 12th—about the time Crabapple was halfway home.

His mother was sitting next to him, holding his hand and talking to him like the nurses had suggested, just as she'd done since that first terrible night.

He was already in a coma when Lois and Paul Roth got the horrible call from the sheriff's office in October, saying Johnny had been taken to the hospital in Breckenridge. They were offered no other news in that call, but you don't get a call from the sheriff without knowing it has to be bad.

Paul drove like a maniac the thirty miles, Lois crying all the way, expecting to find a body when she got there, rather than a son. Paul never cried—hadn't even when his dad died—but Lois thought his eyes looked moist.

Nettie Schlener was the first person Lois Roth saw when she ran into the emergency entrance. Oh my God, Johnny and Amber had an accident, she instantly thought as her mind conjured up twisted metal and broken glass and maimed children. The two women embraced. Lois knew Nettie was less than happy that her perfect daughter was dating Lois' imperfect son. But Lois herself was as pleased as pie about it. Amber was such a good, solid girl. She was no lightweight when it came to brains and the Good Lord had given her an extra dose of common sense. When you've got a rebellious son, you couldn't ask for anything better than an Amber.

"What happened?" Paul was frenzied, looking for anyone with news. But the emergency waiting room was empty except for nurses and Nettie, and she didn't know, either. None of them knew that most of the class of 2000 had been here earlier, but had slipped away so nobody had to face these parents.

"The doctor will be out shortly," the nurses said, as though speaking from a script.

So the three parents sat on the plastic molded chairs in the waiting room, wondering if they still had teenagers to raise. Lois thought she should call the other boys, but Paul said that could wait until there was something to report. Her youngest son in the hospital was enough for her, but Lois didn't contradict her husband. Nettie borrowed the front desk phone to call her brother and her sisters, and Arlene was there within a half-hour.

There's no way to describe the kind of dread a parent feels at a time like that, although every parent has a good idea what it feels like. They get enough practice those nights when they sit up, waiting for the family car to come home with the kid who, on second thought, never should have been given the keys. Teenagers always think curfews are meant to limit them. They don't understand until they're parents themselves—curfews just limit the hours of fear for the folks sitting at home.

And too many times, the fearful hours end in terror.

Paul Roth was prepared for that, as he sat in a room that could use a paint job. He was quite sure his wife wasn't, but Lois had always been frail. That's probably why he fell in love with her in the first place—he was strong and would take care of her. Hadn't done a bad job, either, although riches would never visit the Roth household. Paul never cared much about being rich. He never knew an honest man who was, and he was perfectly comfortable making a comfortable living, although the Good Lord didn't always let that happen.

Paul Roth had always provided a solid roof over his family's head and the cupboard was never bare, and he and Lois had even taken a trip to see his sister in Florida last year. Paul Roth never expected much else. In their twenty-eight years together, he and Lois had brought three sons into the world. Paul Jr. was in The Cities now, working for Honeywell and making a home for his wife and three kids. Jimmy had settled on the home place, with a trailer not far from his folks for his wife and two kids. And Johnny—Johnny was supposed to graduate high school this year and who knew how he'd end up?

How could his first two boys turn out so good, when the last one was so much trouble? It wasn't that Johnny got into criminal trouble, just nuisance stuff. Speeding. Poor grades. Expelled once for three days. Staying out all hours. That kind of trouble. The kind that Paul Roth's quick tongue and quicker fists couldn't stop. Not since the boy got too big to hit anymore.

Lois Roth would never admit to having a favorite, but in her heart, she knew it was Johnny. Not that she didn't love the other boys, but Johnny was such a surprise. Paul Jr. was ten and Jimmy was eight when Johnny was born and Lois couldn't have been happier. The first two arrived in those awful first years of the marriage, when Paul was waiting for his father to die so he could take over the farm. They lived in a trailer with nothing more than what Old Man Roth handed out. He was never known for his generosity

But by the time Johnny came, they were in their own house and Paul was the sole owner of the farm—brother LeRoy got land nearby—and Lois had the time, patience, and money to handle a baby. She fantasized that Paul would take a softer hand with their surprise child. Certainly he must share the joy of raising a child now that things were so much easier. And the first two were turning out so well—nice, respectful boys who did their chores and never talked back to their dad and weren't a bit of trouble, considering they were normal boys. Surely Paul wouldn't have to be so heavy-handed with Johnny. Maybe he could even show this boy some love.

Lois never understood that Paul was convinced his first two had turned out fine because his heavy hand kept them in line, so he saw no reason to abandon his winning streak.

Nor did he see the need to say out loud what must be obvious. He wouldn't work his ass off on the farm if he didn't love his family. He wouldn't be so strict if he didn't love his boys. He wouldn't hammer them on their studies if he didn't care. He'd be out spending his money at Jerry's Bar if his family didn't come first. Paul didn't think you had to be a rocket scientist to know he was a good, loving father. Actions speak louder than words, wasn't that the saying? Paul Roth had never been very good with words anyway, at least not those soft ones like Lois dished out. The softest words he ever used came every Sunday during mass, when his silent prayers thanked the Lord for giving him his boys.

If Lois Roth lived to be a hundred, she'd never understand why her husband saw his first parental responsibility as punishment. To her, it was natural to hug first, comfort first, and then dish out whatever penalty was due. Her approach worked—Paul's didn't—because unlike her husband, she knew the sweet joy of hearing her children say, "I love you."

Even she found it hard to love Paul at times, for a whole list of reasons. The worst one still played out in her memory from ten years ago, when Johnny was seven. His arm got caught in the thrasher and only by the grace of God, did he escape with no more than a gash that thirty stitches repaired. He bled all over the pickup as Lois and Paul rushed him to this hospital, and during the entire drive, Paul never let up on what a stupid mistake the boy had made to get injured in the first place. Lois wanted to tell her husband how heartless he sounded, but of, course she didn't. She joined Johnny in resenting every word.

And now who knew what the boy had done that landed him in the emergency ward? How mad would Paul be at yet another stupid mistake?

It took forever for the doctor to finally come out, looking for the parents that must hear bad news. Nettie's sister, Arlene, had arrived by then and all four adults jumped to their feet when the doctor walked in.

"I'm Doctor Clark. And you're...?"

"I'm Paul Roth and this is my wife, Lois, and our son Johnny is here. And this is Nettie Schlener and her daughter, Amber, is here. The sheriff called and told us to come."

The doctor asked Nettie and her sister to wait in a side room, as he pulled over a chair and sat close in front Johnny's folks. "I'm sorry to tell you, Mr. and Mrs. Roth, but your son is in a coma."

Lois nearly fainted from panic and shock.

"We believe he overdosed on drugs."

Lois didn't hear anything else. She didn't hear that Johnny also had a broken leg—that was irrelevant. She didn't hear her husband let out a stream of blasphemes. She didn't hear anything as she lost consciousness.

Later, Lois would be grateful that fainting kept her from the worst part of all. But Paul heard it, when the doctor left them to join Nettie and deliver the words of death. She was grateful she never heard the screams from poor Nettie and Arlene. She was grateful she didn't hear the hateful words Arlene spit at Paul.

A nurse was with Lois when she came to. She broke the news gently. Lois couldn't believe it. The nurse said the hospital would provide a cot if she wanted to stay in Johnny's room, and certainly, Lois Roth wanted to stay. In fact, she had to stay. By the time she'd regained consciousness, her husband had driven off like a bat out of hell.

Lois Roth had been sitting next to Johnny, holding his hand and talking to him like the doctors and nurses suggested, for most of the sixty-eight days he was in a coma. The first break was when she went home to attend Amber's funeral, but at the last minute, she couldn't face everyone and went back to the hospital. Her cousin told her Nettie let Amber wear the corsage that Lois had sent.

She had to break for Thanksgiving, as her other children and grandchildren wanted her, but thank the Lord that Jimmy's wife stepped up and cooked the turkey dinner. Lois adored her sweet daughter-in-law. But she found no relief from the annual dinner of family and abundance. All the healthy faces around the table couldn't erase the image of Johnny, pale and still. All the laughter of children couldn't overcome the silence of that hospital room. Even the mincemeat pie—made in her honor, as she was the only one who liked it—went uncut when Lois passed on dessert. As soon as dishes were done, Lois returned to her son's bedside.

Paul didn't share the vigil. He came back the day after "the accident," as Lois demanded it be called, and stayed an hour. But he couldn't abide sitting there when the farm needed attending. Johnny's brothers and their wives each came once, but it was pointless.

So Lois sat alone, willing her son to wake up. She convinced herself he could hear her, so she talked about the people he knew. She read him the *Fargo Forum* every day and the *News-Monitor* from home every week. The nice librarian from Hankinson brought her a pile of books Johnny would like, and Lois cried for an hour at that kindness.

She'd never been much of a reader herself, but she dived into the books and found some comfort for herself. *The Call of the Wild* by Jack London. *Treasure Island* by Robert Louis Stevenson. One day Lois picked up a thick book with an interesting cover and by the time she'd finished *Harry Potter and the Philosopher's Stone*, she was hooked. Thankfully, the librarian had brought the next two in the series, and Lois knew she'd read the rest of the books when they came out. The first time she smiled—a real smile over a pleasant thought, not a forced smile to be pleasant to the hospital staff—was when she realized she'd been looking for Platform 9 3/4 her entire life.

Lois was watching *I Love Lucy* reruns and relaying the story line to her son when Paul surprisingly walked in the door.

"No change?" he asked his wife.

"Nothing yet," she said. "You look tired, Paul. Here, sit down by him and talk to him. The nurses say that's the best thing we can do."

"No, you stay there."

Paul walked around the bed as though he were seeing the scene for the first time. "What are these machines for?"

"They're monitoring everything—his heart and brain and blood pressure. That other tube is the IV feeding. I think it's sugar water."

"Hum. Did the doctor say anything?"

"No, he says we just have to wait. He still thinks Johnny is going to come out of it."

They both were quiet for a long time.

"So, how you doin'?"

It didn't surprise Lois that her husband had taken so long to ask. "I'm fine. I'm tired. And the food here isn't anything to brag about. But I'm fine."

Another man would have taken his wife in his arms. Another man would have comforted her with whispered words of encouragement. But Lois Roth didn't expect that and as usual, her expectations were met. It was a relief when Paul said he was going to the cafeteria for a cup of coffee and a smoke. Lois went back to Lucy, like she was rejoining an old friend.

The credits were rolling when Johnny opened his eyes.

Lois didn't see it at first. She was looking at the TV screen and repeating the dialogue and all of a sudden, she felt pressure on her hand. It took her a few seconds to realize Johnny was squeezing it—not much, but a definite squeeze. He was looking at her when she turned her head away from the TV.

"Johnny!" She sucked in her breath. "Oh, Johnny. Oh, my boy. Oh, honey. Oh, God. Oh, thank you, God. Oh my God. Johnny."

She sprang up from her chair as she chanted the words, leaning over to kiss his cheek. "It's okay, honey. It's gonna be okay." She'd been instructed to alert the nurses if there was any change, but she forgot all that now as she clutched her son's hand and stared into his open eyes. Johnny kept blinking, trying to get a clear image and Lois kept talking: "You're going to be okay now. Don't worry. Everything's going to be okay. Don't move, honey.

You're hooked up to machines and there's a lot of tubes. Don't move, but you're going to be okay."

What Johnny first heard was this: "oin. be. ow. do. ked." It sounded like a radio station that keeps cutting out. It took a while before the words started to make sense. By then, the smoke that had covered his eyeballs was gone and he could easily see a woman—she's so familiar, I know this….Mother!

He opened his mouth, but the sounds that came out didn't resemble words, even to his own ears. His tongue felt thick and covered with cotton; his throat was raw, there was a bell ringing in his ears, his right leg felt like it was weighted down with an anchor. He kept trying to say, "Where am I?" but it came out as just a guttural noise.

Mothers may be the only ones who can understand the noises of their children, and Lois knew enough to ground her son to this moment as he came back to life. "You're. In. The. Hospital. Honey. In. Fargo. You're. Going. To. Be. Alright." She forced herself to say the words slowly, letting them sink in.

Another guttural noise that was supposed to be "Why?"

How many mothers in the world faced the task ahead of her? How do you explain what's happened? How do you tell your child that he might get out of this bed, but things are never really going to be okay again? How do you account for sixty-eight lost days, and the horrible night that started it? Carefully. Slowly. Prudently. She'd practiced it a million times as she sat here at his bedside, how she'd parse out the information. He didn't need to know much at first. First he had to get strong. Then they'd tell him. Then he could grieve. Lois planned to have the minister here when she finally told him the last awful truth he had to know. But that was way down the line. Right now, he didn't need to know any of that.

"Johnny, you overdosed at the barn dance, but the doctors say you're going to be alright. You'll be okay, son. Just stay quiet."

Lois finally remembered she was supposed to alert the medical staff, and she tried to pull away to go to the hall and call for help, but Johnny's grip tightened.

"Am I going to die?"

"No, sweetheart. No. No. No. You'll be okay. Don't worry. Just stay calm. I have to go get the nurses. Just stay quiet and I'll be right back."

Johnny hung on even tighter. "Am...Am....Amber?" he stammered as though a memory had been pricked.

Lois went from her joyful crying to anguish in a second.

"Oh, honey," she whispered. "Don't think about that now. Just think of waking up. Please, just wake up all the way. I'll get the nurses."

And that's when Paul Roth walked into the room.

Lois didn't know what she feared most, having to tell her son that Amber was dead or watching her volatile husband do it. Her worst fears were standing there, his fists clutched and his jaw working in anger. In her dreams, Lois had prayed this brush with death would touch Paul enough to show compassion, but one look and she knew she'd fooled herself again. Still, she tried her best.

"Look, Johnny's woke up, Dad. Isn't that wonderful?"

Paul never once looked at his wife.

"Well, you did it this time, you no-good, son of a bitch," Paul started, and even men more hard-assed than Paul would have flinched at the attack.

"I shoulda known you were into drugs. Anything to get in trouble. You've been trouble all your life. You had to be a smart ass, didn't you? You had to mess with stuff that could kill you. Bet you thought you were something. A big man! Well, it didn't kill you. But it sure as hell killed Amber. What that pretty little girl saw in you, I'll never know. But you know what it got her? It got her buried six feet under. And it got your whole family tarred like we were some no-goods. You should see how the men in town look at me now. And your brother. Like we're dirt! All because of you. Now how the hell you going to live with yourself?"

Lois was flailing her arms at Paul, trying to push away the words, trying to use her body to shield her son from this diatribe, but it did no good.

The monitors hooked up to Johnny's body went crazy.

Paul paced the room, continuing his verbal assault, as nurses and orderlies and doctors came rushing in, panicked by what they were seeing.

For once in her life, Lois raised her voice to her husband. She screamed at him with a force that astonished them both. "Stop it! Stop it! He just came out of a coma. My God, he's your son and he's alive. How in God's name can you be so damn cruel?"

Paul was stupefied that his wife would challenge him. He was so stunned, he didn't have an instant retort. He wouldn't get another chance this day, as the room filled with people in white who pushed him and Lois aside.

To a trained eye, the heart rate and blood pressure inside Johnny Roth's body were heading toward a stroke. Nobody could even interpret what the brain monitor was showing. But you didn't need medical training to see this boy was in utter agony.

He didn't so much scream as burst with a sound both frightening and pitiful. One hand was making a slow journey toward his face. The other was stretching forward, like he was warding off a knife attack. All ten of his fingers were frozen in a curl that reminded one of the nurses of her spastic patient down the hall. He tried to pull his knees up to his chest, as though it were imperative that he return to the fetal position. While all the time his vocal chords made the scream-moan of a dying animal.

Lois feared she was watching her son die.

Paul turned away, finding the sight and the sound unbearable.

"What happened?" the doctor demanded in his sharpest tone. "What the hell happened?"

"I told him his girlfriend was dead," Paul Roth said, as though that benign explanation characterized the words he'd just uttered.

As an orderly held Johnny's convulsing body, the doctor jabbed him with a hypo that sent him back into that gray world where unconsciousness and comas are first cousins.

Lois slumped against the wall, making herself as small as possible, determined to stay put. Paul turned, and left without a word to his wife. She didn't see him go because she wouldn't take

her eyes off Johnny. But she was relieved when she finally realized he was gone. She knew she'd never share a loving moment
with Paul Roth again.

This place is familiar.

It isn't quite the same, but it's close.

*Lighter. Airier. Is that a fog machine kicking up all this mist? Is
it smoke? Why doesn't it smell?*

*I can move more now. Have I lost weight? Was I unshackled? It's
better here. No wait. No wait!*

As Johnny rethought the situation he realized that before,
there was nothing. He couldn't remember thinking a single thing
in all that time when he didn't even wonder where he was. But
now lots of thoughts swirled around like the fog.

*I'm not dead. I'm not going to die. My mom is here. She's by me. This
is going to end. This isn't permanent. My dad...I'm not going to die.
My dad...OH HOLY GOD, MY DAD SAID AMBER IS DEAD.*

Johnny Roth tried to go back to that heavy, dark place where
such a thing wasn't possible. But no matter how fast he ran, or
which direction he turned, he couldn't find the entrance to the
tunnel of that place. His dad's angry words kept ringing out
over the loudspeaker hidden in the fog. The man wasn't lying.
The man was a lot of things, but he never lied. And his mom's
face—for a brief moment as he heard the words, he looked to
that kind woman and saw in her eyes that truth was being told.

*He said I killed Amber. I didn't. I didn't. That's a damn lie. I
wouldn't have done that. I couldn't have done that. I didn't mean
to do that. We were just going to try it. She didn't want to, but I
thought it would be fun just to try it. Everybody did. Just a little.
To see what the big deal was all about. How can you die from that
stuff? You're not supposed to die. It's supposed to be fun. It was our
senior prank. It was just for fun. I didn't kill her. Oh, God, Amber.
I didn't mean it. I love you. I love you more than anything. I'd
never hurt you. Never.*

As this pitiful confession broadcast through the fog, Johnny
knew only one thing. He never wanted to come back.

Chapter Twelve

Thursday, December 16, 1999

Alice Peters started another pot of coffee and smiled to herself that things were finally going back to normal. Any minute now, the men would come into her bakery for their afternoon card game.

It was December 16, 1999. There was a healthy mound of snow outside, left behind by the city's snowplow, but the temperature was kind—forty-six degrees, what passes for balmy in North Dakota in December. The bakery felt especially cozy today and the smell of cupcakes baking for tomorrow's baby shower made it inviting and homey. She looked around the free-standing two-room building with only two more years of mortgage payments, pleased that she was a businesswoman in a town with the slogan, "Kindness is Our Way of Life."

Officially, this was the City of Northville—an honorific the state conferred on every community, no matter how big or small. Some thought that helped compensate for the bad self-image North Dakota was supposed to have. Alice thought it was an acknowledgment that every settlement in the thirty-ninth state was important.

Some might think of Northville as the middle of nowhere, but here, folks saw themselves in the middle of everything. Alice often heard, "We know when we have it good," and the nine hundred forty-seven residents—especially the six hundred seventy-eight who got Social Security checks every month—knew what good looked like.

You wouldn't call it a quaint town. The gingerbread of New England never made it to the plains of Dakota Territory, where German practicality outscored English fussiness. But it was a pretty little town on the prairie of the Red River Valley, founded over a hundred years ago to serve the homesteads that made North Dakota part of the breadbasket of America. It never grew much bigger than it was today and never attracted many outsiders. Farms or the railroad brought people here and kept people here. The only real growth now was the farmers who retired and left the family farm to their sons—the Mrs. especially thrilled because she got a dream house in town as reward for all those years making due in that old farmhouse.

Alice heard it every day—wouldn't it be nice if the town could hold onto more of the young ones, like it had hung onto her?

But the jobs were elsewhere, the excitement was elsewhere, the world was elsewhere and most of the kids who graduated every May were anxious to be elsewhere. They came back only for a visit. This town held onto your heart, if not your hide.

Her own cousin, Joya, was a good example. She was home every year to spend part of her three-week vacation with her folks. Alice loved visiting with her big-city cousin over a cup of strong, black coffee.

"Girl, you make me tired just telling me what you do every week," Alice chided. "You must think we're as dull as dishwater."

"I do not," Joya always objected. "No, this isn't like Phoenix, but it's nice. I wouldn't come back if I didn't like being here. Mom and Dad come out to visit me, you know, so I don't have to come here to see them. But I like it here. Sometimes I wished I'd stayed."

Alice laughed. "You'd have died of boredom. No, you belong in Phoenix. But glad we're a nice break for you!"

Over the last two weeks, the cousins had burned up the phone lines. Alice reassured her cousin more than once that what her parents reported was all talk and bluster. There was nothing to worry about. Yeah, everyone was riled up, but Crabapple had split, and he had to be smart enough to know he could never come back. Alice promised Joya that by the time she came home for her next visit, all this would be history.

Alice prayed at night that she was telling the truth. Not just to cover her promise, but to quell the butterflies in her stomach. The town needed to put all this behind it and get back to being the safe, secure place it had always been.

Alice Peters was as invested in Northville as anyone—had been since she graduated high school in 1959 and got married that summer. The marriage didn't last and he split, but she raised her three kids here. One daughter stayed on and had Alice's two grandchildren, hardening the cement. At forty—still pretty, with a taste for tight jeans—she was happy with her decisions.

Alice wiped off the large table in the middle of the front room and passed the sign her dad made when she opened this business eight years ago: "The hurrier I go, the behinder I get." Right on cue, the bell on the front door jingled and the men walked in.

"There you are," she announced. "You know, we could set a clock on you guys!"

The men laughed. Of all the regular-as-clockwork routines in this town, the men's Monday and Thursday card game topped the list. The group fluctuated, with some guys showing up now and then, but it always included the unofficial leaders of this town—Ralph Bonner, Bernard Stine, and Earl Krump.

On Tuesdays, Wednesdays, and Fridays, the Senior Citizen Center served a hot noon meal that was usually above par, and these men and their wives ate there. This was the meal called "dinner"—a nod at how important it was to fuel up at noon for the afternoon's work in a farming community. The evening meal that was called dinner elsewhere was "supper" in these parts. Before any meal in Northville was a prayer, and at the Senior Citizen Center, it was sung.

*"Praise God from whom all blessings flow, praise Him all crea-
tures here below. Praise Him above the heavenly host. Praise Father,
Son, and Holy Ghost."*

They all stayed to spend the afternoon playing cards or domi-
noes with the widows who dominated the center's membership,
and after "lunch" at four—coffee, a sweet—they went home to
spend the night in front of the television.

But Monday and Thursday afternoons were devoted to the
men's-only game at the bakery—poker or smear—where the
coffeepot was never empty, and there always was a gooey treat
handy.

If she were pushed, and the day was fast coming when Alice
Peters was pushed plenty, she'd give chapter and verse about
what fine men these were.

Ralph is "my favorite uncle, and he was on the City Council
for four years," she bragged, mimicking the admiration of her
mother. "Bernard is Santa Claus at Christmas, for God's sake!
And Earl practically built the city park by himself. These are
good, honest, honorable men."

The three had been friends since grade school—none actually
finished high school. Bernard was an orphan and had to work
to help support himself; Earl was a farmer's son—ducks don't
take to water like Earl Krump took to farming—and Ralph
got a railroad job through his dad. The only time they'd ever
been separated was during World War II. All three had gone to
Wahpeton to sign up to fight Japs the day after Pearl Harbor.
Bernard and Earl went into the Army, but by the time Ralph
got to the front of the line, the recruiter said the country needed
Marines and so that's where he ended up. He went to the Pacific
Theater while Bernard was sent to Germany. Earl's eyes were so
bad he couldn't go into battle, but spent his hitch doing office
work in Minneapolis.

All three came home to marry their sweethearts, raise their
children, and take care of their hometown. They joined the
American Legion—their wives belonged to the Women's Aux-
iliary and Maggie Bonner was president for eight years. Most of

the scars of the war were inside their heads, although Bernard had frozen his feet in Germany and suffered for the rest of his life.

Ralph ended up selling farm equipment. Bernard bought the grocery store. Earl farmed until he retired and moved into town. They were so active in the church—each one tithed—that whenever a new priest came to town, these three filled him in on the lay of the land.

The question wasn't if these men belonged to the NRA but how long they'd been card-carrying members, and the first time Ralph voted for a Democrat the other men made him buy a round at Jerry's Bar as penance.

If you wanted something done in Northville, the short list included these three men. All were retired now, enjoying their mid-seventies with pensions and Social Security and the respect of the community.

These were men who knew they'd someday have a big funeral in the Catholic church where they'd worshiped all their lives. After all, in a town where everybody knows everybody, it's only decent to say goodbye when it's your time to go. They knew their families would eat funeral hotdish after they came back from that pretty cemetery outside town, where they laid near their parents, their grandparents, and their great-grandparents.

Alice could recite chapter and verse about these fine men, and except for Earl's temper, there was little to list as faults. Stubborn, sure, but then, they were Germans and you expect that of German men. "You know what they say," Alice often joked out of their earshot: "You can tell a German, but you can't tell him much."

So Alice kept the coffeepot full and welcomed them every Monday and Thursday, blending into the background as they played their games, gossiped and told their silly jokes.

For some reason, Alice would always remember the groaner joke on this particular day—an Ole and Lena joke that poked fun at Swedes: "Ole left Lena at home one day and went fishing with Sven when he caught a magic walleye. The fish looked up at him and said, 'I can give you anything you want,' and Ole said, 'By jimminy, I want a million dollars,' and the boat filled up with hundred-dollar bills. Sven's eyes were as big as saucers and he jumped right in, 'Well, I want the lake to be all beer,' and wham, the water turned to Schlitz. Ole glared at his friend: 'Oh, Sven, how could you do that? Now we've got to pee in the boat.'"

Alice's eavesdropping on this December day paid particular attention to the key phrases that signaled a serious topic: "You know what a guy could do" or "A guy wouldn't be wrong if..." or "It wouldn't be right for a guy..."

It was normally just conjecture and thinking out loud, but since Amber died, those words often had a sinister tone. "This was not Amber Schlener's time to go—not by seventy or eighty years. Not her. Not like that. Not here. *Got im Himmel, not here!*" She heard oaths of vengeance that scared her and pledges of retribution that she prayed were just big talk.

But that wasn't the worst part. The worst part was what she couldn't hear when the voices got so soft, she knew the words were private. Or when the men decided to take a break from cards and walk outside and huddle in a little group. Through the big picture window she could see they sometimes got animated, their arms flying. That never lasted and before they came back in, she'd see heads bobbing in unison as a great agreement was reached.

"You guys have a secret?" she dared ask one day.

Ralph said, "No, just a medical problem that's personal."

Alice wished she believed he was telling the truth. Underneath it all, she saw the guilt. Three men around that card table felt a responsibility for Amber's death. One day she tried to relieve their remorse.

"You know, you guys tried your best to get rid of that kid. A lot of people would have just turned away and not done anything. But you guys went to the sheriff. You went to the school board. You alerted everyone. I'm proud of you for that. The whole town is. Everyone knows how hard you tried. That's a lot more than most people would do. None of this is your fault. Uncle Ralph. Bernard. Earl. You hear me? Jelly donuts on the house today."

Of course, she thanked the Lord that Crabapple had left town the night Amber died—was it really two months ago already? She prayed every day she'd never see him again.

After the funeral, Alice had waited for the wound to start healing. But then, Sheriff Potter showed up and it got ugly.

Like everyone else, the sheriff knew exactly where to find the men who held sway in this town. A week after the funeral, there he was, adjusting his holster belt and swaggering into the bakery with his usual air of authority.

"I knew I'd find you boys here." He pulled up a chair and sat on it backwards. "I'm sure you're aware I'm in town investigating the death of that girl…"

"Amber," Earl spit out. "Her name was Amber."

"Ya, sure, Amber. Sorry. I've had two deputies going around collecting evidence. We're talking to everybody and I knew you guys would be here so I am here to personally get what you know."

"We know that Darryl "Crabapple" Harding sold the drugs that killed Amber," Earl declared, like he was on the witness stand.

"Did you personally see this man sell drugs?" The sheriff asked in a tone that told everyone he already knew the answer.

"No, but everyone knows," Earl shot back.

"Well, then it must be true," the sheriff dripped sarcasm, and Alice could imagine Earl decking the SOB.

"Well, boys, I'll tell you. We searched his house and we didn't find any drugs. And we talked to the kids at the high school and none of them know a thing. Funny how that happens. Not one of them says they saw him sell the drugs. Not one. Of course, none of them admit to taking any drugs, either. Isn't it amazing? Must have been only Amber and the boy, that's all."

"Johnny Roth," Bernard injected. "He's not just the boy. His name is Johnny Roth." Alice was proud they stood up for Johnny, even though they all cursed him for buying drugs in the first place.

The sheriff ignored the scolding and waded into the weeds.

"Well, it looks like this Crabapple kid skipped town. Or disappeared. Or something. Any of you know anything about that?"

"Now what do you think we would know about that?" Ralph Bonner asked in his most incredulous voice, his brown eyes flashing. "Sheriff, you have a tendency to look everywhere except at what's in front of your face. Now you're asking about *us*? What the hell are you thinking? We came to you with this problem and you couldn't be bothered. Now, look what happened. We told you so. I'll tell you this—we don't know where he is but he better not come back to this town."

"Now, son, don't get riled. We're doing everything we can to find out the facts in this case, I can assure you. You need proof, boys, not just gut instincts. Proof. Now, if you have any proof to give me, I'd sure like to hear it."

Nobody said a word. The sheriff hoisted himself up real slow. He adjusted his holster belt again and stood over the men like he was the king on the hill.

"You boys just take it easy and let the law do its job. If you hear anything or know anything, you know my number. I don't like drug dealers any more than you do, but I've got to have evidence. So take care and stay calm and let's see what happens. Hell, maybe the kid is gone forever and your problems are over."

Alice remembered him sauntering out of her bakery—pulling the door back and forth to make the bell sing its head off—and she felt the same contempt the men did. She didn't turn around as she went back to the kitchen, so she wasn't sure which one spewed out, "I haven't been called a boy for fifty years."

But she was sure this proof-versus-know argument held no more sway with these men than the first time they heard it a year ago, when they'd tried to prevent a tragedy like Amber's death. These were men who watched enough cop shows on TV—there's not a lot else to do on a cold North Dakota night—to know that good cops go out and GET the proof they need. They don't sit on their fat asses and complain that it didn't walk in the front door. Besides, these men had lots of personal experience in proof-versus-know—all were the law in their own homes and all had raised children. When they were convinced, that was proof enough. And as any child knows, the threshold for proof is far lower for fathers than it is for mothers.

But since Sheriff Potter's awful visit, things were slowly working their way back to normal. Johnny had woken up—again. His broken leg was healing inside the thick cast that demanded he use crutches. His folks brought him home over the weekend and the word was he was going to be alright. Everyone was nervous to see him. What do you say to the boy? How do you treat him?

Alice hoped people would be kind—kinder than Johnny's own father, from what she heard. Everyone knew the boy would be scarred—you don't have a loss like this without consequences. Her own cousin, Mary, was proof. Years ago she was babysitting and the poor little girl fell out of her highchair and landed on her head. The girl was never right after that and Mary entered the nunnery to do penance for her mistake. Alice knew the religious life wouldn't be where Johnny Roth found his solace, and she worried what was waiting on the other side of the road. More likely, he'd move away to avoid a whole town that knew what he'd done.

Johnny was one of the threads of today's slow conversation. How was he? Was there any brain damage? Was he going back to school? How did he look? How did he sound? What would become of him? When was the cast coming off?

"I hear his classmates all went out to see him at home," Bernard offered. "He's not strong enough to get around yet."

"They're standing by him," Ralph noted. "That's good. The boy needs support."

Another hand of Smear was dealt. All attention was on the trick-taking game as Earl's team won the bid. The game was almost over when someone offered, "Yeah, the poor kid needs support. It's a helluva thing to go through life with that hanging over your head."

Two games later, Earl said, "I hear he said he's going to kill Crabapple." Alice stopped kneading her Dakota Maid dough and held her breath.

"Yeah, I heard that too," Bernard chimed in, letting out a deep sigh like it had been weighing on his shoulders.

Alice stayed transfixed as the game finished and points were counted. It wasn't until she heard the cards being shuffled that Ralph spoke the words that gave her chills.

"It wouldn't be right for a guy to let that happen."

The next "oh, no" moment came when Alice heard the bell and looked up to see LeRoy Roth walking through her front door. There was no one she hated more seeing in her bakery—or anywhere else, for that matter.

"LeRoy Roth is certifiably nuts," she often declared, and there wasn't a person in Northville that didn't agree.

Johnny's uncle was the only card-carrying member of the extreme right-wing group called the Posse Comitatus. They hated Jews, Blacks, Mexicans, gays, women's libbers, and anyone associated with the government. They saw a communist under every tree and thought Hitler wasn't that far off. LeRoy was always trying to recruit new members, but thankfully, hadn't found any takers.

The man had quit paying taxes years ago, claiming the federal government was operating under the Communist Manifesto rather than the U.S. Constitution. That was the same reason he opted out of Social Security, informing Washington in a letter address to "The Synagogue of Satan." He recognized only "township government," which didn't exist anywhere except in his head. Even free public schools were a communist plot, and he believed America got into World War II because the feds lied about Pearl Harbor. That thought alone was enough to turn off the men at the card table.

If there was one subject on which LeRoy Roth was absolutely obsessed, it was the fate of his idol and fellow North Dakota farmer, Gordon Kahl. Some call the 1983 tragedy "North Dakota's most notorious crime," and LeRoy never got over it. The way he told the story, Kahl and his family were ambushed by evil federal agents who got themselves killed—what they deserved for going after an honest patriot. The way the FBI told it, Kahl was an armed and dangerous fanatic who killed two federal marshals who were trying to arrest him for probation violations.

And then there was Ruby Ridge in 1992 and Waco in 1993, and LeRoy kept stepping deeper and deeper into the fanatical world of the ultra right-wing—so much that his brother, Paul, hardly talked to him anymore. These days, the communist conspiracy took backstage to the "Zionist conspiracy," and just mention a homosexual and LeRoy might shoot on sight.

So Alice Peters wasn't the only one who got nervous whenever he crossed the threshold.

LeRoy Roth burst into the bakery. "The Bastard's Back," he announced, like it was the title of a play.

Chapter Thirteen

Thursday, December 16, 1999—Wednesday, January 5, 2000

As Christmas approached, the wiretaps secretly invading Sammy Gravano's life counted in the thousands.

Joya was ashamed that she didn't worry about how many of these were illegal, how many calls had nothing to do with drugs and everything to do with the daily life of a family. She knew the cops weren't supposed to listen to everyday conversations, but you never knew when one thing began and the other stopped. It made her uncomfortable that she was so ready to give the cops a pass on what was legal and what wasn't.

It was a long-established problem of the press that reporters assigned to cover the "cop shop" got too cozy with the police they were supposed to be watch-dogging. They ended up seeing the cops' side of things, even when the cops were wrong. Joya now realized how easy that was. But she'd made a deal with the devil, so she stuffed away her qualms.

She couldn't ignore the problems at home that easily.

Joya hated it when the cracks started showing up. Not the creases—his inability to put down the toilet seat or throw away his own beer cans—but the cracks that let in light.

The first crack was predictable. Joya had dated enough divorced men to know that the ex never liked the new girl-friend—"Get your fat ass out of my husband's apartment!" or

"Help yourself to my leftovers, honey, but he'll never stay with you over me!" But those calls and ex problems usually rose at the start of the relationship, so she got agitated when the call came to her house six months after he'd moved in.

"Is Rob there?" The female voice on the other end sounded official and impatient.

"Who may I say is calling?"

"It's Rose. I need him." There was such entitlement in the voice that Joya felt like yelling, "Fucking Heavenly Queen, Mother of Your Children is calling." But she didn't. Maybe one of the kids was hurt. She announced the call and even Rob looked a little startled that she was calling *here*.

He rushed to the phone and listened a minute. "I'll be there as soon as I can."

On his way to the bathroom, he told Joya, "Her sinks are all plugged up. I need to go help her."

"She couldn't call a plumber?"

"Our house is old and the pipes are touchy and I've fixed them a dozen times."

"And a plumber couldn't?"

He gave her a dirty look and jumped into clothes to rush out the door.

She watched the back of the door for a minute, mulling over his exit. To Rob, it was still "our house." He jumped when she called. What could possibly go wrong here?

The second crack was a surprise. She came home one Friday afternoon to find a woman with legs up to here and tits hanging out of her velvet shirt walking through her living room.

"Hi, Joya," the fancy lady said over her shoulder as she walked into the kitchen.

Joya wouldn't have been more surprised if she'd encountered a giraffe in her home. She followed the woman—there was a hint of recognition—but before she could ask the obvious question, the woman started laughing.

"Don't recognize me, do you?"

The voice gave her away. "Mary Kay? Is that you, Mary Kay? Holy shit, what have you done to yourself?"

The last time Joya saw Detective Mary Kay Grimes, she was sitting at her desk on the fifth floor, discussing the value of the wiretaps with Joya. Mary Kay was a passably-pretty woman and a little skinny. But here she was, dolled up like a hooker, standing in Joya's kitchen.

"What's going on?"

"We're going undercover tonight to the clubs in Scottsdale. Detective Cope needs us. He's been buying Ex for months— nothing big, twenty-five, fifty pills at a time—but tonight he's going to try and make a big buy and hope that smokes out Mike Papa and the Gravano kid."

"Wow. That's big. They hang out at these clubs?"

"Oh, sure. You should see Papa—he's the king of the hill. Silk shirt open. Gold necklaces around his hairy neck. He looks ridiculous, but he thinks he's cool. He's a real bad-ass. Comes out of the East Valley. He headed some racist gangs out there—the Devil Dogs, White Power. He's a mess. Sammy's kid follows him around like a puppy dog. We hope they got the word a big buyer's in town and they show up. But you never know about undercover work."

What Joya knew about undercover work was that you needed to be young, with a smokin' body. It wasn't work for her.

"Well, you look…"

"If you think I look hot, wait till you see Sandy."

"Sandy's going too? Where is she?"

"She's in the bedroom getting ready."

"Where's Rob?"

"He's back there, too, getting into his get-up."

Joya blanched. Sandy wasn't passable, but a flat-out fox. Even in the police uniform of polyester pants with shirt tucked in, she looked hot. And she was back in the bedroom with Rob? Joya could imagine how she'd gussy up, but when Sandy walked into the kitchen, she realized her imagination was lazy.

Sandy's black satin pants were so tight, she couldn't be wearing underwear. Even a thong would have shown. Her boobs were up high and perked, and she had a red flower in her blonde hair. There was enough makeup on her face to open a counter at Macy's.

"Holy shit."

"She says that a lot," Mary Kay laughed. Sandy laughed back, already showing the confidence of a woman who can look like that.

And then Rob appeared—or someone who resembled the man who lived here, in a creepy way. He looked a decade younger than his thirty-nine years in his weight-lifting body and black leather jacket and silver chain around his neck. His pants were the kind of tight meant to show off his package, and even though Joya knew that part of his anatomy quite well, she was still impressed at how absolutely well it showed itself. His hair was slicked back. His hands held a wad of hundred-dollar bills that could have paid cash for a house.

"Did you see the 600 SL convertible outside?" He was trying to ignore how she kept muttering "Holy shit." Sure, she'd seen the snazzy car, but had guessed someone was visiting a neighbor. "That's our ride tonight." Rob was eager to get behind the wheel.

The three of them started a checklist of names and info they'd pass out tonight as they posed as a high-rolling party from Paradise Valley. Mary Kay would be known as Katie. Sandy would be known as Susy. Neither needed a last name. Rob would be Deacon, but they argued over what his last name should be.

"How about Goldwater?" Sandy suggested, and the other two said that was too familiar a name in these parts to be safe. "How about Goldberg?"

"Too Jewish."

"How about Martinez?"

"Do I look Mexican?"

"How about Sinclair, like the old oil company?"

"Perfect."

Deacon Sinclair didn't even give his girlfriend a kiss as the three waltzed out the door for a night of drinking and snorting—sometimes undercover required it—and dirty dancing.

Joya stared at the back of the door. She felt incredibly plain and undesirable. She stuffed it down with a bowl of ice cream.

She tried waiting up for Rob, but by one a.m. she was snoozing on the couch and by four a.m. she was in deep REM sleep. He woke her up with a sexy, heavy kiss. He wrapped her in his arms and cooed at her. His arms were too rough and his kiss tasted too much like scotch and weed.

Rob led her to bed and almost tore her dressing gown off her. They had furious, almost violent sex. At first, Joya tried to match his passion before sensing it didn't make any difference. He didn't need a partner, he just needed a warm body. She laid under him and wondered which one of his undercover hotties he was balling in his fantasy.

By the time Rob woke up Saturday morning, Joya was on her regular walk. She marched down the historic streets of Phoenix, talking herself out of her anger and angst. Did he use her last night or was it her insecurity? Should she be worried or was her imagination working overtime? Sure, things were tough right now. This case was wearing them both out. Just fatigue, she argued to herself. Don't jump to conclusions. Yet she couldn't escape the fact that with every step, she felt blinded by the sunlight pouring through this crack in their relationship.

Rob was nursing a cup of coffee when she came in. He wasn't going to see his kids until later in the afternoon, and she agreed that had been a smart move. She pretended everything was okay.

"So tell me what it's like," she asked in her best reporter's voice.

"I think we made contact. At least, we let them know we were in the market. We asked for five hundred pills, and nobody would hand them over. But everyone kept warning us that if we went that big, the 'New York guys' would think we were dealing and then they'd want a 'tax' on every pill. We told them, no way. We just liked to party. Tell the New York guys that."

"That's good, right?"

"That's fuckin' good."

They didn't talk about last night and never would. Rob left soon with an excuse he had errands to run and Joya was frankly happy to see him go. She curled up on the couch and ordered a science fiction movie on pay-per-view.

On Monday, Joya stopped by Mary Kay's desk to get her impressions of the night of sin.

"You're not going to believe this." She leaned in. "I was dancing with this yo-yo who kept trying to kiss my tits and this kid is gyrating like he's a spaz. It's really hot in those clubs and this music was really making us move and this kid pulls up his shirt to cool off and guess what—he had a baby bull tattooed on his stomach!"

"You're kidding. Was it Gerard Gravano?"

"Sammy's son in the flesh! Sandy danced with him once."

"Was Mike Papa there?"

"No, he didn't show, but I bet he got our message."

"You guys going out again?"

"Oh, yeah, get used to it. We've got to keep showing up until Papa comes to us. But I don't think it will take long. That Gravano kid was already trying to seduce Sandy, bragging he could get her all the drugs she wanted. But that kid's too dumb—he may be a little 'slow'—to be the brains of this. He's doing somebody else's bidding."

Joya took notes. This would be a great tidbit in her piece.

The wiretap chatter kept up, nothing big enough to send someone to jail, but big enough to add later, after the "big score." Joya found it amusing that police looked on arresting Sammy with the same words Sammy's people looked on a big drug deal. A Big Score.

Christmas became the third crack. The one that broke everything in two.

Her hometown was hurting because of this horrible drug problem, and Cousin Alice kept her informed on how unsettled the town had become. Joya's original plan was to go to North-ville for Christmas and check it out for herself. Maybe visit that stupid sheriff and demand an update, throw her investigative reporter weight around a little. But as the brick wall of Sammy's story kept stacking up, she knew she couldn't leave. It shocked her that Rob couldn't see that.

"I really think you should go home for Christmas and see your folks," he offered one night over dinner. "I think they need you. I think you need to see for yourself."

"Oh, for God's sake, Rob, there's no way I can go home now. What if the Sammy story broke and I'm halfway across the country? You think I'd jeopardize all this work to go home for Christmas? Don't be an idiot. I'd never forgive myself if I was that unprofessional. I'd never let that kind of sentimentality get in the way of this story. And my editor would kill me. Would *you* take off now to visit your folks? Of course not. And if you think for one second I don't take my job as seriously as you take yours, well, you're wrong, buddy. Rob, this might be the biggest story of my life. Reporters don't get inside police investigations every day, you know. With a famous Mafia snitch. With a huge drug ring. Jesus, this is a reporter's dream come true and I'm on top of it. No, I can't go home. I wouldn't dream of going home. My feet are nailed to the floor here. Now, if you guys do your job and nab him before Christmas, that would be a different story. But I sure don't see that happening."

Rob got up from the table and put his plate in the sink. "I was just trying to be helpful," he said over his shoulder, as he grabbed his jacket. "And if you think we're lollygagging around to make your life miserable..." He slammed the door behind him.

She stewed all night. First she blamed him for a ridiculous suggestion. "So, he thinks my job isn't that important? That I'm not as dedicated to this as he is? Fuck him." Then she blamed herself. "Did you hear the hurt in his voice? Jesus, we can't even talk to each other anymore. Joya, you are such a bitch."

Rob didn't come home that night. The next day at police headquarters, she grabbed his sleeve to pull him aside.

"I'm sorry, Rob. I had no right to snap at you like that. You were trying to help. I'm so on edge, you know? And I'd love to go home, but I just can't risk it. And I didn't mean that shit about you guys—I know you're working your tails off."

"I know," he said. He gave her hand a half-hearted squeeze. "We're all on edge. This case is driving us nuts. We thought we'd have him by now. Don't worry about it."

"I won't worry if you don't worry. We're okay, right?"

"Sure. We're fine."

"I know, let's go out tonight and not say one word about this case."

"Sure. Maybe. Let's see how the day goes." He winked as he walked away.

Joya could recognize whistling in the wind when she heard it. They were both whistling their hearts out.

It was all downhill after that.

Rob traded off with the single detectives so he could spend Christmas with his kids. But Joya never expected him to move home with Rose and spend *all* the time with his family. He promised he was staying in the guest room and the kids were so little they *needed* him in the house over Christmas.

Wait for New Year's Eve. That will be *our* night.

But New Year's Eve was a bust, too. The one big "date night" of the year—and this one the turn of the century!—found her dateless. Rose called with an "emergency" and Rob went running. Joya went to dinner with friends, but was home so early, she saw the ball drop in New York, two hours ahead of Arizona.

Joya started the year 2000 knowing it was hopeless. Hell, it had been ridiculous to think she could date a cop in the first place. But Rob was different. She felt so safe with him. They'd had such fun in the beginning. He was helpful around the house. He had a great sense of humor—she could run that list in her mind all day and still come up with the same conclusion. They'd tried. They'd failed.

There was no final scene. No screaming and crying. No lies about how this isn't your fault, it's mine. No soft talk about how you deserved more. Someone special. I'm not the one. She came home one Tuesday and his clothes were no longer in the closet.

A note sat on the kitchen counter under the salt shaker. "I'll always love you. Sorry it didn't work out." He didn't even sign it.

She got her back up and refused to cry. "The only good thing to come out of this relationship was the Sammy story," she said out loud, sounding every bit a bitch. She drank one scotch after another that night. The liquor finally broke down the locked door of her heart.

"Rob, oh Rob. We were so good together until this goddamned Sammy thing came up. Good men like you don't come around every day. I loved you. Man, I loved you. Why wasn't that enough? Why couldn't that keep us on track? I tried. I really tried."

She cried herself to sleep. In the morning, her eyes were swollen. She put ice packs on her face and laid down an extra half-hour before she dared go to police headquarters.

But the break-up gods were kind to Joya. The next day she heard about the twenty-five thousand pills the Arizona ring was buying out of California. She was so busy with this incredible news, she didn't have time to mope.

The code was thick, but by now, Phoenix PD had it down pretty pat, so they knew the pills were coming and they were going to be dropped at University and Mill in Tempe, catty-corner from P.F. Chang's restaurant.

Joya wanted to go along on the surveillance, but this is where the police chief put his foot down. She stayed back in the wiretap room, monitoring the progress of the drop from police radios.

Sergeant Cope and Rob were hiding on the top level of a two-story parking garage practically on top of the drop. Rob took pictures as one guy handed over money in a red backpack, while the other guy swapped a black sack with the Ex pills. Neither guy was Sammy. Nor were they any of the principals the cops were following. No Mike Papa. No Gerard Gravano.

"Where are they?" Joya almost screamed the question, thinking this was going to be *it*.

"Those guys don't get their hands dirty on deliveries," the captain told her, more kindly than he would have when she first showed up. "Now we follow the money."

"Great," Joya thought to herself. "More delays. More stake-outs. More sitting around waiting for something to happen. God, this is never going to be over!"

She was never so happy to find herself wrong the next day. Joya was doodling in her notebook and wondering if she could get away for a haircut when she heard Mike Papa scream into a tapped phone, "My Godfather gave that money to me and he counted it himself. No fuckin' way it's ten thousand short."

The captain didn't have to snap his fingers for Joya to alert the others. Within minutes, the room was filled with officers listening as a drug courier insisted the money from the Tempe drop was ten big ones shy.

That wasn't the only call. Another just like it came the next day. Papa was even more belligerent. "The Big Man" himself had made sure all the money was there, and that was the end of it.

And then another tap caught Sammy's daughter, Karen, speculating about the missing money with her boyfriend, David Seabrook. David thought Papa had taken the ten-G, and Karen said he'd better tell her dad. When Seabrook showed up at Marathon Construction, to the delight of the cops staking it out, the blinds were open. They clearly saw Sammy waving his arms.

"You could tell he was really ticked," Cope told Joya. She'd never seen such a big smile on his face before. Because now police had "probable cause" that Sammy was holding drug meetings in his office. They went to court and got an order to expand the wiretaps to Marathon Construction. And Cope assured her of something else that now was clear: This wasn't an important drug case only because Sammy was involved; this was an important drug case because it was enormous. Thousands of pills were running through this ring every week.

"Is there any way those pills are being sent to the Midwest?" she asked the captain one day when they were alone in the wiretap room.

"Like where?"

"To Minneapolis?

"Why?"

"Captain, there was a girl in my hometown in North Dakota who died from Ex. Is there any way that could have been Sammy's Ex?"

"It wouldn't surprise me. Minneapolis is a big drug hub. It's the biggest west of Chicago until you get to Denver and Phoenix. But what's a nice girl in North Dakota doing taking Ex?"

"It was a senior prank, they say. The whole class took it. I know. Stupid. Her boyfriend was in a coma. They were the only ones hurt. Why would that be?"

"You can never tell with Ex. A thousand kids can take pills and nothing happens. Then a kid dies. Another goes into a coma. It's the luck of the draw. Sorry about that girl."

"Thanks. It's tearing my town apart. I didn't even know they had Ex back there until this. Don't think the adults in town did, either. Will you keep your eyes open, in case there's a connection? Please? I'd sure like to know."

"Sure." The captain sounded sincerely sorry.

Unbeknownst to her, he took it upon himself to do some digging—he hadn't wanted a reporter around, but if it had to be, he was glad it turned out to be Joya. He called the Ransom County Sheriff's Office, but surmised quickly they were clueless. He called the Fargo Police Department to find they hadn't been called into a case in Northville, North Dakota. But their drug enforcement unit dropped a bombshell.

"We think the Ex coming into Minneapolis originates in Phoenix," he was told. "You guys working anything?"

The captain lied and said they didn't have anything right now, but what did Fargo know?

"We're picking up a lot of chatter. A big buy is coming up. Thousands of pills. We've never seen this much at one time. We're thinking somebody big is involved."

The captain promised to keep his ears open. He hated lying to another officer, but he couldn't reveal the Sammy connection and expect that would stay secret. He made a note to call Fargo as soon as Sammy was in custody.

He shared the news with Joya.

"Oh, God," she cried. "This drug stuff really is like a virus, isn't it? Here's this Mafia killer in Phoenix dealing drugs that probably killed a nice girl in North Dakota—doesn't seem possible, does it?"

"Yeah, Joya. It's not only possible. It happens all the time. Drugs are destroying this country. You're only getting a little taste of it."

She'd come to admire the captain, even like him. He took his job seriously and she was touched that he went the extra mile to find the Midwest connection.

After three months of tedium—one revelation here, another there, a wall growing brick by brick—it was all over within hours.

If Joya hadn't been monitoring the wiretaps that day, she wouldn't have believed the end would be so ridiculous.

It started when Gerard called his dad the night of January 4, 2000. Sammy must have been snoozing in his five-hundred-ninety-dollar-a-month, one bedroom Tempe apartment. He sounded sleepy. "Mommy wants me to ask you to lend Mike seventy dollars for gas receipts," the boy said.

A drowsy Sammy told him, "Have your mom bring the money to work tomorrow."

Around the room, officers were slapping each other on the backs and dancing around like fools and laughing and calling out. "We're gonna get him. We're gonna get the son of a bitch."

They knew the code meant that Debra Gravano wanted to take seventy thousand dollars from her home safe to loan to Mike Papa to buy drugs. And the money was on its way in the morning to Sammy's office at Marathon Construction. Now police just had to follow the money to the drug buy and they'd tie it all up in a pretty package.

Joya was right there, laughing and congratulating with the rest of them. Rob even gave her a hug, although it had none of the sexual tension his hugs used to have. She was ready to celebrate.

"So, who buys when you break a case like this?" She was laughing when she asked it.

All of a sudden, the room got quiet. Everyone looked to Rob to deliver the news.

"Um, Joya, it's a tradition. Boys only. Sorry."

He watched her face fall, and tried to soften the blow. "We don't even ask Mary Kay or Sandy. Just the boys. You understand."

"Oh, sure." She went home with a bruised ego and poured herself a stiff vodka. For good measure, she knocked back a shot of tequila.

The next morning everyone was there early, even though they knew this wasn't a family that roused much before ten a.m. First thing after she finally got up in mid-morning, Karen Gravano delivered the money to her dad.

Both eyes and ears were on Sammy—Rob was hiding nearby with a telephoto lens to shoot whatever he could see, and the wiretap room was as quiet as a church to catch every word.

Sammy picked up the phone and called his ex. "Hey, you short me five thousand?"

"What you talkin' about? I packed that money myself and all seventy thousand is there."

"No it ain't. I just counted it and it's five short!"

"Can't be, Sammy. I was careful. Count it again." Debra hung up, obviously perturbed.

Rob could see Sammy through his lens and the man was painstakingly stacking up the bills into thousand-dollar piles and he was shaking his head in anger.

Sammy called Debra again.

"I counted it again. It's five shy. You know, Deb, this is the second time a bundle is short. Now I'm thinking it was you that ripped off the money the first time around."

Joya heard grown men suck in their breath like they'd just gotten an electric shock. Sammy the Bull had just tied himself to the drug deal out of California that was ten thousand dollars short. And was well documented by the cameras and eye witnesses of the Phoenix Police Department.

"That's it," one of the officers declared. "We got him cold."

The captain picked up the phone to county prosecutors, who were waiting to fill in the blanks of the indictment of Sammy and his entire family. Chief Tomayer rushed up to dole out arrest honors to cops who'd been on the case from the start. They weren't even out the door when Sammy called Debra again.

"Hey, hon, forget it. I miscounted. It's all here."

Everyone froze. And then started laughing. Some so hard, they wet their pants.

Joya issued her trademark, "Holy shit."

She couldn't have wished for a more juicy detail to end this story.

◇◇◇

Joya was standing in the booking room of the Maricopa County Jail when Sammy "The Bull" Gravano arrived in handcuffs at 4:47 p.m. on Wednesday, January 5, 2000.

"Sammy, what do you have to say for yourself?" she yelled at him.

He looked at her and snarled, "I was stupid. You can say, 'Sammy, you were a fucking retard.'"

She pushed forward and Phoenix cops knew better than try to stop her—this was her payback for holding the story all these months.

"Why did you do it, Sammy, why? You had a whole new life. Why?"

He looked at the ground, but turned so she could hear every word. "You ever have a son that's going wrong and you're trying to help him? I know you won't believe this, but it was my love for my son—Gerard was in deep before I knew anything about it. Instead of squashing it, I decided to help him. I wanted to stay close to my son. I wanted to be sure he didn't get hurt."

Joya heard officers laughing at Sammy's words, but the way he spoke—the simple, clean way he said those words—made her believe him. It wasn't an excuse that would keep him out of prison, but it was a reasoning that made sense.

She rushed back to *Phoenix Rising*, to bang out the last chapter of her all-time best scoop, while the production staff tore apart the paper they thought they were publishing on Friday to replace it with a story that shocked the city and made the daily newspapers look like amateurs.

While the Thursday morning *Arizona Republic* was breathlessly reporting the first words revealing Sammy was even in town—to say nothing of what he'd been doing—her upstart weekly newspaper came out twenty-four hours later with the complete inside story. It was a journalist's dream come true.

"Bringing Down the Bull" covered the entire front cover, printed over a picture of Sammy. "The EXCLUSIVE, inside story of how the Phoenix Police Department broke the biggest Ecstasy Ring in the Southwest—and nabbed the Mafia boss under the noses of the FBI." Joya's byline was an inch tall.

> By the time he got to Phoenix, Sammy "the Bull" Gravano had killed nineteen people, spilled his guts on the witness stand about the Gambino crime family, served just a few years in prison to pay for his sins, and was given a new life under the federal Witness Protection Program.
>
> Few people get such a spectacular second chance, but it was probably apropos that the affable, charming Sammy— the highest-ranking Mafiosi to ever break the "blood oath of silence"—was one of the few.
>
> Within five years under the Arizona sun, it was all over. In that time, Gravano opened a construction company, became a popular cult figure among the students at Arizona State University, and, oh yes, went into business with his son running an Ecstasy drug ring. The FBI, which still counted on Sammy's

```
testimony in prominent Mafia cases, knew
about the first two. It didn't have a
clue about the drugs.
    When Sammy was finally busted, he said
the reason he went back into crime was
to get closer to his son—that his sin
was a father's misguided love. The state
of Arizona said he was running one of
the biggest drug rings in the country
and was plotting a new crime family
called the Arizona Mafia.
    This is the inside story of how Sammy
the Bull was brought down, right under
the noses of the FBI.
```

It had ended in such a ridiculous way. Joya's story dripped with delicious irony:

```
There are thousands of pages of court
documents that lay out the Ecstasy ring
hung around Sammy's neck, but police
got him because of one simple reason:
Sammy can't count.
```

At the last second, Joya had called Attorney General Janet Napolitano for comment. She hailed the "extraordinary efforts" of the Phoenix Police Department in busting "Arizona's largest-ever Ecstasy drug case."

The story got Joya invited to every morning show on television, and to Pat McMahon's celebrated talk show. Her paper would submit it for the Don Bolles Investigative Reporting Award given every year by the Arizona Press Club.

Professionally, she was at the top of her game. Nobody knew the stiff price she'd paid to get this story. She never mentioned Rob or the breakup. She never told anyone she'd traded warm arms and soft kisses for a byline.

Her boss took the whole staff out for dinner and drinks to celebrate the scoop. Everyone was anxious to hear all the inside stuff that doesn't quite make it into a story—the war stories journalists tell each other. Everyone was there to celebrate. Except Peter Roman.

"Wonder why Peter couldn't make it," Joya cooed at her editor, as though she didn't know the answer.

He laughed and shook his head, putting an arm around her shoulders. "You got him good, girl."

"I know," she said, more smug and happy with herself than she'd ever felt.

She had no idea what was going on back home.

Chapter Fourteen

Wednesday, January 5, 2000

The same day Sammy "the Bull" Gravano was being booked in Phoenix, Arizona, the three leaders of Northville, North Dakota, kidnapped Crabapple.

It was Wednesday, January 5, 2000.

It was the day Johnny Roth went in to have his cast taken off.

There had been a day-by-day vigil since Johnny came home, with each man taking on a job. It was Bernard's task to keep tabs on the boy who was bursting with revenge; Earl's to get the silo ready; Ralph's to watch the comings and goings of Crabapple.

Bernard was the one who kept arriving with bad news. Johnny's leg was healing and he'd be up and about pretty soon, but it wasn't just him that they had to worry about. "I think his dad and uncle are as determined to kill Crabapple as Johnny is," Bernard whispered at a regular card game. "Wouldn't surprise me if all three of them went hunting the punk."

"Think we should move it up?" Earl asked. Nobody had to him what "it" was.

"No, I think they'll let Johnny take the lead," Bernard said. "Paul thinks that's how his son is going to redeem himself. The man has gone as batty as his brother."

"I'm ready," Earl offered, to be sure they knew the silo was prepared. He'd attached steel chains to the rings in the wall and soldered handcuffs on the ends. He had a kerosene lantern and gas-powered space heater in place and borrowed one of Angie's old quilts. When the time came, he'd add a jug of clean water and fill the bucket with water to make do as a toilet. He'd already bought a sackful of junk food and soda because, after all, they weren't barbarians.

"No, we'll wait," Ralph decided. Crabapple was predictable as the fall harvest. He showed up for work five days a week at five a.m., beating the sunrise by nine minutes this time of year. Ralph saw that Huntsie wasn't exaggerating when he said the boy was a natural mechanic and a hard worker. Darryl had lunch at noon at the motel outside town, back to work until five or six—well after the sun had set—a couple beers at Jerry's bar, and then the drive home in the pitch black of a North Dakota winter. He'd turn left at the Sunoco Station and head to his place, turning right at Harding's Corner, and then left on County Road Four that ran in front of the farm.

The last turn is where the men were waiting. Ralph's pickup truck blocked the road, its lights on. Crabapple naturally stopped, thinking there had been an accident. He parked at an angle so his headlights gave him a clear path and yelled out Ralph's name as he sloshed through the melting snow.

"WHAT THE HELL?" he yelled when he was met by three men in ski masks with shotguns. Even if he hadn't been so startled, he could have guessed who they were and he was sure he'd seen those winter jackets. But that hardly counted. "IS THIS A FUCKIN' JOKE? WHAT DO YOU BASTARDS THINK YOU'RE DOIN'?"

He was blindfolded at gunpoint, pushed into the pickup, and taken to a place he knew by smell was a grain silo.

Nobody said a word to him on the drive, and they didn't take the blindfold off until he was chained by his wrists to rings on the silo wall.

That isn't to say Crabapple was a silent hostage. From the moment he realized this wasn't a joke, he'd shouted, using the f-word again and again—a word these captors found particularly offensive. He called out each of their names, reminding them they weren't fooling anyone with their silly disguises and asserting his rights as an American (for all that was worth at this moment).

When the blindfold came off and his eyes adjusted to the darkness of a silo illuminated only by a lantern, he stopped swearing and started begging.

"DON'T SHOOT ME. OH GOD, DON'T SHOOT ME. WHAT DO YOU WANT? WHAT DO YOU WANT?" He'd already asked the question a hundred times and got no answer. "Is it money? I don't have any money. I swear. But my cousin will loan me some. Is it money? I'll get you money." Even though he said the words, he knew damn well this wasn't about money. But he sure didn't want to let on that he knew exactly why he was here.

Nobody answered him. The men stood there with shotguns on their hips and stared at him like he was a strange animal.

"WHAT'S GOING ON? WHAT THE FUCK IS GOING ON?" Crabapple screamed.

The three men turned to leave. The first two were out the door when the last man said a single sentence. "Sold any drugs to kids who died lately, Crabapple?"

"WHAT DO YOU FUCKERS THINK YOU'RE DOING?"

"COME ON, THIS IS ENOUGH."

"YOU'RE GONNA BE IN A SHITLOAD OF TROUBLE WHEN I GET OUT OF HERE."

"HEY, COME BACK. YOU CAN'T JUST LEAVE ME HERE."

"I'LL FREEZE TO DEATH!"

"A couple days there and he'll confess."

"Or leave town."

"Either one's okay by me."

"I want him locked up."

"Even if he confesses, what kind of sentence would he get?

"I don't think it's much. Maybe better he leave town."

"Either way, he's not selling any more drugs to our kids."

Ralph stopped next to Crabapple's pickup. Earl jumped out to drive it to the kid's place. He left the keys under the front seat, then climbed in with his friends and Ralph drove them all back to town. Nobody said a word.

After dropping them off at their vehicles, Ralph drove the six blocks home alone, admitting to himself he felt kind dumb that he hadn't spotted all this sooner. Looking back a year, it took the stammering words of a little kid to clue him in.

Ralph always paid extra attention to his slow nephew, Danny. "Uncle Alph," Danny called him. "Danny Boy," Ralph returned.

Danny had never been quite right, but as his mom liked to say, it's no sin to be slow. Slowness accounted for most of it, although that didn't explain the individual world where Danny spent most of his time. Danny could play by himself for hours in apparent bliss. Good thing, since nobody paid much attention to him in the social world of the fourth grade, where he had a desk everyone knew he hadn't earned. He was passed along every year because it seemed the only thing to do. He wasn't slow enough to be in a special class—even if they had a special class in Northville—but he wasn't fast enough to keep up. He was always caught in the middle.

Ralph had spent more than one sleepless night worrying about what was going to happen to Danny. He had a pretty good idea. Eventually the kid would be pushed through school or drop out, but he'd never be fit for more than sweeping floors somewhere—Ralph always prayed it wouldn't end up being at Jerry's, because he knew how cruel drunks could be.

At every family gathering, Ralph let Danny hang on him.

"Crabapple floats," Danny told him one Sunday in 1998 when they were celebrating a confirmation. "He can float like a balloon way up in the sky."

"Oh, sure," Ralph answered, as though that made sense.

"He says it's lots of fun. He says he can see the top of the water tower from up there. He says you can see all the tops of trees and you can fly with the birds."

"Uh-huh," Ralph said as his brother interrupted to get him a beer.

"Crabapple says if I give him ten dollars, I can fly up there too."

"Oh, good," Ralph said, wondering when dinner would be ready.

"So Uncle Alph, can I have ten dollars?"

"What?"

"Can I have ten dollars so I can fly like Crabapple?"

Danny had never asked for money before. The boy liked the lifesavers Ralph always carried in his pocket—and sucked on since he quit smoking years ago—and once when they ran into each other downtown, Ralph bought him an ice cream cone, but he was taken aback at being asked for money.

"Now, what do you want this ten dollars for?" he asked to get himself focused.

"If I give Crabapple ten dollars, he said I can fly up into the sky."

Ralph wasn't sure how Crabapple had even gotten into this conversation, but Danny now had his attention. All Ralph knew about the kid called Crabapple was that he was a mechanic at Huntsie's who'd had a tough childhood and always had dirty hands.

"Now tell me again," Ralph began. "What did Crabapple say?"

Danny took a deep breath like he was getting tired of repeating himself and repeated himself.

To be sure he got it right, Ralph said the words back to him.

"Exactly how can he make you fly?" Ralph asked.

Danny didn't even hesitate. "He gives you this yellow magic pill and you swallow it and you fly up like a bird."

Now Danny had Ralph's undivided attention. In fact, they had to call twice for the man and the boy to come in for dinner.

"Crabapple says he'll give you this magic pill?"

"Yes." Danny beamed with the enthusiasm of a boy who finally has the right answer.

"And it costs ten dollars?"

"Magic is expensive, Uncle Alph."

Ralph looked at the boy with such intensity, Danny carried on. "He says all the other kids do it and he wants me to have some fun, too. I want to be like the other kids, Uncle Alph. I want to fly like a bird."

Ever since the war, Ralph Bonner knew there was a special spot in his gut that acted up when he was scared. That spot was acting up now. He took Danny in his arms.

"I want you to stay away from Crabapple," he whispered to the boy. "This is important, Danny. I don't want you to talk to him anymore. Okay?"

"But Uncle Alph..."

"No, I've got something better for you—much better than what he has—but you can only have it if you don't talk to him anymore. Okay?"

"Better magic?"

"Oh, yeah. It's really, really good. It's going to take me a little while to get it, but just wait for me, okay?"

"Sure, Uncle Alph. I'll wait for you."

The next day, Ralph started playing detective. He made an unusual afternoon visit to Jerry's Bar to shoot the shit. Nobody got suspicious when he started bemoaning how the kids in town were getting into drugs. Yeah, it's a shame, the afternoon drinkers said, but then it was a problem that went in spurts.

"Remember back in, oh what was it, maybe '96, '97? Remember we had that pot field out by the Colgrove farm? Man, you coulda got high just standin' there while they burned that sucker. Then it seemed to die down. Guess it's back, huh?"

Jerry's daytime bartender, Ruthie, said she heard the school was searching lockers to confiscate the stuff brought into the schoolyard. She wasn't sure that was true, but that's what somebody said.

"You mean it's bad enough that kids are bringing it to school?" Ralph was incredulous.

"Now, that's what I heard," Ruthie reaffirmed. "But you know how the school's always trying to make things worse so we'll pass another bond election. What was it last time? The cafeteria ceiling was falling in? Hell, I went and looked at it myself and it just needed repairs. If you ask me, they always make things worse to soften us up for more taxes."

Ralph didn't dismiss that logic, since he shared the disdain for politicians who always had their hand out. And the schools were as bad as politicians sometimes, although he couldn't remember a school bond he hadn't voted for.

"Well, how are these kids getting the stuff?" he asked.

"Damned if I know," one of the drinkers said. "I bet the high school kids are picking it up in Fargo. Or Minneapolis."

"What about the grade school kids?" Ralph wondered.

"There's drugs in the grade school?" Ruthie hadn't considered that. "Oh, I don't think it's *that* bad. The locker stuff is in the high school. You don't think the little kids...? Hah."

"That's what I hear," Ralph offered. "I was talking to a kid the other day and he told me kids in grade school are getting high."

"Damned if you say," one drinker pronounced, as he downed his brew and, as usual, left Ruthie no tip.

"Who do you suppose is pushing this junk?" Ralph tried again.

"Man, the only idiot around here who'd do that is probably Crabapple," Ruthie offered, but it was clearly a guess.

Ralph left and had a good idea where he could get some real information on the situation. He drove out to his nephew's farm. If any kid in school knew the score, it was his nephew's oldest son, Bobby. Ralph didn't think Bobby was into drugs—the kid was more intent on earning wages for the car he'd get to buy at sixteen, and he had only a year of saving left. But Bobby was one of the cool kids in school—tall, handsome, smart, quick with the tongue, he was the unofficial leader of the kids who weren't athletes. Bobby was never much good at sports, but he was good at making friends and if there was a hot party in town, Bobby was sure to be on the guest list.

Ralph had known Bobby since birth and always had a good relationship with the kid, but you'd have thought Ralph was the FBI the way Bobby backed off from the questions about drugs in school.

"Man, I don't know nothin' about drugs. I don't do 'em. My friends don't. Don't ask me. I dunno."

"I'm not saying you do drugs, I'm just asking if somebody is pushing drugs in school."

Bobby didn't see it the same way his older relative did. As far as he was concerned, opening his mouth made him a snitch. And Bobby was too cool to be a snitch. He even congratulated himself on how well he was playing dumb. It would make a great story at school, where, by the way, everyone should know they were getting wise to Crabapple and they'd better back off. Bobby had no particular reason to protect the guy, but he had no beef with him either. If the guy wanted to make some extra change, well, that was his business. Besides, the adults got just as bent out of shape over the beer that Bobby preferred, and the last thing they needed to know is that Kook Miller was their buyer. You start snitchin' on one thing and who knows who's gonna snitch you off.

Ralph could see the smugness and he let it sink in for a minute before he dropped his bombshell.

"Well, Danny tells me Crabapple wants ten dollars from him for yellow magic that will make him fly."

"That son of a bitch." Bobby didn't even realize his admission as he said the words. As far as he knew, Crabapple only sold to high school kids—kids old enough to make some of their own decisions, even if their folks hadn't recognized that yet. But dammit, what was the asshole doing pushing the stuff to dumbshits like his retard cousin, Danny?

"He's gotta be stopped," Ralph declared. "He's hittin' on little kids who don't know any better. And can you imagine Danny being stoned? Who knows what the kid would do. I could see him climbing the water tower and jumping off, convinced he was going to fly."

Bobby looked at his uncle and he could see it, too. "Yeah, that's bogus, man. He's got to be stopped."

The next day Ralph filled in his buddies and they went to see Sheriff Potter.

Everybody in town knew how badly that went. Their frustration at being turned away empty-handed burrowed into their guts. It ulcerated when Amber died, and bled every day that Crabapple went unpunished.

Ralph Bonner knew they were doing the right thing now because that pain in his gut was gone by the time he got home from kidnapping Crabapple.

Jesus, it's cold in here. A blanket. A space heater. They left me a blanket and a little space heater and they think that's going to be enough? Those fuckers. They can't do this to me. I'll show them when I get out of here. They ain't got nothin' on me. They think I'm so stupid I'm gonna get caught? Hah. I'm showin' them.

They're just trying to scare me. Chain me up for a night and think I'll be scared shitless. Then they'll let me go and think it's all over. In a pig's eye. Their asses are goin' to jail. It's a federal offense to kidnap somebody. Isn't it? The FBI will be all over this town and they'll take care of those shitheads. Who the fuck do they think they are?

They wouldn't kill me. Hey man, don't even think about that. Of course not. It's just a scare tactic. They couldn't kill me. It would be crazy to kill me. They don't have the guts. I don't think any of them have ever killed anybody. Even in the war they think was so high and mighty. No, they're just trying to scare me.

Okay, boys, I'm scared. Wait till you come back and see how scared and repentant old Crabapple can be. I'll promise them I'll never do anything wrong again. Now, don't go admittin' anything, Darryl. They don't have any proof of anything, so don't go giving them any.

What if they're wired, and they want you to confess and they'll take the tape to old Lazy Potter? No, don't admit anything, but let them know how sorry you are. Be real nice and tell them they'll never have to worry about Crabapple again.

And then they'll let you go.

And the first stop I'm gonna make is to the sheriff's office to report a kidnapping. And then they'll never mess with me again.

◇◇◇

The plan was simple. And true to plan, the three men met in the parking lot at the Legion—a place their pickups were familiar and nobody would wonder why they were there—and drove out together to the silo the next night to check on their hostage. They left their ski masks at home because there really was no need for them.

They found Crabapple with wrists bleeding from trying to slip out of the handcuffs. He'd already eaten all the junk food and sodas, and the toilet-bucket had been used.

Ralph put a Tupperware cake pan on the floor and pushed it toward him with his foot. "Supper," he said in a deadpan. "It's left over funeral hotdish from the Mead funeral."

"It's probably poison," Crabapple shot back.

"Well, if you don't want it," Earl taunted, as he took a step toward the food and watched Crabapple scramble to grab it.

"Anything you want to tell us?" Bernard asked, and prayed they'd get the answer they were after. Seeing the boy on the cold cement floor, shivering, even with the quilt and space heater, he felt bad about what they were doing.

"I don't know what you think I did, but I'm just a mechanic. Ask Huntsie. You guys know him. He'll tell you. But whatever you think I did, I want you to know I'm sorry. Don't know what I'm supposed to be sorry for, but whatever it is, I am. Now let's just stop this. Unchain me and let me be and we'll forget all about this."

Darryl "Crabapple" Harding had been practicing that speech all afternoon, and to his ears, it sounded exactly how he'd planned. It was calm, it was clear, it was repentant without admitting a thing, and he fully expected it to bring these men to their senses.

"So tell us about the drugs you sold to Johnny Roth," Ralph said.

"I DIDN'T SELL JOHNNY ANY DRUGS. I DON'T KNOW WHAT YOU'RE TALKING ABOUT."

The calmness and bravado he'd practiced all day disappeared. His stomach growled and he popped off the Tupperware lid to get at the goulash inside. He wolfed down four bites before he tried again: "Listen guys, I'm as sad about Amber as anybody, but I didn't have anything to do with that. It wasn't my fault. I was in Minneapolis with my cousin. I wasn't even there." He hoped they didn't know he was lying. "But whatever happened, you can't pin that on me. I'm not the one you want. Please, stop this."

Earl ambled over and picked up the water jug, going to the far wall to refill it. He put it back within Crabapple's reach without saying a word.

Ralph and Bernard were just as communicative.

"Maybe you need another night to get your head on straight and tell us what we want to know," Ralph said as he turned to leave.

"NO! NO, STOP! I'M GOING TO FREEZE TO DEATH OUT HERE. YOU CAN'T IMAGINE HOW COLD IT GETS. COME ON. IF I DIE, IT'S ON YOUR HEADS. GODDAMN YOU BASTARDS!"

They left him screaming and swearing and drove into town.

"What if he doesn't confess?" Bernard asked on the way.

"Then we'll have to drive him out of town—demand he leave," Earl offered.

"I don't know," Ralph said. They left it at that because they hadn't calculated that the kid would endure another freezing night in a silo rather than fess up.

Their simple plan also didn't include Huntsie getting nosy.

Ralph well knew that Huntsie had been fit to be tied when Crabapple "disappeared" right after Amber's death—because Maggie's Buick was one of the cars waiting for the boy to tune up. Ralph had driven over to check on its progress, when he found that Huntsie was mad as a wet hen and gave Ralph an earful. Huntsie himself had to do Maggie's car—it was more a lick and a promise than the professional job Crabapple would have done, but he got away with it.

Huntsie was mad enough then to drive out to Darryl's farm. The place was empty. Darryl's truck was gone, so obviously, the kid had gone off on a toot and abandoned his responsibilities.

As Ralph told his buddies, Huntsie swore about the kid and declared he was fired, but that was it. The man filled in the best he could and even after he finally heard from Crabapple—a phone conversation that made little sense to the old man—he just shrugged his shoulders whenever the kid was mentioned and asked everyone he knew if they had a line on a new mechanic. It was kind of surprising that Huntsie took him back when he finally showed up in town, but that had more to do with the lack of good mechanics in southeastern North Dakota than it did with any moral compass.

So the men figured Huntsie would just steam and pout again when his mechanic didn't show up for work. They had no idea that on Thursday, Huntsie called Darryl's number a dozen times and never got an answer. When Johnny Roth showed up at the garage asking for Darryl, Huntsie knew that meant trouble. Nor did they know that on Friday, Huntsie drove out to the Harding place again. But this time, he found Crabapple's pickup in the yard, its keys under the front seat.

Huntsie had a terrible feeling about this. He went to the house and yelled for Darryl from the front door—he always called him Darryl and hated the Crabapple nickname. When no one answered, he gingerly walked into the unlocked house and found it empty. It was a mess—a sink full of dishes in the kitchen, some broken; old pizza boxes strewn around, couch pillows on the floor (one of them losing its stuffing), clothes tossed here and there—but Huntsie had assumed Darryl lived in a pigsty. He did think it went beyond slovenly not to sweep up the glass vase that had been smashed against a wall, apparently in one of Darryl's fits of anger, but that was the only thing that he thought twice about because Huntsie, himself, lived the bachelor life and inhabited his own pigsty.

He left the house and walked to the barn that hadn't done its name justice for years, fearing the worse. He wondered what he'd do if he found Darryl hanging from a rafter, and it startled him that he'd even have that thought. But Johnny had been so angry. Thank heaven the barn was empty.

But where was Darryl? He couldn't go anywhere without his pickup, unless somebody picked him up. While he knew Darryl didn't have many friends, he also knew he had enemies. Could this all be an overworked imagination? Could Darryl have bagged out with friends like he did a couple months ago? Back then, Darryl swore that would never happen again, and Huntsie decided to believe the cockamamie story about a "family crisis."

But this was different. Huntsie stewed about the problem all day Friday. What if Johnny had done something? What if Darryl were hurt somewhere? Or what if he decided to start the weekend early? Huntsie wasn't a man who liked confrontation, so he decided he'd just wait and hope the kid showed up for work on Monday.

If Huntsie hadn't waited, things might have turned out differently.

But then, if a ferocious snowstorm hadn't hit Friday night, things would have been different, too.

And if…

A lot of ifs were about to show Northville, North Dakota, that it had gone from the town in a Norman Rockwell painting to the town in a Stephen King novel.

Chapter Fifteen

Saturday, January 8—Monday, January 10, 2000

The snow didn't fall, it dumped. The wind didn't blow, it screamed. This was a doozie of a North Dakota storm and everyone knew to stay put and warm and wait it out.

"I can barely see across the street and I can't get out of my driveway," Ralph said into the phone Saturday morning.

"Me, neither, and I don't see any letup." Bernard sounded worried.

"What are we going to do?"

"He's got heat and we left him enough food last night. Not much else we can do. He's not going anywhere. He should be alright. I bet he'll be ready to confess now."

"I'll call Earl," Bernard offered.

"Is Johnny home? Okay, good. See you Monday." Ralph turned around to see his wife's eyes as big as dinner plates. He thought she was in the backroom with her quilting project, and he'd been speaking softly, but not softly enough for a woman who raised three children and therefore was a champion eavesdropper.

"What have you done?" Her voice was sharper than she ever used on her husband.

"Nothing. Don't worry about it." Ralph turned as though they'd ended the conversation, but Maggie Bonner wasn't letting go.

"WHO has heat and enough food?" Her voice was urgent, climbing the scale of hysteria as she continued, "WHO should be alright? WHO should be ready to confess? WHAT about Johnny?"

Her husband offered nothing but a cold shoulder.

"Oh dear, God, don't tell me you've done something to that boy who sells drugs!"

Still Ralph said nothing.

"I'm calling Angie."

"No you aren't. Don't go calling anybody. There's nothing to get excited about. Just leave it alone. You hear me? Just leave it alone." Ralph used the tone that said, 'I'm the king in this house and that is my decree.' Maggie never liked that tone.

She knew this was all wrong, and it didn't take a genius to figure out what probably was going on.

"You do know this storm is supposed to last a couple days," she told him, as though he hadn't been monitoring the weather all day.

"I know. I know. Don't worry about it. This is none of your business."

"You guys have done something stupid and it's none of my business?" Maggie was almost screaming.

"We haven't done anything stupid and I said drop it. I'm not talking about this with you. And don't you dare talk about this with anybody. ANYBODY. Just stay out of it. I'll take care of it."

Ralph fell into his La-Z-Boy recliner and pulled the lever to raise the footrest. He turned the TV up loud to watch a western—Ralph Bonner loved westerns—and ignore his wife.

Maggie went back to her sewing room and stewed. Ugly pictures kept dancing through her head. She held her head in her hands as she cried. *Oh God, please, please don't let anything bad happen to that boy.* And then she did what Catholics do when they're scared. *Hail Mary full of grace...*

She was halfway through the Rosary when she realized she had to do something. She slipped quietly into the living room to look in on her husband. Ralph was snoozing. She went back to their bedroom, closed the door, and called Angie.

"Angie, can you talk? Where's Earl?" She was glad to hear he was in the basement, working on the cabinets he was making. "Do you know what those fools have done?" she whispered.

"Bernard called and Earl acted like it was the secret service calling or something, and he told me it was a private call." answered Angie's soft voice. "He's never done that in his life. So of course, I went to the extension. They're worried somebody might not have enough food or heat, but they said Ralph thought it would be okay. What are those idiots up to?"

"I think they kidnapped Crabapple and have him somewhere."

"WHAT?"

"Shh, we don't want them to know we know."

"Have you talked to Norma?"

"No, I was going to do that next. Ralph is snoozing right now. I don't want him to know I'm calling. He told me not to."

"Let me call because Earl can't hear anything down there. I'll call you back."

"Yeah, but you can't say what it is," Maggie reminded her.

"Right. Okay, if it's what we think it is, I'll talk about…our circle. If it isn't, I'll—"

"If it isn't, tell me about your grandchildren."

"Yes, that will work."

Maggie hung up and slipped out of the bedroom to her quilting.

Five minutes later, she heard the phone ring and Ralph answered it.

He yelled at her to pick up the call on the bedroom phone. He was listening in.

"Hi, Angie. How are you surviving this storm?"

"Oh, I'm okay. What a mess. Speaking of messes, our circle is getting tapped for two funerals in a row. Did you know that?"

"Two? Why two?"

"I don't know. One of the other circles can't do it and you know how Father is—he always looks to us."

"Well, we won't have to worry about it in this storm. Unless things calm down, we're not even going to church tomorrow. Our driveway is filled!"

"Ours, too. Stay warm. Goodbye." After Angie hung up, Maggie lingered until she heard Ralph holster the receiver. She sat on the bed and finished her Rosary.

Angie and Norma spent some information currency that afternoon.

Nobody said anything ridiculous like "our husbands have kidnapped the pusher and have him hidden someplace," but hints that *somebody* had done *something* to that terrible druggie were whispered by women calling friends to double-check on them in the storm.

Gertie Bach heard and wondered if Johnny were involved. Her sister, Wanda, who often got things wrong, told Gertie that Johnny had "taken care" of that Harding boy. Those were the words she used. Those were the words Nettie Schlener heard. Those were the words that Alice Peters heard, but she knew better.

Although, Johnny was back on his feet, and maybe…Alice didn't want to complete the thought. People better stop speculating because this could mean real trouble for nice people.

When the snow finally stopped late Sunday, snowplows were out immediately. First they cleared the highway from town to the interstate, then street by street. By Monday, if you lived in town, you could get around. But if you wanted to go out into the countryside, good luck. Until the farmers got their tractors out and started clearing driveways and roads, little was moving there until Monday afternoon.

Monday morning, Huntsie was disappointed to find his mechanic didn't show up for work again, and his unease grew over where the boy could be. Maybe he should call the sheriff and tell him Darryl was missing Or maybe he shouldn't be alerting the sheriff to anything about his mechanic. If the kid was in trouble, Huntsie wanted to help, but he didn't want his efforts to get the kid in trouble. He better just wait. The kid had to show up eventually. This time, he really was going to fire him. A man can be disrespected just so much before he won't take it anymore.

Alice's Bakery was extra busy Monday morning, and there was a constant buzz as people gossiped in small groups. Angie came in for bread at about ten-thirty and Alice pulled her aside to ask if anything was going on, which made Angie think Alice knew, so she spilled the beans. In a whisper, of course.

Norma showed up for a cake for her granddaughter's sixth birthday. Angie nodded toward Alice. "She knows. She knew all along. She says we have to be certain not to tell *anyone!*"

The two women shared one of those moments they'd remember all their lives—nobody could ever know their husbands had kidnapped Crabapple. Nobody. This wasn't a currency to spend, it was a secret to hoard. They knew Maggie well enough to know she'd agree.

Alice prayed the men would show up for their one p.m. card game, but when they didn't show, she wasn't surprised. From what she'd heard, from those who actually knew something to those who thought they knew something, she figured that wherever they had stashed Crabapple, they'd be heading that way as soon as the roads were clear.

The men left in Bernard's truck because it had four-wheel drive. They could plow through the deep snow at Earl's old farm. They brought burgers from the Corner Bar, Lays potato chips, and a six-pack of Pepsi. By now, they were certain Crabapple would confess, or would instantly pack up and leave town.

"How much can a man take?" Ralph had reasoned, and everyone agreed.

Bernard started swearing as they pulled into the yard of Earl's old place. "Jesus, there's tracks here." All three men stared in astonishment. I looked worse when they got to the silo. The fresh blanket of snow had been trampled, like someone walked through here and then tried to sweep out the footprints. Bernard had pretty much driven over the tracks that had been left by—WHO? A car? A truck?

"What. The. Hell?" Earl said the words with the same reverence he used in church.

They climbed out of the truck and went to the door. It wasn't locked because there was no need for a lock—the hostage inside couldn't get to this door. The chains weren't long enough.

Earl opened the door and all three walked inside.

The only sound was a whimper as the scene before their eyes sunk in.

Most of Crabapple's chest was gone.

A shotgun blast had torn it apart, spreading bits of his body against the steel wall. Splats of blood had already dried.

Blood, more brown than red, puddled under the body. Sticky. Smelling bad.

"Oh, my God," Ralph moaned. Bernard started to cry. Earl kept whimpering.

They had to turn away because the scene was so ugly, and as their eyes met, each one looked at the other with astonishment. With questions. With suspicion.

"Who did this?" Ralph demanded, as though the killer would speak.

"Well, it wasn't me," Earl screamed back. He turned to Bernard: "Was it you?"

"Are you out of your mind? I didn't do this." Bernard turned to Ralph: "You didn't, did you?"

Ralph backed up as though distancing himself from the corpse would answer the question, before he slowly shook his head. "No."

Nobody seemed satisfied with the answers, even as they were ashamed of themselves for thinking the worst.

Before this moment, each man would have sworn he knew the others to their core. That moment was forever altered. A lifetime of trust was shattered. They prayed they were telling the truth…but not completely sure.

As though someone had fired a starting pistol, all three ran out of the silo. Ralph threw up. Earl hunkered down on his haunches and rocked like a little kid. Bernard walked around his truck, again and again, and he never stopped crying. Two of these men had seen battle during World War II, but they'd never been this petrified. Nothing in the life of the third prepared him for such terror.

It was Earl who finally took charge. "We've got to get him out of here. We've got to clean this up. They can't find him here or they'll finger me. It's my silo."

The other two quickly agreed, Ralph reassuring with the Marine code of never-leave-a-man-behind.

"Earl, we're all in this together. If one goes down, we all go down."

Bernard agreed. "Earl, we won't let you get stuck with this. If we have to, we'll explain that we kidnapped him, but we didn't kill him. We might have to do that."

"Let's hope not!" Earl begged. "Who's going to believe that? If I was on a jury that heard that, I wouldn't believe it. Our only hope is to get him as far from here as we can and clean up this mess and then deny everything."

But knowing what you had to do and doing it were two different things. The largest corpse any of these men had ever handled was a ten-point deer. Not one had ever had to move a human body.

And where? What do you do with a body? How do you get rid of all this blood? Those questions had never been discussed. They weren't imaginable in a plot to scare this kid and save Johnny from doing something else stupid.

They were punting now, making wild guesses about how to dispose of this body without getting tied to it.

They worked all afternoon and all night. They drove into town to get bleach from workshops, tarps from garages, plastic gloves from under kitchen sinks, rags from utility rooms. They knew enough not to buy anything incriminating. They avoided spouses and everyone else. They missed their suppers and worried their wives.

When Ralph finally made it inside the safety of his home—exhausted and depleted—he realized they hadn't even said a prayer for the kid they got murdered.

Chapter Sixteen

Johnny Roth was a mess.

He now knew he could survive a coma and heal a broken leg without surviving or healing.

He had a limp—the doctor said there always would be—but he hardly cared. If he'd had his way, he never would have woken up a second time. But he did. At least he could complete the mission he'd been planning since he regained consciousness.

Johnny Roth was going to kill Darryl "Crabapple" Harding. He would shoot him with a shotgun so his guts sprayed out. Then he'd leave him where the foxes and wild dogs would have a feast.

He told his best friend, Kenny Franken. But if he expected encouragement, Kenny disappointed him. "Man, don't make things worse—you'll go to prison! Everyone will know it's you. They won't care why. They'll just lock you up for the rest of your life."

"No, they won't." Johnny left it at that.

His dad pulled him aside one day, when Lois was busy cooking dinner. "I'm hearing you're going to kill Crabapple." Paul Roth used his low voice.

"Yes, sir."

His dad looked him in the eye—the first time Johnny had seen anything but hatred in the Old Man's eyes since this nightmare began—and patted him on the back.

Uncle LeRoy came by to welcome him home and mentioned more than once that he had weapons, if anyone needed any.

"No thanks, I'm fine," Johnny told the wild-eyed man who'd become such a loon. Johnny would never use a weapon from Uncle LeRoy to kill Crabapple because Amber had been afraid of LeRoy.

Lois drove Johnny to Fargo on January 5 to get the cast off, but they had to stay over because the pickup overheated and couldn't be fixed till the next morning. Thankfully, Lois' sister lived in Moorehead, and she drove over to get them for the night.

They had just gotten home Thursday morning when Johnny snagged his car keys off the hook in the mudroom and drove himself into town.

"Crabapple here?" he yelled to Huntsie as he entered the mechanic's garage. "No, I've been callin' him, and he's not answering," Huntsie said, before he put two and two together and realized Johnny was a threat.

"Now, son, I think everybody should calm down. It's a real shame what happened to that nice Amber. But you can't think it was your fault. And I don't know just what Darryl has to do with this, but people talk and they think he owns some fault, too. It's not going to do any good for anybody to turn on anybody."

Johnny didn't wait for the lecture to end. He jumped in his car and took a left at the Sunoco Station.

Crabapple's pickup was in the front yard, and Johnny ran from his car into the house. But it was empty. Damn. His truck was here but where was he?

"The son of a bitch is lucky he's not home," Johnny spat out as he walked around the house, looking at how his enemy lived. It wasn't that bad, actually—far neater than Johnny would have kept a place—but it got messier as Johnny explored. He swept some dirty dishes off the counter into the sink, breaking some. He turned out the trash can and threw pizza boxes around like Frisbees. He grabbed the pillows off the couch and tore a hole in one before throwing them on the floor. He went into the bedroom and tossed around clothes and boots. When that didn't give him any relief, he grabbed a glass vase sitting on the TV and threw it against the wall, breaking it to smithereens. But his rage seemed childish.

"When I hurt you, Crabapple, it's really going to hurt." He shut the door on the empty house.

He drove into town and found Kenny. He knew nothing of Crabapple's whereabouts, and therefore was worthless to Johnny. Kenny could see it. He was scared, thinking, "I've got to get him off this track, get him back to reality." But his small talk of high school was no longer relevant to Johnny.

"Hey, we've got a basketball game Friday night. You should come. We're playing Rutland. Everybody would like to see you."

Johnny looked at Kenny like he had two heads. "Yeah, sure. Hey, I gotta go. See you later."

Kenny Franken would always remember that moment because it was the last one he ever spent with his best friend.

On Friday Johnny was back in town and hounding Huntsie. Crabapple wasn't to be found. What Johnny did find was the always reliable Kook Miller, who took Johnny's fifty dollars to cover two big bottles of eighty-proof Windsor, with a ten-dollar tip. He would have preferred Crown Royal, but it was too rich for his pocketbook.

He took his Canadian whiskey and went home, shutting the door to his room and telling his mom he needed to sleep, so please leave him alone. He drank half the first bottle that night. It wasn't so much sleep as it was stupor that put him in bed.

He woke up Saturday morning to a world painted white. The snow had been piling up all night, and if Johnny hadn't been so drunk, he would have heard the howling North Dakota wind that always sounded so angry. He was surprised to see the farm shut down by the continuing storm that left drifts climbing up the side of the barn and a driveway that stopped any driving.

He pulled on a pair of jeans to eat a breakfast of pancakes and bacon. Lois Roth tried to make small talk with her husband and son, but neither was talkative. As soon as he'd finished, Johnny begged off, complaining he was so tired he wanted to rest all day. Lois didn't push her son these days, and with nothing to do but hunker down until the snow passed, Paul didn't care what his son did.

Johnny went upstairs to his room and finished off the first bottle.

When his mother called up that Kenny was on the phone, Johnny was already passed out.

He awoke Sunday morning with his head doing the drum solo from *Wipeout*.

"Johnny, it's Kenny again. He says it's urgent."

Johnny didn't know what "again" meant, but he lumbered down the stairs and picked up the phone to hear his best friend raging.

"What did you do?" Kenny screamed into the phone. "Did you do something to Crabapple?"

"What you talkin' about?" Johnny mumbled into the phone, still not completely awake.

"Did you snatch Crabapple and hide him away somewhere?"

Now the words started getting through the fog of hangover. "Crabapple? What about Crabapple?"

"My mom and dad are frantic. Somebody kidnapped Crabapple and hid him out somewhere and now they're all worried because of the storm. Was that you?"

Johnny made him repeat the words to be sure he heard right. "How do you know that?"

"My mom got a call and she told dad and they came to me and asked if you'd done something to Crabapple. Everybody's worried you're going to get in real trouble and end up in prison. Johnny, everybody knows you want to kill him. Please, talk to me."

"So just how in the hell does everyone know?" Johnny spat into the phone.

"Well, I didn't tell anyone," Kenny snarked back to defend himself from the obvious accusation. "But your crazy uncle sure has. He's even threatened Crabapple himself. Everybody in town knows. You know how rumors spread around here. So when LeRoy's running around saying how Amber's death will be avenged, what do you expect them to think? If something happens to him, the sheriff will be at your door in ten minutes. So please, my friend, tell me what's going on."

"So everyone thinks it's me? What if it wasn't? Who else would they suspect?" Johnny was fishing, but Kenny didn't see it. He took it as a cover-your-ass question.

"Well, the mighty three, I suppose. Those guys have been stewing ever since…they've been mad as hell. You know how they tried to stop Crabapple last year. They're taking this real personal. And, pal, I know they're worried about you. They don't want you to get into any trouble, either."

Kenny didn't have to spell out who the mighty three were. Johnny was well aware of the three town leaders who had gone to the school board to force a school-wide lecture against drugs last year.

"Don't worry about it, Ken. Everything's going to be okay."

Johnny hung up and swore a string that made his mother cringe and his father demand he "clean up your mouth." He ran back upstairs and slammed the door to his room.

"Don't you want any breakfast?" his mother yelled, praying to get things under control.

"NO," he screamed back, as he broke the cap seal on the second bottle. The whiskey loosed up his mind and his mood. He rolled around in his head everything he knew about the three men who must have snatched Crabapple. All three lived in town, but where could they secretly hide somebody? He couldn't think of a place. Okay, did any of them have a fish house out at Lake Elsie? That would work. Or maybe they put him in the cemetery's storage house—nobody would look for him there. Bernard used to run the grocery store. Is there a warehouse somewhere? He didn't think so. Earl used to farm, but his son was there now and certainly he'd know if his dad had a hostage. Johnny mulled possibilities around in his mind until he passed out.

He had a dream. He saw himself in his dad's barn, pitch-forking hay into the milk cow's stall—but they'd gotten rid of the herd a couple years ago to concentrate on the wheat and oats. Johnny always considered that the happiest day of his life, because if you've got dairy cows, you're chained to your farm. They needed milking twice a day, and there was no way around that. He always thought the most thankless, dumbest job in the world was being a dairy farmer.

But in his dream they still had dairy cows and he didn't mind. He was laughing as he did a job he had always hated. He was happy. He was talking to the cows and singing under his breath. He felt a hundred pounds lighter. He wasn't limping. "This is nice," he said in his dream, and then the image of Amber jumped back into his head.

He found the rope hanging off a nail and threw it over the rafter. Climbing on the bails, and using the top of the stall wall for the final step, he could get himself up high enough to slip it over his head....

Johnny woke up and it wasn't a second before the dream and Amber were front and center in his mind. As he'd often done the last couple months, he hid his head in his pillow and wept like a baby.

When he pulled himself back together, he went to the kitchen and wolfed down leftover waffles and ham. His dad sat in front of the TV, watching a fishing show.

"Hey, you know that Earl Krump?"

His dad raised his eyebrows like it was a strange question. "Yeah, so what?"

"His son has the farm now, doesn't he?"

"Sure."

"So if he wanted to hide something, where would he hide it?"

Paul Roth eyed his son. Clearly something was wrong, but he couldn't put his finger on it.

"Like what?"

"Oh, anything. Something he didn't want anyone to find."

"Well, he wouldn't put it on the farm. That's the first place anyone would look."

Johnny already knew that and saw he'd been stymied again. He was halfway back to the stairs when his father added, "The other place, I suppose."

Johnny sucked in his breath. "What other place?"

"He used to rent land down the way from his farm."

"Nobody's living there now?"

"No place to live. No house."

"A barn?

"No."

Johnny thought, "Oh, shit."

His foot was on the first step when Paul Roth remembered, "But it does have a silo."

Johnny's heart stopped. Perfect, he thought. Perfect. He went back to his room, put the cap on the whiskey bottle, and hid it under his bed.

It stopped snowing late Sunday and Johnny hurried to the barn, a flashlight showing the way. He fired up the tractor, already fitted with a bucket loader. He had to get out of this yard…down that snow-packed road. He had to clear the way so he could get to Crabapple.

About the time Johnny had pushed and bladed and shoved the snow aside to open the driveway, Lois Roth got a call from her second cousin, twice-removed.

"Lois, there's something you have to know," the woman began, her voice soft but urgent. "If it was my son, I'd want to know." A long pause, as Lois held her breath. "Somebody kidnapped Crabapple and everyone thinks it was Johnny."

Lois started to cry and when Paul finally came into the kitchen to see what was wrong, she blurted it all out. Paul Roth moved faster than Lois could ever remember, grabbing his jacket and running out of the house.

The tractor was parked near the barn. Johnny's pickup was gone.

"Goddammit," Paul swore as he ran to his truck, not needing to search for keys because, of course, they were in the ignition.

Chapter Seventeen

Wednesday morning after Mass was a safe time to meet in the church basement.

Father would be next door in his parsonage, the daily celebrants would have gone on to their routine, and this quiet, holy place would work for a "come to Jesus" meeting.

Maggie, Angie, and Norma desperately needed to talk.

The three women sat around a small wooden table, wishing they had made coffee, and faced one another, like sizing up a firing squad.

"We can never tell anyone." Maggie was insistent.

"Of course not."

"Absolutely."

Nobody spelled out what they could never tell and not one of these women knew what the others knew. But when you're a wife and your husband has done something that turned out as bad as it could, your pledge of silence covers everything.

"Has Ralph said anything?" Angie fished.

"Not much. How about Earl?"

"You know how Earl is. He never tells me anything."

"And Bernard?"

The two women turned to face Norma, who wanted to vomit.

"Bernard told me everything." Norma covered her face with her hands and started wailing.

Maggie stood to put her arms around her old friend, her own tears dripping down her cheek. Angie laid her head on her arms on the table and looked like she'd never rise up again.

"But Bernard didn't kill him!" Norma declared through her sobs.

Maggie took a step back in shock. "Well, Ralph sure as hell didn't kill him."

Now Angie's tiger-mama instincts kicked in. "If you think they're going to hang this on my Earl, you're all crazy. Of course Earl didn't kill him."

"Calm down, calm down." Maggie tried to calm down. She went back to her seat and pretended she was the adult in the room. "Let's go through this logically, girls. Remember, everything we say here goes no farther. We'll never speak these words to anyone else. You can never tell anyone. Agreed?"

Nods around the table reaffirmed the pledge.

"Now, Norma, tell us what Bernard told you." That would be the best place to start.

Norma looked suspicious, as though Bernard's version could come back to bite him.

"I'd rather hear what Ralph told you," she answered in a shaky voice.

"Me, too," Angie threw in, signaling they thought Ralph was the ringleader.

With all her heart, Maggie Bonner wanted to trust these women she'd known since they were girls. With all her heart, she wanted to share what she knew so they could sort it out together and decide what to do next. With all her heart she wanted to be anywhere but here, talking about anything but this. But this was her private sorority now. This was the coven that must hold this secret to their graves to protect the men they loved.

"It was never supposed to end up like this," she began, choking back her fears. "They wanted justice and they couldn't get it

and they thought if they forced him to confess or leave town...
that was all. That was ALL."

"Earl said they gave him food and water and they were trying
to scare him. Oh yeah, and one of my quilts."

"Bernard said he stayed belligerent and they thought just
one more night in the cold and he'd come clean but then the
storm hit."

"Something else, too." Maggie's voice was thick with phlegm.

"They were trying to protect Johnny. He said he was going
to kill that boy. Everybody knew. They thought if they could
stop that, Johnny would have a chance."

Angie for one didn't buy that part of the story—it was the
men's egos that drove them, not some do-good instinct to help a
boy they all blamed for Amber's death. But it was a good excuse—
an added point in their favor—so she kept her doubts to herself.

Norma jumped on the Johnny angle like it was a life raft.
"Yes, Bernard said that, too. They didn't want Johnny to kill
that kid and go to prison. But they couldn't just order that boy
out of town. They had to scare him out of town. Or get him to
confess so he'd go to prison. That's where he belonged—prison
or out of this town. But not here. Not in Northville."

"It was probably Johnny, anyway." Angie sighed, defeated.

The other women nodded, more in sorrow than agreement.

"I know my Ralph didn't do it."

"My Earl, either."

"Not Bernard. I know that in my soul," Norma said. "Ladies,
we have known these men our whole lives. We've raised families
with them. We've helped them bury their parents. We've been
through tough times together. We've been happy, too...." Her
voice trailed off.

"Never in a million years did I ever think..." Maggie started.
"No way. This is unbelievable. This is a nightmare."

"It was a stupid plan from the start," Angie pronounced, like
she was a Supreme Court judge.

The other two looked at her like she was a traitor. "Now
Angie..."

"You can excuse them all you want, but my God, kidnapping a human being and leaving him in a silo? What kind of idiot comes up with a plan like that? That's what got him killed. Whoever did this had an easy kill. *Oh, don't look at me like that. You know it's the truth.* The killer could do this because our husbands kidnapped that poor kid and chained him up. You don't have to pull the trigger to be a killer, you know. We have to live with the fact that our husbands are accessories to murder. That is a terrible, terrible thing. Whatever that boy did, he didn't deserve this. When did our men get so goddamned arrogant they thought they could be judge, jury, and executioner?"

Angie's diatribe ended in pathetic sobs. Norma was already so distraught she could hardly speak. Maggie's eyes were closed in pain as tears trailed down her cheeks. Nobody said a word for a long time.

"And it's my Earl's silo! If they tie this to anybody, it's him!" Angie spit out the words in a rage.

"You know the men have pledged to stand together," Norma jumped in. "Nobody's going to let Earl take all the blame."

"Well, they're all to blame for hiding the body." Angie made the point like she'd just won a debate.

That horrible fact circled the table.

Kidnapping the kid was one thing.

His death was another.

But hiding the body—trying to cover up that he ever was in that silo? You didn't have to spend the winter on a diet of television cop shows to know that had "guilty" written all over it.

"How could they ever explain that?" Norma wondered. Nobody had a clue.

"If they'd have left the body where it was, and gone right to the sheriff, and told him what happened…"

But nobody thought the outcome would be any better.

"Nobody knows for certain it was them who kidnapped the boy. They might suspect, but nobody knows." Maggie hung on to that thread of hope.

"Somebody better tell Alice to keep her mouth shut, too."

"Don't worry about Alice. My niece knows when to stay quiet," Maggie offered.

"But we must never tell. Never." Norma pleaded.

"Never," Angie agreed.

"To my grave, I will never tell," Maggie vowed.

Finally, Maggie said the words that didn't need to be spoken. Words that each knew in her heart. Words that came from years of loving a man and relying on a man and trusting a man and now, protecting a man.

"We have to stand by them. That's all we can do."

Each one felt older as she walked out of that meeting.

Each one felt sadder.

Each one was more scared than she'd ever been in her entire life.

Chapter Eighteen

Thursday, January 13, 2000

Deer-hunting season was well over. So was elk. Pheasant season had closed last week. Nobody should have been out in that tree claim chomping through snowbanks to shoot at anything, but the Anderson boys were, and that's where they found Crabapple.

The body had been half-covered with snow—probably completely covered at one point, but it hadn't snowed for three days and the wind had blown away some of the burial shroud. If the Anderson brothers had any knowledge of crime scenes, they wouldn't have tromped all over the place, sometimes twirling in circles in their fright at finding a dead body. By the time they were done, few of the tracks left behind were useful. But you couldn't really fault them, for as soon as they ran home and their folks called the sheriff's office—then called friends in town—word spread and a half dozen townspeople beat the cops to the site.

Sheriff Potter's boys weren't experts on crime scenes either, but they certainly knew one that had been "contaminated" when they saw it.

It was about ten a.m., Thursday, January 13.

Somebody had turned the body over so it faced skyward, rather than lying on its stomach. Nobody ever fessed up to it and it hardly mattered who'd done it. But now that the full horror of the corpse was visible to anyone, there were several who wished nobody had done that.

Fear had been growing in the silence of Northville for the last few days, that things would end up badly. Huntsie was telling everyone he feared for Darryl's safety. Johnny Roth was seen around town looking wild and angry. After a no-show at the bakery for their Monday card game, the Tuesday dinner at the Senior Citizen Center also missed the Ralph Bonners, the Bernard Stines, and the Earl Krumps.

Wednesday morning, Huntsie gave up waiting, so he called the sheriff in Wahpeton to report Darryl missing.

The officer who took the report was new to the job. A mechanic missing in a small town nearby was hardly something to get excited about. But a day later, an excited Mr. Anderson reported his sons had found a dead body in a tree-claim four miles outside Northville. The chagrined officer now showed Sheriff Potter the missing person report.

The sheriff exploded. He pounded his fist on his desk and let out a string of swear words. "Those Rambo wannabes are in a shitload of trouble now!"

He headed to Northville, fully expecting to arrest three smart-ass bigshots by the day's end. And he would have, too, if he'd had any evidence to pin on them.

But forget tracks or boot marks around the body—all those were trampled by looky-loos. Forget shell casings, as none were found around the body. Forget imprints in blood, for there wasn't much blood out here. That was the main clue.

One of the Anderson boys announced to Sheriff Potter, as though the lawman wasn't smart enough to see it, "This body was dumped here." The twelve- year-old said it with such pride, knowing his notoriety had just soared. He'd be telling this story the rest of his life.

"I see that," Sheriff Potter shot back, a little too sharply, some felt. He tried to recover: "But I thank you for your fine police work, son."

Mr. Anderson grabbed his boy by the neck of his jacket and yanked him back to the sidelines with the look of "stay out of this!"

Sheriff Potter wasn't as kind to the adults in the audience. "Now folks, you see how you've all been walkin' around here and drivin' your trucks up here, and you see how we no longer know YOUR tracks from those of the killer who dumped this body here? You see that? That doesn't help us one bit. Now please leave so we can do our jobs. Thank you very much. And goodbye."

The chagrined audience—realizing what they'd done—peeled off and went home to speculate about who had done this and when would Sheriff Potter figure it all out.

For his part, Sheriff Potter saw that mangled body as a personal insult. "Those sons of bitches," he swore under his breath. "They think they can take the law into their own hands and made me look like a fool."

To his men he announced, "We need to find out where this man was killed. We find the kill site and we've found the killer. Now I've got some strong suspicions about who that might be, so let's nail this down. Benson, call the coroner's office to come get this body. Stephens, take pictures of this corpse."

His men looked at him with admiration—maybe Sheriff Potter wasn't as lazy and clueless as he seemed. Right now, he looked and sounded very much like a lawman who knew how to solve a murder. And his men were proud of him.

He could see it in their eyes and it gave him a jolt of confidence.

"Nobody's gonna make a fool of Sylvester Joseph Potter," he silently vowed. "I'm gonna show this town and those assholes what it means to mess with the law."

LeRoy Roth was one of the spectators that day—several looked at him askance—and he hightailed it to his brother's when the sheriff turned everyone away. Paul had just heard the news from the frenzied grapevine, which was working overtime.

One look at his brother and LeRoy knew something was terribly wrong. Paul hadn't slept for days, and the red rings around his eyes made him look like a raccoon.

"What's the matter?" he asked.

"We can't find Johnny. He's been gone three days. He left here like a bat out of hell on Sunday after the storm, and he hasn't come home. I've looked for him all over. He's disappeared. His mother is beside herself. And we just heard about the body. I don't want my boy to go to prison."

Now you're concerned, Lois thought as she angrily bit her lip. *NOW!*

"Calm down, calm down," LeRoy said. "You don't know he's the one who did this. You don't know, Paul. And he could be anywhere. Maybe staying with a friend. Maybe he went away for a few days—you know how hard it is for him to come back here. Now calm down, man."

The phone rang and Lois Roth ran to it. A cousin was calling to report she'd seen Johnny's pickup parked at the Catholic church. "I think he's talking with Father, and that's a *good* sign, Lois. It's really a good sign."

Maybe the only sign of hope Lois had for a long time.

When she told Paul, he and LeRoy dashed off to town to see if Johnny was still there. But his pickup was gone.

Paul walked up to the two-story parsonage that stood next to the church and rang the bell. Father Singer was distressed to see the Roth brothers on his stoop.

"Is Johnny here?" his father asked, with hope.

"No, he's gone." Father Singer had so much more he wanted to say to this man who was about to grieve, but he couldn't. The words spoken in a confessional are sacrosanct in the Catholic church, and no matter what the consequence—*no matter what*—a priest cannot reveal what he's been told.

"Johnny came to confession," the priest explained—that at least he could say, but that was all.

"Father, I hope you helped him. My boy is so lost."

"I hope so, too, Mr. Roth. Do you want to come in and we'll pray?"

"No, that's alright. I'm going to look for him. Any idea where he's gone?"

The priest could honestly—and legally—admit he had no idea.

The sirens on the sheriffs' cars blared as they blasted through town at about three p.m., turning left at the Sunoco to rush to Darryl Harding's farm. It was the obvious place to start, Sheriff Potter had instructed, knowing none of his deputies had ever investigated a murder before. He neglected to mention that he never had, either.

Two pickups were in the yard. One had keys still in the ignition. The other one's keys were under the front seat.

The officers went into the house, looking for clues. At least these men knew enough about forensics that they wore gloves and were careful what they touched. One whipped out a finger-print kit and started dusting items. The splay of broken glass along one wall looked particularly suspicious, and a few shards were big enough to hold at least a partial print.

In a closet, they found drugs hidden under a loose floor-board—marijuana, Ecstasy, a small vial of cocaine. Here was the evidence the town had been begging them to find. But now it was way too late.

"I've got a bootprint on the carpet," one man yelled. Someone cut out that piece for testing.

Along with all the photographs they'd taken at the dump site, Sheriff Potter guessed they probably had something. He wasn't sure what, but something had to make sense. Clearly, Darryl Harding had not been killed in his home. There was no blood. No pockmarks from a shotgun's pellets. Nothing here but a trashy house occupied by a young man who'd never come home.

On the way out of the house, Sheriff Potter told one of the officers to double check the barn. "Sheriff, you gotta see this," he yelled. Sheriff Potter ran—as fast as he could with his belly flopping.

Hanging from the rafter was Johnny Roth. His body was still warm.

Chapter Nineteen

Saturday, January 15, 2000

Joya Bonner was on the next plane out of Phoenix when she heard the news.

It took awhile to understand what was happening, for her mother's weeping over the phone. That kid they thought was the pusher was dead, and poor Johnny Roth had hung himself. The whole town thought Johnny had done it and then couldn't stand the guilt. But the sheriff was still sniffing around because he thought her father had something to do with all this.

"What?" she cried incredulously. "What would Dad have to do with this?"

Her mother sobbed all the louder, while Joya waited for the woman to compose herself. Her mother never acted like this, even when there was a death in the family. She was far more likely to call with a calm, motherly voice of comfort to break bad news, like when Grandpa died. But this was different. This was her mother in turmoil and terror.

"Your father…your father…I can't say. But it's bad. And the sheriff has gone nuts trying to pin it on him."

"Pin what?" Joya couldn't picture what was going on.

"Pin Crabapple's murder. And he's not sure Johnny really killed himself."

"FUCK," Joya yelled, a natural response that her mother wouldn't appreciate. "Sorry, Mom. What in the world is going on back there? The sheriff thinks Dad killed that kid and Johnny? What possible motive would he have?"

Later, Joya would realize that when you hang with cops for months, you get to talking like they do.

"They knew he was a drug dealer and tried to get the sheriff to arrest him, but he wouldn't. And then Amber died. And…"

"Who's 'they'?" Joya asked. She was reminded about the three musketeers of Northville. "So the sheriff thinks all three are involved?"

"Well, they are," Maggie said through hiccups that often came on her when she bawled. "But I can't talk about it. Oh, it's so awful. And your dad isn't sleeping."

"Dad's involved? How? What did he do? This isn't even possible. My dad is no killer."

"I know that, Joya!" It was the first clear sentence Maggie had uttered.

Joya instantly regretted her words. "Mom, I know. I know. I'm sorry."

The horrible reality of the sheriff's thinking was becoming clear to Joya Bonner and she had to get home. She quickly calculated if her bank account could handle it—she lived paycheck to paycheck like every print journalist—and knew it was shy. But she had a good friend who would float her a loan.

"Mom, I'm coming home."

"Oh, Joya, I don't know. Do you really think so?"

That was mother-code for "please hurry."

When Ralph and Maggie Bonner met Joya at Hector Field in Fargo the next day, the mother embraced the daughter with relief and joy while the father gave a perfunctory hug as if to say, "Why are you sticking your nose in this?"

The greeting didn't surprise Joya. She'd always had a standoff relationship with her father. She knew she should be gentle with him, completely supportive, not pushy, but that wasn't how she played cards. They got off to a bad start.

"Tell me what happened." She asked her father the same way she'd question someone like Sammy the Bull. It was the worst approach she could have taken.

"If you think you're going to stick your nose in this, I'll tell you right now, you are not," her father exploded. "This is none of your business. I don't want you digging around in this. You'll only make things worse. If you came home to visit, fine. But if you came home to mess in this, then I want you to get back on that plane and go home to Phoenix."

Joya had stood up to governors and mayors and richer-than-God land developers and even the self-proclaimed "toughest sheriff in America," but standing up to her father was far harder. He could hit that spot in her gut that none of the others even knew existed.

"Dad, I don't want to mess anything up. I want to help." Her voice sounded too much like a little girl's.

"I don't want your help and I don't need your help. So god-dammit, stay out of this!"

The first half-hour of the trip to Northville was noisy in its silence. Maggie tried to make small talk, but it was lame. Joya waited, anxious that she didn't know what she needed to know—how in the world was her dad involved in a murder-suicide? Why was the sheriff after him and his buddies? How could any of this be happening to her church-going-upstanding-community-leader father?

Something was horribly wrong and her dad would never fess up. Hopefully Mom would come clean when they were alone. She counted on that, just as she counted on her dad stonewalling her unless she got him to see she could be a help.

They were forty minutes into the ride when she started detailing her recent scoop on Sammy the Bull.

She told the story with flourish and excitement, noting how he was going on trial and could face decades in prison.

"You know," she finally said, taking aim, "he ran a big Ecstasy ring that focused on the Southwest, but his dope went all over.

The Phoenix Police Department says the Ecstasy that killed Amber came from Sammy's ring."

That wasn't exactly true, but it could have been. Even if it wasn't, Joya needed her dad to believe it. It was the only way she knew to get through his wall of hands-off. Funny, she thought to herself. For the last few months, I was praying they'd build the wall that would get Sammy. Now here I am trying to tear one down.

"Why does the Phoenix Police Department know anything about Amber?" her dad asked, too sharply.

"Well, I've made a lot of friends in the department as we were working this Sammy thing, and when I first heard about Amber, I mentioned it and they came back to me and told me how she was connected to Sammy." Joya knew her dad respected law and order—Sheriff Potter notwithstanding—and she hoped that would help her now.

"How are they connected?" Ralph showed guarded interest.

"They've traced the stuff to Minneapolis and that's where North Dakota dealers get their Ecstasy," she said, as though all those dots had been connected. It was an educated guess and that was good enough for now.

"That's where Crabapple went when he ran," her dad mused.

"Really? He went to Minneapolis?"

"Yeah, to a cousin's or something. Huntsie told us."

Joya had a toe in the door. "Make sure your attorney knows that," she offered, "and I can give him anything he needs about Sammy's operation in Phoenix. I can put him in touch with the detectives who worked that case—I have their private numbers. And I brought copies of my story home, so you could give that to him—it might be helpful."

"We don't have an attorney," Maggie said.

"What? You don't have an attorney? Isn't that sheriff snooping around like he suspects you of something?"

Ralph shot a nasty look to his wife, but she glared at him in defiance. "This is no time to stick your head in the sand," she declared, knowing Ralph's was already halfway there. To her daughter in the backseat she announced, "I've been telling him he needs an attorney."

"Dad, even though you're innocent, you need an attorney. I've watched innocent people go to prison because they didn't have anyone to protect them. You know, the police aren't always after the truth. They're really after a conviction—closing a case and sending someone away. Sometimes they don't care who that someone is. And if this sheriff has his sights on you, well, that's bad."

Ralph didn't say anything, although he was glad to hear she thought he was innocent. And his daughter was making sense. That pissed him off, because of all his children, this was the one he usually disagreed with the most.

Maggie would say that was because father and daughter were frick and frack. Both were stubborn to the point of pigheadedness. Both were mouthy. Both naturally thought they should lead. Both were chauvinists, with Ralph believing males were superior to females and Joya believing it was the other way around. She even had a quote on the wall of her study at home from folk singer Louden Wainwright III: "…and the world is a place of horror because every man thinks he's right."

For his part, Ralph actually relished the verbal sparring that came home with Joya every year—once telling a visiting son he couldn't get into issues with him because "I've got to rest up for Joya." But in the end, he thought his daughter was almost always wrong and always, always, too liberal. He couldn't figure out where he'd gone wrong with her.

"What do the boys say?" Joya knew her father put more stock in his son's opinions.

"Oh, they agree with me." Maggie turned in the seat to look her daughter in the eye, signaling that the boys might agree, but they weren't pushing. The look pleaded, "PLEASE PUSH."

"I know lots of lawyers in Phoenix, Dad, and I could ask one for a recommendation here in North Dakota."

"We don't have money for attorneys." As though that really was a factor.

"I'll help you find one that isn't expensive," she replied. "Somebody from this area would be good. It doesn't hurt to just talk to an attorney." She'd have to find a male attorney because her father would never trust a female.

"Maybe you and Earl and Bernard could all go in together," Maggie suggested now.

Joya opened her mouth to object, but her mother threw a look that said "back off." Still, if her mother's bawling recitation on the phone had been accurate, each of those three men needed their own attorney.

She gambled and took one more step she prayed would work. "Dad, I've investigated a lot of crimes and one of the things that's important is what the sheriff knows and what he doesn't know. There's ways of finding that out. The police report is a public record and anyone can read it. The autopsy report is a public record, too. I could get those for you, without any problem, and you'd see what kind of evidence they think they have. Or maybe the sheriff is just bluffing, trying to make you guys nervous enough to fess up to something. It's important to know what the sheriff knows."

Ralph had to admit this was one of the most practical sentences his daughter had ever uttered. As he pulled into the driveway of his home and hit the automatic garage door opener, he could see the wisdom. Maybe it wouldn't hurt if she did this *one thing* and got those reports.

It took him most of the afternoon to revisit their conversation. "Is it hard to get those reports?"

"Oh no, it's easy-peasy. I can go next week and get them."

Ralph Bonner's silence let the words hang there. He gave a little shudder, amazed he was talking with his daughter about records in a murder case. *How the hell did I get here?*

Joya had his tacit approval—since she was a rebellious teenager, when her dad meant no, he said no, but silence meant it was okay.

They'd just sat down for supper—Mom's famous pot roast—when a loud pounding on the front door startled everyone.

Joya jumped up to answer it and was swept aside as this overweight, huffing man pushed his way in and announced he was there to see Ralph Bonner. She didn't have to ask to recognize Sheriff Potter.

"I need your shotgun and I need your shells," he bellowed at Ralph, standing with his legs spread shoulder-width as though he were on the shooting range.

"Why?" Ralph's voice didn't sound as strong and sure as he usually did.

"You know why," Sheriff Potter answered. Joya was sure she saw a smirk.

"No, Sheriff, I have no idea why you'd want my gun."

"The game's over, Bonner. We found the silo."

Ralph paused, and then punted. "What silo?" He'd later be incredibly grateful he'd remained calm.

Silo? Joya thought. What's a silo got to do with any of this?

"The silo where you three Rambos chained up Darryl Harding before you killed him. We've already arrested your co-conspirator. Earl Krump."

Joya stopped breathing.

"Sheriff, we did not kill that kid!" Ralph now was on his feet, and he stood toe to toe with the sheriff. "Don't you come in my home and make wild accusations. I am not a killer. Neither are my friends. But if you want my gun, you can have it because I have nothing to hide."

Joya's mind was racing with the ridiculous image of her father and his friends chaining up a kid in a silo. They really did that? What were they thinking? What in the world were they doing?

Ralph started to take a step toward the gun cabinet. If she were ever to help her dad, Joya needed to help him right now.

"Wait, Dad!" She was screaming.

She turned and threw back her shoulders to make herself taller. "Sheriff, do you have a warrant?"

She said the words with clarity and force, looking him right in the eye. Sheriff Potter stared and stayed quiet.

As though she were teaching a tutorial in basic police work, Joya lectured, "You know, you can't just waltz into somebody's home and demand they hand over anything without a warrant saying you've got probable cause. You've got to convince a judge that you have cause to believe this man committed a crime. You can't just run around like you're the Gestapo. So I ask again. Do. You. Have. A. Warrant?"

Nobody had ever spoken to Sheriff Potter that way. Ralph and Maggie were mortified that their daughter would be so obstinate. After all, he *was* the sheriff. But they quickly realized she was standing up to a man who had already made up his mind that Ralph was a murderer.

"And who do you think you are, young lady?" the sheriff asked with disgust.

"I'm Joya Bonner, an investigative reporter from Phoenix who just worked hand-in-hand with the Phoenix Police Department to break up a major drug ring. So I know how these things work. And they don't work with a sheriff who doesn't know the constitutional rights of American citizens, waltzing into my parents' home and making wild accusations against my father. If you can get a warrant, we'll be glad to give you the shotgun and you can see it has nothing to do with anything. If you can't get a warrant, then we're done here. I'll show you the door, Sheriff."

Joya threw out her arm in the direction of the door. Sheriff Potter looked at her like he was seeing a unicorn. "Now listen here…" but he got no farther as she flicked her hands to shoo him away.

"Sheriff, our attorney can be here in fifteen minutes if you don't leave us alone. Now, either do this legally, or you're not going to do this at all. You realize, of course, that if you illegally confiscate this gun and then find something, it wouldn't be permissible in a court of law. You do know that, right?"

Now she was showing off. Some would applaud her "gotcha moment." Others would despise it. But Joya didn't care. This felt good. She was racking up points with her father.

Sheriff Potter threw a dangerous look at Ralph and pointed his finger. "You're not going to get away with this," but his legs were doing the real talking as he headed out the door.

Joya slammed it behind him. He never saw that she had to brace herself against the jam so she wouldn't collapse from her false bravado.

When she turned, her parents stared at her as if they saw a person they didn't recognize. *This is who I am*, she thought, as she sat down at the table and demanded, "What in the world is going on here?"

"Oh God, thank you, Joya," her mother finally said as she began to cry.

Joya got up and put her arms around the woman she adored. "Don't worry, Mom, it's going to be alright."

Ralph had to give it up, too. "Yes, thank you. You know, I could have given him my gun because it has nothing to do with this." He had to underscore the point that he wasn't a total idiot.

"That wouldn't have mattered, Dad. He could have done anything with that gun—he could have shot it to make it look like it was the murder weapon. Did you see how gleeful he was when he rushed in here? He was ready to arrest you for murder. Do you understand that? He could have hauled you off in handcuffs and thrown you in jail. That's just what he wanted to do. A guy like that could easily fudge the evidence to get what he wants. He didn't have a warrant because he has nothing to get a warrant with. You've got to convince a judge that you've got real evidence that points to someone in particular. You can't just go on a Walmart shopping spree."

Ralph Bonner saw his daughter through new eyes that night. He never thought he'd say this, but the girl was right. And she'd probably just saved his neck.

"So tell me about this silo."

Ralph had to come clean. He told the story in shorthand, with Maggie jumping in now and then to add a detail. He said the words with his head lowered, like he now realized how foolish it had been.

"We kidnapped him, but we didn't kill him." Ralph sounded very certain, hoping it wouldn't allow any more questions. But Joya needed more.

"Dad, I'm sure you didn't do it. But are you completely convinced one of the others didn't? Nobody knew where he was. How would anyone find him? Nobody even knew he was kidnapped, right? Being missing isn't the same as being kidnapped. For all anyone knew, he'd left town with a buddy or something. I know they're your best friends, but the three of you were the only ones who knew where he was. And now the sheriff knows it was Earl's silo and he thinks he's got you guys."

"I don't know what the sheriff knows," Ralph admitted in defeat.

Joya took over. "I'll go get those reports so we know what's going on. And let's find you an attorney."

Ralph got up to go to the phone and Joya stopped him in his tracks. "Dad, who are you calling? You can't be calling Bernard or Earl. That's exactly what they'd want you to do. Oh God, they might have a wiretap on your line! Dad, don't say anything on that phone that you don't want the police to know. And if anyone calls you, play dumb. You have no idea what that son of a bitch is up to. That's how they caught Sammy. It was the wiretaps."

Later in bed, she'd fantasize that Sheriff Potter had stormed in on a bluff, betting Ralph didn't know anything about the necessary warrant, unaware he had a daughter who knew the law, certain he'd call his buddies and spill the beans—everything caught in a wiretap. But then she thought, Naw, the guy's a two-bit backwoods hack. He's not smart enough.

How she wished she was right.

Chapter Twenty

Tuesday, January 18, 2000

Government offices were closed on Monday for Martin Luther King Day, so Joya had to wait until Tuesday to get the records. She drove to the beautiful historic courthouse in Wahpeton, where the sheriff's office and jail occupied the lower level.

"I'm here for a copy of the sheriff's report on the murder of Darryl Harding and the suicide of Johnny Roth," she announced to a skinny woman with thin hair and a cardigan sweater.

"Oh, I don't think you can have them?" The woman intended it to be a statement, but her voice made it a question.

"Yes, ma'am, they're public records," Joya said. "And you should know that, since they did the North Dakota Public Records Test last year. Remember, the one that you guys failed? And a district judge told you to comply with the law in handing out public records. Remember?"

The clerk well remembered that embarrassing "test," in which North Dakota reporters posed as ordinary citizens to test the availability of public records. And just like in other states—Iowa, Indiana, South Carolina, South Dakota—they found that while most public departments were good about sharing records the public had every right to see, law enforcement departments weren't. In every state, they found police and sheriff offices made it tough, if not impossible, to get public records. In North Dakota, one reporter had been followed by a sheriff when he left the office in Jamestown. From this very office in Wahpeton, a reporter was interrogated and detained when he tried to get records on a shooting. And that brought national news organizations to North Dakota to help clean things up—including an appearance in front of a district judge who demanded compliance.

Joya had watched this test in her home state with interest, since Arizona wasn't the easiest place to wrest public records from some law enforcement units, either. She'd thought of suggesting they do a test in Phoenix, but she'd never gotten around to it. That information about North Dakota's test sure came in handy now.

"Remember," she repeated, and the clerk looked at her with disdain.

"It will be one dollar a page." The clerk thought that would stop this nonsense.

"Isn't that a little pricey for a five-cent Xerox?" Joya asked. "You know, you can't make copy costs prohibitive."

"We don't think a dollar a page is prohibitive," she answered back, determined to get the upper hand.

"Fine. I'll pay it. And I'll wait right here for my copy."

Joya sat down in a wooden chair against the wall and pulled a book out of her big bag, making it clear she was ready to settle in until she got what she wanted. She'd had the book on her pile for a while. She brought it along from Phoenix, because now seemed like a good time to read about investigating a murder case.

"October 16, 1931, was a bloody Friday night in Phoenix, Arizona," she read, as she began *The Trunk Murderess: Winnie Ruth Judd.*

It took more than an hour for the clerk to come back with a ten-page report. Joya flipped through it, screwing up her nose as she came to the end. "How about the report on the silo?" She looked the woman straight in the eye.

"That report isn't ready yet," the woman lied, and Joya called her bluff.

"Sure it is. Your sheriff is running around arresting people because of the silo, so there's got to be a report. I'll wait."

She sat down and reopened the book, picking up at the end of Chapter Three: "The very first thing you notice is that she was cut apart so precisely the coroner was able to stitch her back together."

When the silo report was finally added—all three pages of it—Joya paid her thirteen-dollar fee and left the office.

"What a bitch," she heard the clerk say as she walked out the door. Joya beamed.

The sheriff's report showed that everything they had so far pointed to Johnny Roth as the killer. It was his bootprint on the carpet in Crabapple's home, his print on the smashed vase. And of course, it was in Crabapple's barn where they'd found his hanging body.

From the silo, they'd found specks of Crabapple's blood—and plenty of evidence that someone had tried to clean it up—but no other blood. Okay, that was good, Joya thought.

They knew the silo was owned by Earl Krump. "Krump is a known associate of Ralph Bonner and Bernard Stine, all of whom have approached the sheriff's office over the last two years to arrest Darryl Harding. Sheriff Potter has heard these three men threaten the life of Darryl Harding and vow revenge against him, claiming he was responsible for the death of Amber Schlener."

Joya read those words in the police report with her mouth open. The sheriff was a witness to a death threat? That's why he was ignoring the evidence that Johnny did it? It was absurd. Who goes around telling a sheriff they're going to kill somebody? But Joya knew that the word of a law enforcement official held great sway, not only with a judge and jury, but with the general public. After all, in Arizona a woman was sitting on death row solely on the word of a police detective that she'd "confessed" to having her son killed—a confession neither recorded, witnessed, nor attested. His word against hers. If a cop's word alone is enough to get you a death sentence, imagine what happens if an officer says you personally told him you intended to kill somebody! Everyone would accept it as gospel. This wasn't good.

Another bit of bad news was that the silo had yielded one possibly fabulous clue: a spent twelve-gauge shotgun shell. It had rolled into a crack in the cement floor, and whoever had cleaned up the place had overlooked it. Joya instantly saw the problem. If they could tie this shell to one of the shotguns owned by her father or his friends, they'd be in real trouble. That's why the sheriff had tried to bluff her dad into giving up his shotgun on the spot. She bet that he'd tried a similar tactic with the other two, and hoped they were smart enough not to comply.

If, on the other hand, the shell was from Johnny's gun, that would be the end of this.

She prayed it was Johnny's.

Joya Bonner was used to a coroner's office that occupied a two-story building in the heart of one of the nation's largest cities—a first floor with refrigerated rooms that could hold dozens of bodies, which it sometimes was called to do, and three "operating theaters" on the second floor for multiple autopsies at a time.

So what passed for a coroner's office in Wahpeton, North Dakota, seemed amateurish. Two rooms. Not a refrigerator in sight. One room was the office. The other was the autopsy room. One steel table to hold a body. No communication system to record the report—just a tape recorder on a nearby shelf. No viewing room for visitors to monitor the autopsy. Here, if you wanted to observe, you sat on a chair in the corner of the small room as the body was cut apart inches away.

Joya walked into the office and smiled at the plump woman who was eating lunch from a Tupperware bowl.

"Oh, sorry." Wiping her mouth, she set the bowl aside. "We've got a lot of work to do today so we're staying in for lunch."

"Well, it looks good," Joya offered, smiling her friendliest smile. "Leftovers?"

"Yeah, meatloaf."

"Oh, I love meatloaf. Nobody makes it like my mom. You're making me hungry!"

The two women laughed and Joya always loved it when there was a connection.

"How can I help you?" the woman asked.

"I'd like a copy of the autopsy report on Darryl Harding," she said. "The boy from Northville?"

"Oh sure, I know who you mean. We don't have a lot of murders, you know, and this one was so yucky. That poor kid. Somebody just blew him away. Can you believe it? That kind of thing doesn't happen around here."

"I know. I grew up in Northville and the whole town is in shock. You wouldn't think North Dakota would have to worry about stuff like this."

"You sure wouldn't." The clerk reached over and pulled a file from her "in" basket. "Do you want a copy?"

"Yes, please."

The woman got up and took the file to a Xerox machine in the corner, copying the six pages as she continued her testimony about the value of living in North Dakota. "You know, my husband wanted us to move to Odessa, Texas, because they've found new oil down there and he says it's going to mean lots of easy money. But I said, Petie, I'm not moving! I don't know what Texas is like, but I bet it's not as nice as North Dakota and I don't want our kids to grow up somewhere that isn't safe. That's what I told him. And he finally agreed, and we stayed here. That will be a dollar-fifty—we charge twenty-five cents a page."

Joya stifled a laugh and handed over the money. "I thank you so much, and now I'm going to go out and find myself some lunch, and then call my mom and tell her I want meat loaf for dinner!"

Both women were giggling as Joya left the office.

She sat in her dad's car and gobbled up the report.

Darryl Harding was killed by a single shotgun blast to his chest, the killer so close, the steel B-B's hardly fanned out. The shooter was standing over the body when the trigger was pulled, probably holding the gun at the hip, rather than on the shoulder, according to the angle of the pellets. The wound was contaminated with plant material that was not identified.

The body's wrists were raw, as though he'd been chained. His clothes still held remnants of straw and wheat shaft, suggesting he was in a grain silo.

The stomach was clear, signaling he hadn't eaten in a day or so.

The body was moved after death, as much as a day after, according to postmortem lividity.

Joya closed her eyes, imaging how devastating this information could be in a news conference that went to the worst possible scenario—the kind she was used to hearing from her own sheriff back in Phoenix.

If Sheriff Potter were the publicity hog that Sheriff Arpaio was, he'd have already called a news conference to decry that this poor boy was chained up and starved to death before being blown away by a Rambo with a shotgun. How soon before some reporter came calling for this very report and reached the same conclusions?

She didn't have all day to get the help they needed.

Joya next stopped at the office of the attorney who'd been recommended by a friend in Phoenix. He wasn't a seasoned criminal defense attorney, but then, Wahpeton didn't have any. Violent crime wasn't a profitable specialty around here, since there was so little. For that, Fargo attorneys were needed. Around here, the money in lawyering came from the civil cases—more leases and rental disputes than kidnapping and murder.

But Dolan Lowe came recommended with enough experience to know the ropes. Besides, her Phoenix friend said, this guy hated Sheriff Potter.

Joya laid a twenty-dollar bill on the desk and said, "Let's call that a down payment on a retainer so my father is officially a client, and I'm his representative."

Lowe saw what their mutual friend in Phoenix had meant when he said, "Don't bullshit this woman. She's smart, and she knows the law."

Under the attorney-client privilege standard, she filled him in on what had happened in Northville, stressing that while her dad and his buddies had kidnapped the kid to get him to talk, she was completely convinced none of them had killed him. She handed over the police and autopsy reports she'd gathered that morning and suggested he make her a copy and he keep the originals, and she noted the points in the reports that worried her.

"The sheriff thinks he's got them because they kidnapped the kid," she told the attorney, sounding anxious.

"So what evidence does he have that they kidnapped him?" the lawyer asked. Joya laid out the facts as she saw them.

"That's not evidence. That's circumstance." Lowe was glad he was smarter than a journalist. "So what if it's Earl's silo? Ownership doesn't mean anything in this case. It doesn't mean Earl had anything to do with a kidnapping. I don't see that they found a lock. Did they find a lock on the door?"

Joya noticed for the first time that the police report said nothing about a lock.

"Well, if there had been a lock, they sure would have mentioned it, because they could have traced that back," Lowe stressed. "Found out who purchased the lock. Found out who had the key or the combination. And that would limit access. But if they didn't mention a lock on the door, there probably wasn't one and that makes ownership even less important. Anybody could have had access to that silo. Anybody could have kidnapped that kid and put him there. There's nothing to tie it to your dad or his friends. Unless they've admitted they kidnapped him. They haven't, have they?"

"Oh, no," Joya assured.

"Fine. Let's keep it that way."

Joya gave a great sigh of relief. She'd totally missed the lock. She'd put too much strength in Earl's ownership. She'd accepted that they'd have to answer for the kidnapping, and now she could see there was nothing that proved her dad had kidnapped anybody.

"The only thing they found in that silo was a shotgun shell, and if they can't tie it to your dad, they've got absolutely nothing," Lowe concluded.

Joya already knew that, and it scared her. "I know, that would be so bad." She relayed how the sheriff already had come for her dad's shotgun, but she'd stopped him.

"Good work," the attorney said with real admiration. "But you know it's almost impossible to trace a shotgun shell, don't you?"

Joya perked up. "Really?" She hadn't known, but then, guns weren't her strong suit. She didn't like them, didn't own one, and since she'd left home, hadn't shot one, although her dad had made sure all his children were gun savvy.

But in all the lessons Ralph Bonner gave his children, he never discussed the traceability of a shotgun shell. Attorney Lowe now gave her a CliffsNotes version.

"Shotgun shells are anonymous. They're not like bullets that get marked up as they go through a barrel of a rifle or a gun. You can trace bullets to a specific weapon. It's very hard to tie a particular shell to a specific shotgun. Plus we have no evidence that the shell they found has anything to do with this murder. Maybe it had been there a long time. Having a shotgun shell in the same place as a shotgun murder doesn't mean much. Especially not on a farm in North Dakota."

Joya was thinking of all the nice things she'd do for her friend back in Phoenix for finding such a smart guy to save her dad's ass. This was exactly why he needed a good attorney. This was the kind of clear thinking she'd seen defense attorneys in Phoenix do again and again. And here was a clear-thinking, answer-for-everything defense attorney that was taking her dad's case.

"So what do you think?" she finally asked.

"I think one of your dad's friends killed that kid."

"WHAT?"

"You heard me. What makes you think they didn't?"

"I know these men. I've known them all my life. The town knows them. They're not killers. They were trying to save the town—to force him out, or to confess. Or to save Johnny. They never intended him to die!"

"Are you sure?"

"Goddamnit it, yes, I'm sure. Listen, maybe you don't understand Northville. This is a nice little town. Families have lived there for generations. Everybody knows everybody. They take care of one another. It's a wonderful place to raise children. It's not some cesspool where people going around murdering somebody."

"I might have bought that before somebody turned it into a cesspool where people go around murdering somebody." He said the words slowly, quietly. He was surprised a seasoned reporter couldn't see through the disguise to what the town was really like.

Joya refused to be swayed. "My dad and his friends thought they were helping the town. They aren't murderers. If you can't believe that, if you can't get up in a court of law and argue that, I'll have my twenty dollars back and we'll forget this."

"Oh, I can get up in a court of law and argue your dad is a saint, but it doesn't mean I have to believe it. But I'm keeping your twenty dollars because I don't believe your dad is a killer. Now his buddies, I don't know. But here's the thing…if one of them did kill that kid, all three are culpable. It's called 'felony murder.' If someone dies in the commission of a felony, every-one involved is as guilty as the one who pulled the trigger. So the only way to save your dad is to pretend all three of them are saints. So here's my first piece of legal advice: tell your dad and his friends to keep their mouths shut and they'll be okay."

Joya nodded in great relief.

"Why don't I come down next week and talk to your dad and I'll lay it all out for him?"

"He'll want his buddies there, too. I know you can't represent all three, but would it be okay if they all listened?"

"Sure. Let's see, I'm in court on Monday. How about Tuesday?"

They made an appointment and Joya left feeling hopeful. This man knew what he was doing, and anyone who's ever needed a good attorney knows how great that feels.

She stopped at Econo Foods to pick up greens for a salad—with diverticulitis a problem for both her mom and dad, their idea of salad was Jell-O. She left the store at about four p.m. and decided to take the back way home, rather than drive out to the interstate.

She was feeling so proud of herself, so happy to take such good news home. The country music station her dad favored even sounded good today. She didn't notice the pickup until it was beside her, forcing her off the road.

Joya screamed as she pulled the wheel to the right and went into the ditch that was half-full of snow. She was amazed how the car plowed through the white snowpack, and for a second she thought it might just keep moving forward until it went up into the barren field on the other side of the ditch. But suddenly, the car came to a jolting stop as it smashed into something solid, hidden beneath the snow. Only her seat belt kept her from flying through the windshield, but it didn't stop her head from crashing into the steering wheel. When she opened her eyes, she saw blood.

"Oh my God, oh my God, I'm bleeding," she cried out. Who would come to help her? There was no one on the road. The pickup was gone. The wind was blowing and it was eighteen degrees outside, and she was alone in the last minutes of light on a North Dakota winter's day. She started to cry.

"He ran me off the road. Who was that? Why did he do that? What kind of car was it? No, it wasn't a car, it was a pickup. What color? Black. No, not black. Dark blue. Why? Who would do that to me? Oh God, I've smashed Dad's car."

She unhooked her seat belt and tried to open the door, but it couldn't push against the snow. She was tilted downward, so it looked like the passenger door might be freer. She pushed and shoved and angled and tried to get herself up to the passenger side, but she couldn't. All the time, the light was fading.

If she'd been on the interstate, somebody would have stopped by now and rescued her. But she was on the back road. It was a good road, used mainly by the farmers who lived off it or the railroad workers who had a depot up the way. Joya calculated that not many of them would be driving by soon. If she was to get out of this, she had to do it herself.

And then the dark blue pickup came back.

She stopped breathing as she looked in the rearview mirror and saw a man get out of the pickup and start down the ditch slope. He was carrying something in his hand and Joya feared it was a gun.

Oh God, he's going to kill me. Right here. Who is he? Why? Why? Why?

The man reached her door and she saw he held a shovel. He used it to clear away some snow so the door could open. "Push," he yelled, and she pushed on the door while he yanked, and their combined effort opened it enough that she could slip out.

He grabbed her coat and helped her get out of the car. She finally had a chance to look at him. He was wearing the badge of the Richland County Sheriff's Office.

Her first instinct was to scream at the man who'd run her off the road and demand an explanation, but first instincts are best corralled when you're facing a badge.

"So what happened?" He asked like he didn't know. He was looking her straight in the eye, but there was a smirk around his lips.

"I, I, I, don't know," she stammered. She felt her palms sting, just like that day at the library.

"You probably hit ice and went off the road," he coached, saying the words as though he were talking to a child.

"I guess...I hit...hit ice and...went off the road?"

"That sounds about right." The deputy grinned. "You've got to be more careful, girly. Roads like this can be dangerous at night. You shouldn't be fooling around out here. You know, it's never good for your health if you're foolin' around in stuff you shouldn't be. You're not from these parts, are you?"

"I...I...I'm from Phoenix."

"It's a lot nicer in Phoenix these days than it is in North Dakota. Think maybe you should head back home?"

Joya's mind was recording every word, even through her fright. She looked at his badge, No. 329. It was a number she'd never forget. She looked at his face—blue eyes, sandy blond hair under his ear-flap cap, a mole on his right cheek, thick lips that knew how to sneer.

"Yeah, yeah, sure." She was getting her bearings but careful not to let on that she was regaining her equilibrium. "I think my car is smashed. Can you radio for help or something?" She thought to herself, *No way am I ever getting in a pickup with this man.*

"I can pull you out. Put it in neutral."

He climbed out of the ditch, backed up his pickup and uncoiled the chain. It took him only a few minutes to hook onto her back bumper and pull her out. There was a dent in the front bumper, but no real damage. When she turned the switch, the car came alive.

"Think you can make it home without any more accidents?" Like he was concerned about her welfare. "Wouldn't want any-thing to happen to a visitor who's not staying long."

"I'm sure I can," she said. "Thank you, Officer."

"Yes, ma'am. Just remember, I pulled you *OUT* of that ditch." He smirked at her again and drove away.

Joya drove home, plotting her revenge. That stupid son of a bitch. He thinks he can scare me and make me run away. He thinks he's so goddamned smart. Wait till I get him. The asshole called me 'girly'!

She decided to tell her folks she hit ice and went in the ditch and a nice farmer pulled her out. She couldn't admit what had really happened or they'd make her stop working on this case. No, she'd lie to them, but she'd sure as hell tell that smart defense attorney in Wahpeton. He'd know how to handle this. Badge 329 had pulled his last stunt.

Chapter Twenty-one

The next day, Joya stayed close to home, helping her mother make pierogies and enjoying a day of being the woman's daughter.

Maggie signaled first thing that she wanted no discussion about "the case," and that was fine with Joya. She was ready for a break.

When Maggie sent her uptown for more dry cottage cheese, Joya made a side stop at Leona's Flowers to buy her mom a bouquet.

"How about those two pink roses and some white ones?" she asked.

"Sorry, the pink ones are spoken for, but I've got some nice red roses that are as big as cabbages."

Joya bought a dozen—no baby's breath because her mother was allergic—but rich greens and a satin gold bow. Maggie loved them, but scolded her daughter for spending so much money.

"You should go visit Gertie," Maggie suggested after lunch. "I don't think we'll have her much longer."

"Great idea." Joya was chagrined to realize her promised call to Gertie months ago had never happened. "When's a good time?"

Maggie called the house to ask Wanda when Gertie took her nap and if today would be okay for Joya to visit. "Oh, I think that would be fine. No, she'd love to do that. I'll send her over at three."

Joya nodded. Her mother was the only person she'd allow to set a schedule without checking. "Wanda's got an eye appointment in Wahpeton at three-thirty, so you'll go over at three and stay with Gertie till she gets back."

That "babysitting job" would be about one and a half hours. Fine. She'd always loved Gertie. The woman was her late grandmother's best friend, and she told great stories.

She arrived early at the neat, small house that Gertie and her sister shared. She liked its screened-in front porch—not usable now in the snow, but the unofficial "living room" for the women all summer. Today, for the first time, Joya realized the front porch was the largest room in the house. The rest was two tiny bedrooms, a closet of a bathroom, a one-butt kitchen and a living/dining room just big enough for two recliners and TV-tray side tables that held books, magazines, mail, and a space big enough for a cup of tea or glass of milk. Both recliners faced the television, encased in a cabinet that must have been here since these women were girls.

Gertie was in her recliner. Joya figured that was where she spent most of her waking hours. The first thing she noticed was that the woman was skin and bones. Her collar bone was so sharp, Joya thought it would rip through the neckline of her dressing gown at any second.

"When did you get so skinny?" she joked with the woman.

"I don't have much of an appetite these days."

"Wish I had that problem."

"Don't worry, you look fine. A couple extra pounds never hurt anybody."

Joya saw that Gertie's eyes kept darting to the television and realized she'd been in the midst of watching *Oprah*.

"I love Oprah," Gertie whispered, admitting a guilty pleasure.

"Oh, me, too. Let's watch."

"Oh, Amber, I was hoping you'd say that."

Joya was stabbed with sadness that this dear woman was not only wasting away, but losing it. What did she expect? The girl had been like a granddaughter to her, and to lose her like that!

During a commercial break, Joya offered to make tea.

"That would be lovely, Amber, thank you."

She went to the kitchen and knew her mother was right— they weren't going to have Gertie much longer. She wondered if the woman remembered her own sister. But when she came in, she was sure Gertie knew who she was, so she used an old trick on the woman.

As she settled the cup and saucer on the only clear space of the side table, she said, "I was just saying to myself the other day, 'Joya, you've got to drink more tea.'"

Gertie blinked twice, looked her in the face, and smiled, recognition in every wrinkle. "That's a fine idea, Joya. I can't tell you how much pleasure I get from a good cup of tea."

After Oprah, Joya worried how they'd spend the time, but Gertie was now anxious to talk.

Joya had never expected *this* conversation.

"You can't worry about your father, dear," she began. "He didn't kill that boy. You do know that, don't you?"

Joya blanched. "Yes...yes, of course. I don't think my father is capable of killing anyone. He's a good man, Gertie. A decent man. He might have made some mistakes, but I'm certain he couldn't kill anyone."

"No, he didn't. Neither did his friends. You know, that Earl blows up now and then, but he's a real softy. You know what he told me one time? He told me he had two moments of every year when he was happy 'from the top of my head to the bottom of my toes.' One was the early spring when he got on his tractor to face a field to plow. The other was the end of harvest when he turned off the combine. Now somebody who loves the earth that much is no killer. No, Earl didn't do it.

"And Bernard. I've never seen a man who can cry so easily. He couldn't hurt a flea. He's so quiet—Norma is perfect for him. No, he didn't kill that boy. What was his name?"

"Crabapple."

"Don't call him that. Call him by his real name."

"Darryl."

"Those men didn't kill Darryl, and the whole town knows it. If we have to, every single person in this town will get on the witness stand and swear on a Bible that we know these to be good, honest men. Father Singer will certainly stand up for them, and I bet we can get the Bishop down here. He thinks the world of your dad because he paid him back. When they redid the church roof, they borrowed money from the Bishop and your dad saw that every cent was repaid. Nobody ever repays the Bishop, so he loves your dad. No, don't you worry. We have plenty of wonderful things to say about those men, and no jury would ever convict them."

Joya was amazed at how Gertie had put all this together, mentally making a list of character witnesses. She was glad that Gertie was so certain of their innocence.

"Johnny didn't kill that boy, either." Gertie spoke as though it were common knowledge.

"He didn't?" Joya almost yelled.

"No, he didn't."

Joya waited for more explanation and when none came, she gingerly asked, "Gertie, how do you know Johnny didn't kill Cra….Darryl?"

"Because a boy who's about to kill himself does not lie in his last confession."

Joya hadn't felt an electric charge up her spine like this since she'd discovered Sammy the Bull was in Phoenix—and that one had been mild, compared to this shock.

"You, you, you heard his last confession?"

"Wasn't 'sposed to. I was in the sacristy polishing the brass candlesticks and Father was out in the church with his paint kit, touching up the stations of the cross. Johnny came in and said he needed to make his confession. They sat in the front row, face-to-face, and Johnny told him. You know how sound bounces in that big church. I could hear them plain as day."

Joya's breathing had become irregular.

"What did you hear Johnny say?" She used her most gentle voice.

"He was crying and carrying on. He confessed to Father about giving Amber that pill that killed her. And he said he wanted to kill that boy. He intended to kill him. He even figured out where he was, and he went there but somebody had beat him to it, and the boy was already dead. Johnny said it was probably just as much a sin to want to kill so badly, so he wanted that off his soul. He wanted a clean slate. He wanted a chance. I'll never forget him saying, 'I know I have to go to Purgatory and I'll probably be there a long, long time, but maybe someday I can get to Heaven and be with Amber.'"

Gertie started crying softly as she shook her head at that memory and the heartbreaking admission of a boy in his last hours.

"Father knew then that Johnny was going to kill himself. I knew it too. And Father tried so hard to talk him out of it. He talked and talked, but it didn't do any good. Johnny kept crying and begging for absolution and Father gave it to him, but he never stopped begging. Maybe I should have run out of the sacristy and tried myself, but it didn't seem right to interfere with his last confession. Poor Johnny, oh, that poor boy."

Joya realized she was crying. She tried to speak, but sometimes when she cried, her voice got very high and squeaky, and it did that now.

"That's okay, dear, it's a sad story," Gertie said. "It's a very, very sad story. But now everyone thinks Johnny killed that boy. The sheriff doesn't. He's out to get those guys. But everyone else is happy that this is almost over. And nobody else is going to suffer." Gertie reached over to take Joya's hands.

They were ancient hands, veined and purple—the skin so thin that any pinch or bump left a bruise. But they were strong hands as they enveloped Joya's and Gertie raised herself up to her full height and looked the girl in the eyes.

"Joya, do you know what it means to let 'sleeping dogs lie'?"

Joya nodded, not secure that her voice would be more than a shriek.

"I haven't told this to anybody else. Not even Wanda. I won't. And I didn't tell you so you'd go tell someone. I just told you so you'd know. I think somebody should know before I go, and you're the one I'm trusting. I've spent a long time thinking about this and we must keep this secret and let sleeping dogs lie. Johnny will get the blame for this and that's sad, but God knows the truth and He's the only one who counts. If Johnny gets the blame, everyone else goes on their way and our town can heal."

"But the real killer…" Joya finally found her voice.

"That's not important." For a woman who believed in her God, that shocked Joya. "There's been enough pain. There's been enough agony. It's time for it to stop. So promise me you'll let sleeping dogs lie."

Joya didn't think that was a promise she could keep, but Gertie's hands tightened around hers.

"It gets your father off the hook," the old woman said, like that should be the end of it.

"Gertie, do you know who killed that boy?"

"I wouldn't tell you if I did."

Wanda walked in the front door, announcing herself and putting an end to the conversation. She apologized for being so late and it was only then that Joya realized she'd been here three hours. She'd have stayed three more if Gertie had kept talking.

"Time for a little supper and the news is on," Wanda said, dismissing Joya and getting her sister back on schedule.

Joya reached over to kiss the old woman goodbye. Gertie threw her arm around her neck and gave Joya a big hug. "Sleeping dogs," she whispered.

Joya felt it would be the last time she'd see the woman. She vowed, no matter what, to come home for her funeral.

She drove to the city park that was such a point of pride. When city fathers couldn't come up with the money to grade the site, Earl Krump drove his tractor from the farm and bladed the ground himself. Somebody wanted to name it Krump Park after him, but of course, they settled on something inspiring. Northville Public Park.

Joya parked and kept the engine running so the heater would continue to blow, and thought about the afternoon of revelations. Her training as a reporter kicked in and she could almost recite the woman's words verbatim.

She knew a secret that only three other people in the world knew. One of them was bound by Canon law to forever stay silent. Gertie would take her knowledge to the grave. The real killer certainly wasn't going to fess up. Joya was the only one who could tell the world Johnny was blameless.

But if he didn't kill Darryl, who did? Joya felt certain Gertie either knew or had a good idea. Whoever it was, Gertie was willing to give that person a pass. Joya was astonished.

Part of her—the girl who grew up in Northville—wished she didn't know this information. Part of her—the daughter of a man in the cross hairs of a vengeful sheriff—wanted to forget everything she'd heard this afternoon. Part of her—the woman who was an investigative reporter—wanted to track down the real killer.

The reporter part first took the upper hand. Staying quiet went against every fiber of her being. Her mind reeled.

"In my world, you don't excuse murder, no matter what. You don't say one life isn't important enough to care about. You don't let a killer walk free. You don't let an innocent boy be scorned as a murderer because the town finds it convenient."

Anyone peeking in would have wondered why this girl was screaming out loud to herself in a parked car with the engine running.

"Nobody's going to be held accountable for Darryl's death? Nobody but a kid so wracked with guilt, he hung himself? That's what they call justice in this nice town? That's okay?"

She punched the steering wheel, again and again, like she was boxing with someone.

"Why doesn't anybody care about Darryl? I never knew the kid. All I know about him is he sold drugs and he worked at Huntsie's. I don't know what he looked like. I don't know if he had a girlfriend. I don't know if he had dreams for the future. I don't know what he wanted out of life. I don't know what he cared about. What made him happy?"

Joya Bonner didn't need to know any of those things to know it wasn't right that he ended up dead.

She started imagining his last moments. The image was so painful, she howled. "No!"

She covered her eyes with her hands and wept.

The daughter part took over.

"My dad isn't a killer. Gertie stressed that. The whole town knows it. Yet he's the one the sheriff wants to nail. Goddamn sheriff and his ego. He wants to be the last one standing. I hate men's egos. They're never under control. Oh, Dad. Why couldn't you guys have left this alone in the first place? Why did your egos have to get in the way? You *kidnapped* that kid. Left him chained up. Cold and hungry. He couldn't even defend himself. He might not be dead now if he'd had a chance against his killer. But he didn't. God, what were you guys thinking? You thought you were above the law. Just like Sammy…Stop it, Joya. Your dad is nothing like that Mafia goon. Nothing. You hear me?"

The little girl who grew up here made an appearance.

"How could all this happen in this wonderful, little town? Good people. Strong family values. Honorable people. Respectful. Kind. Friendly. Helpful. Honest."

She almost choked on the last one.

"They're so honest they're ready to swallow a lie to get back to their tidy lives. It's like Johnny is the scab over their wound and they're pleased as punch. I'd never have believed that. I'd have bet that this town would demand justice. But hey, it's just a druggie that got murdered in a most gruesome way. It's just a disturbed high school kid who offed himself. How inappropriate that this tragedy should visit here!"

She grabbed the steering wheel with both hands and rocked back and forth, trying to dislodge her demons.

It took another hour, but before she allowed herself to get too high and mighty, Joya Bonner found her own scab.

"You have to protect your family, no matter what. I'm not here to solve a murder case. I'm here to save my dad. Let sleeping dogs lie."

Chapter Twenty-two

Friday, January 21, 2000

Dolan Lowe impressed the three musketeers of Northville as he sat at the Bonners' dining room table and laid out all the things the sheriff didn't have. Joya had already told her father these points, but he listened more carefully to the attorney, since it was a man telling him that made him believe they were safe.

Joya swallowed her anger at this slight, but she should have expected it.

"As long as you three keep your mouths shut, you're okay," Lowe declared.

"Now, do we have any problem with that shotgun shell?"

He looked at each of them. One by one they swore it couldn't have come from their weapons.

"So what if they find it was packed in a special way? Any of you guys pack your own shells?"

All the heads turned toward Ralph. "Yeah, I do."

"And who do you pack shells for?"

"Anybody in town. Probably a dozen guys have my shells."

"Great, that's great."

"What's great about that?" Bernard asked.

"Because if it was one of the shells Mr. Bonner packed, there are a dozen suspects. And if you're certain your guns didn't shoot that shell, it means nothing that he packed it. At least, that's what I'll argue if we have to go there."

For men who normally saw things in black or white, this gray area was a new sensation. But they had to admit, it looked pretty damn good right now.

"Okay, so what's this statement that the sheriff claims he heard you three threaten the kid's life?"

"That's bullshit!" Earl yelled.

"Yeah, he's lying. We never said that. We did tell him to do his job, but he didn't." Ralph couldn't believe anybody in town would believe that sheriff over him.

"We are not lawbreakers," Bernard said, ignoring that kidnapping was against the law. "We are upstanding citizens in this town. Ask anybody. If you need—what do you call those people who speak up for you?"

"Character witnesses."

"Yes, if you need character witnesses, we've got a whole town that will speak up for us."

Joya felt the need to interject. "I think you should ask the Bishop to say something, too."

The men looked at her and then remembered the church roof payback and started smiling. Lowe didn't get the joke, but the idea of a Catholic Bishop as a character witness was farther up the food chain than he'd ever been.

"And you might want to stop at Alice's Bakery—she knows everything about this town and she knows all about these men. Her bakery is like party central—everyone hangs out there. She's my cousin."

"Good suggestion," Lowe said. "How about we go there after this meeting? I hear she makes a killer donut!"

Everyone laughed. He was in for a treat.

"So nobody in town knows for certain that you three were the kidnappers," Lowe asked, to be sure this wouldn't come back to bite him.

"The only ones who know are our wives, and they will not tell," Ralph said with certainty. "They know if they do, we'll go to prison. Because who's going to believe we kidnapped him but we didn't kill him? We wouldn't want anyone in town wondering if…No, nobody in town knows and they aren't going to know."

"Good," the lawyer said. "Keep it that way. You've already won the first round. Earl, you're sitting here, rather than in a jail cell, because there wasn't anything to hold you on. The courts clearly saw that. I believe I can get them to see the sheriff is off on a fishing expedition with you guys when the real killer is obvious. I'm going to argue that Johnny Roth is the killer here and there's physical evidence to tie him to the Harding kid. He was disturbed and depressed over the death of his girlfriend. I want to talk to the prosecutor this week and lay this out for him to see, and maybe this harassment can be over real soon."

Joya didn't say a word.

It sounded so completely logical and honest—Lowe sounded so confident and competent—that all three men bobbed their heads in ready agreement.

Joya was always grateful that Bernard looked over at her. "And thank you, Joya. You saved us. Thank you."

Earl also grumbled, "Thank you." Ralph looked away because he'd already said it once and that was enough.

"Yes, you have quite an investigator here, Mr. Bonner. You should be real proud that she knows so much about evidence. She kept you from handing over your gun and she got the reports and she found me. We all owe her our thanks."

Joya knew she'd never hear words like that from her own father, but she knew he'd heard them. She decided to believe he would have said them if his German stubbornness had let him.

Joya and Lowe went to the bakery and Alice vouched for each man with certainty and passion. "I'll testify if you need me," she said. "I'll tell how these men are pillars in our community and would never do something reckless and illegal."

Lowe guessed she knew the truth, but was a good liar. He liked that in a woman.

"Should I tell how that sheriff came in here and tried to browbeat me into saying those men killed Crabapple?" Alice added, and Lowe looked at her like she was the biggest prize in Crackerjacks.

"What?"

"Yes, he was in here the day after they arrested Earl. Wasn't that ridiculous? He didn't even spend the night. And the sheriff told me he had evidence those men kidnapped Crabapple and then murdered him and he knew for a fact that I had knowledge of these crimes and if I didn't come clean, I'd end up being charged as an accessory to murder."

"You never told me that." Joya looked at her cousin with new eyes.

"I knew he was bluffing, so I just blew him off."

"You know what one of his deputies did to me?" Joya was anxious to share. "He ran me off the road—but don't you dare tell my folks. I made up an excuse."

"Oh, my God," Alice shrieked. "Both you and me? That's harassment, isn't it?"

"It certainly is, my dears," the attorney said with a self-satisfied sigh. "I'll need an affidavit from each of you to present to the court, and we'll put an end to this right now!"

Alice treated everyone to donuts, then excused herself to get back to her chores.

"I don't want Mom and Dad to know about this affidavit, but it will help Dad, won't it?" Lowe reached across the table to squeeze her hand as he bobbed his head and filled up his face with a smile.

A week later—Friday, January 28, 2000—the district attorney of Richland County announced his investigation had concluded Darryl "Crabapple" Harding had been murdered by Johnny Roth in retaliation for the death of Amber Schlener. Northville's 104-day nightmare was over.

Lowe was laughing when he called Joya to say the entire courthouse could hear the district attorney ripping the sheriff a new asshole. And he demanded Badge 329 be fired. "I'm betting somebody's going to run against that sheriff in the next election, if the DA has anything to do with it."

It seemed amazing that it was finally over. Ralph Bonner didn't even make a fuss when he wrote out the check to pay Lowe's fee.

Throughout Northville, there was a giant sigh of relief. People felt bad for poor Johnny, so bad that many went to his funeral at St. Vincent's and ate funeral hotdish afterwards. Cissy German was there, of course, leaving her dime.

Johnny was buried on the backside of the Catholic Cemetery, where the suicides are relegated.

The town mourned for his folks and his friends and that the Class of 2000 had lost yet another member. Even Kenny Franken understood that his best friend had become a killer and then hung himself in guilt.

Darryl Harding didn't belong to any church in Northville, but a country church held a simple funeral for him. There was no meal afterwards. Huntsie paid for the funeral and the burial plot at the back of the Protestant cemetery.

To be honest, some people thought that three town leaders had *something* to do with all this, but whatever they'd done was nowhere near as bad as what Johnny did, so "let sleeping dogs lie." The first time Joya heard someone use that phrase, she feared they knew the secret, but then realized it was simply the phrase that fit the moment.

At Alice's Bakery, the gossip died down quickly because it was such an ugly thing, and ugly gossip didn't go well with sweet donuts.

Maggie, Angie, and Norma kept their secret pact. Each of their men had cried in their arms at night in bed, sorry the boy had died, sorry Johnny was gone. "We just wanted justice," each one had said, and each wife believed her man.

Joya flew home to Phoenix, deciding that someday she'd write a book about the time she saved her dad. She had a lot of work to catch up on. The Sammy trial was gearing up and, of course, she'd cover that. She ran into Rob now and then and they were polite, but neither wanted to try again. She started dating a lawyer, but he was a Republican, which didn't work.

From her Sunday calls home, she heard Northville was grateful it was all over.

Sadly, it wasn't.

Chapter Twenty-three

Father Singer knew Ralph Bonner hadn't killed Crabapple.
He knew Earl Krump and Bernard Stine were innocent, too.
He knew the three had kidnapped the boy.
All three men had come today to confess their sins.
All spoke with dismay and remorse at what they had done.
All declared what they hadn't done.
Catholics know they can confess murder and be safe—their secret will never leave the priest's lips. And a Catholic who has killed knows the only way to erase that horrible sin is to confess and do penance.
So Father Singer was certain that the men who swore they were not murderers were telling the truth. Because they believed, as the church teaches, that their confession wasn't to the mortal man standing in, but was to Jesus Christ himself.
Knowing the three town leaders weren't killers was a great relief. Father had a harder time with knowing that Johnny Roth didn't kill Crabapple, either. Most of all, the priest mourned that he couldn't stop Johnny from killing himself.
Father Singer would spend months on his knees, saying one Rosary after another, trying to reconcile the rules of his faith with the holes in his heart.

"If only I could have done something. If only I could have gotten help for Johnny—called his mom, he loved his mom She could have talked him down. She could have made him see there was still a life for him."

But he couldn't call Lois Roth. The sanctity of the confessional forbade him from doing anything but listening to the boy's sins.

He could only plead with the boy, trying to slice through his fog of depression and shroud of hate. He had tried. God knows, he tried. But nothing in his training had prepared Father John Singer for a moment like that.

He was a simple man, a disciple of the rituals and rules of his church. He studied the Bible with an intensity most don't expect from Catholics. He lived in the parsonage next door. He refused a housekeeper so he made his own meals, washed his own clothes and cleaned his own house. He wasn't the best cook, so he ate mainly soup—cereal was supper some nights. He ate little meat, didn't drink or smoke—all due to his pledge of humbleness.

He was a man educated in the ways of the church, the ritual of mass, the management of a parish. He had never had a single second of training in what to do when a parishioner comes to confess and almost screams that he's going to commit suicide.

If Father Singer thought his simple, humble life would impress God enough to help out at a time like that, he was sorely disappointed.

"Please son. Please. Call your mother. You don't want to hurt her like this. You know she loves you. Please don't make her grieve. She sat at your bedside every day when you were in the coma. She prayed every day for you to come back. I was there many times at her side and we prayed the Rosary over you. Please don't hurt her. Please, son, Please."

But his begging did no good. As he gave Johnny the absolution he was due, Father Singer prayed with all his heart.

"Lord, watch over your son who is troubled and in great pain. Help him see that his loving mother and father and friends would mourn forever if he were not here with them. Help him find his way to you and your grace and forgiveness. And help him face another day with the knowledge that You are by his side and You will never abandon him.

"For your penance, say six Our Fathers and six Hail Marys."

Father Singer heard Johnny weeping as he said his prayers. He heard the boy's footsteps echoing off the marble floor of St. Vincent's Catholic Church. He prayed to hear God's whisper that he had done what he could. But he heard nothing more than his heart breaking.

He was shocked when he walked into the sacristy and found Gertie Bach, holding a polishing rag full of Brasso. He'd forgotten she was there. Their eyes met.

"I tried to stop him," Father blurted out before realizing he was breaking an oath.

"I know, Father. I know." They cried together.

Later that day when his fears were confirmed, Father Singer needed an hour to compose himself before he drove out to the Roth farm to comfort Lois and Paul.

Now today, he again was reminded of that awful day as he heard more confessions.

It vexed him that there was still a killer in town that nobody suspected, because they believed Johnny was the guilty one.

There is a burden in carrying around knowledge that can never be shared, but is carried on your shoulders alone, just as Jesus carried that cross. It didn't help Father Singer to think of the Passion of Christ to ease his burden. He lost weight, suffered through sleepless nights, and he wondered if he could live the rest of his life with such horrible knowledge.

In the fourteen years he'd been a priest, he'd heard thousands of confessions. He'd heard a little girl at her first confession screaming out her sins as her classmates tittered and he whispered, "Whisper, Janney, whisper." He'd heard grandmothers admit they were being abused at home by grandfathers who were ushers on Sunday morning. He'd heard boys admit they masturbated and stole apples, and men admit they cheated on their wives. He'd heard a woman admit she didn't love her children.

As he was trained, he said a Rosary after every session of confession and then parked what he'd heard in a closed vault in the far corner of his mind. He knew confession was there, not to punish, but to forgive. It was a sacrament that allowed Catholics a do-over. *Any* sin could be forgiven. *Any* sin was forgiven.

But the words he'd heard in the wake of Northville's tragedy refused to be parked. The vault refused to close. It plagued Father Singer that he kept hearing the words again and again.

He thought that was the greatest burden he'd ever carry.

Until the day the killer confessed to murdering Crabapple.

Chapter Twenty-four

Tuesday, July 4—Wednesday, July 12, 2000

The Fourth of July parade in Northville is something to behold.

Almost every fire department in the county sends its cleaned-up trucks—most red, some yellow. A couple antique pump trucks have been restored to go down Main Street to the cheers of townspeople who bring their lawn chairs and blankets and perch themselves on the sidewalk bordering the street.

Local businesses turn flatbed trucks into crepe-paper fantasies. The big rig company in town sends its purple and green semis down the street, riders throwing out hard candies to the eager hands of children. The Shriners drive crazy little cars and spray water at the audience, and in an election year, politicians in convertibles wave as their volunteers hand out campaign literature.

But most of all, everyone loves the high school band that marches down the street in its new uniforms and plays great patriotic songs. Most people in the audience have someone in that band they call their own.

The bang-up, grand parade starts a day of celebration that includes a cookout at the American Legion and fireworks at the casino. In between there's a baseball game in one corner of the town park and a crafts fair in the other. Out at Lake Elsie, there's a picnic in almost every yard. Those without lake houses cruise by on pontoons to admire the gracious homes with water views.

Someone once said that if you can't find something to like about Northville's Fourth of July, you must be a communist.

Joya Bonner was always home in time because Northville knew how to celebrate the nation's birthday, and here she was on Tuesday, July 4, 2000.

Northville looked so different from when she'd been here in January. It felt so different. It was so different.

Her cousin, Alice, described a pall over the town since Amber's death.

"We'd never been through anything like that, and you know, it changes a place," Alice explained. Joya knew exactly what she meant. Her laugh sounded too loud in a town where mirth now was reserved. Her glee at the annual parade wasn't obvious on other faces. Her aunts and uncles gathering for dessert in her parents' backyard seemed subdued.

Anyone peering in would have recognized a new resignation in Northville. Like a dog that's been beaten and is careful not to get hit anymore.

Three young people were dead. The Class of 2000 had memorialized Amber and Johnny on graduation day, tarnishing a moment that should have been reserved for joy and hope. Maxine left for The Cities the day after graduation, saying she couldn't wait to be rid of this town. Some of her classmates wished they'd had the guts to join her.

Alice Peters worried that the story of Amber and Johnny and Crabapple would become one of the town legends people would tell again and again—like the brave father who faced the storm and the brave men who stopped the robbers. She prayed it wouldn't, but she bet it would.

And Gertie was gone. She died in early June and there was no way Joya could come home that early. How she'd wanted to honor the woman by being there when the town said its final goodbye.

Her mother told her it was an even bigger funeral than Amber's. The Judith Circle was excused from kitchen duty so they could sit in the front rows, as part of Gertie's "family." The

Esther Circle took over and they barely made enough funeral hotdish to feed everyone. (How Maggie and her circle clucked about that one!) Cissy German only got two plates that day before they ran out. But she obviously loved Gertie, too. She left a quarter.

Joya was hanging out in the kitchen of Alice's Bakery the day after the parade when she asked out of the blue, "Do you think he did it?"

"Who? Did what?"

"Do you think Johnny killed Crabapple?" Joya knew she was on tenterhooks, but she had to know if her cousin knew.

Alice stopped stirring her batter and didn't look up. "I don't know. I want to believe it. Because I want it over."

Then Alice looked at Joya and declared, "You know, I never believed your dad had anything to do with his death. The town didn't. But I know he was proud that you came home and helped them prove it. The nice thing is, people have stopped talking about it and I want it to stay that way. So don't stir anything up, okay?"

"Oh no, I wouldn't do that. I was just wondering."

She left the bakery to continue her morning walk in hopes of taking off the ten pounds she'd put back on over the winter. Her goal was to walk the whole town over her two-week summer vacation. One day she'd walk out to the cemetery to visit the graves of her grandparents and the three aunts she'd already lost. And Gertie.

On her way back to her folks' house, she stopped at Leona's to buy her mom flowers. "I'll take four pink roses, please," she told the clerk.

"Oh, I'm sorry, two of those are spoken for. You want the other two?"

"Sure, and put in two white ones, too."

"It's a standing order, so we can't sell them," the clerk explained, as though it needed an apology.

"Who's got the standing order?" Joya asked.

"Nettie Schlener. Do you know her? It was her daughter that died last fall. Such a shame. She gets two pink roses every

Wednesday and puts them on her grave. She's done it since the funeral."

"During the winter, too?" Joya wondered.

"Oh yeah, EVERY Wednesday. That poor woman hasn't moved on. She's so sad all the time."

"That's too bad." Joya took her four roses in their waxed-paper wrap and continued her walk home. How long had it been now, since Amber died? Joya couldn't remember exactly, but thought it had been in October, and now here it was, July 5 and she was still doing it? That was, what, thirty-nine, forty weeks? Man, that was a lot of pink roses.

She handed her mom the roses with a flourish as Maggie squealed with exaggerated delight. "There would have been four pink ones but Nettie Schlener has a standing order for two pink roses every Wednesday for her daughter's grave. Did you know that?" She saw a look of panic cross her mother's eyes.

"What's the matter?" Joya asked.

Maggie tried to recover. "Oh, nothing. Hey, go to the garden and pick me some green beans."

Joya knew a dodge when she saw one. It perplexed her. Her mom's reaction didn't make any sense.

She put the dirty beans in the sink to wash them and walked down the hall to the bathroom to hear her mom on the bedroom phone.

"I don't think she knows, but she's so damn nosy. Okay. Just be careful."

Joya dashed back to the kitchen and stood washing the green beans when her mother came in. "These okay?"

"Just perfect," her mom sang, giving her daughter a hug.

A good investigative reporter doesn't let a lot pass her by. Joya had once helped solve the murder of a woman shot in the back of a pickup truck because she asked the question—how tall is the accused? Only a very tall person could have held the gun at the angle that inflicted the fatal bullets. The accused girl was only five-foot-three and her defense attorney got the case thrown out of court.

Another time she'd help stop three units of a controversial nuclear power plant outside Phoenix when she asked the simple question. "Do we have enough water in the desert for five nuclear units?" Turns out the answer was a resounding "no" and that's why the Palo Verde Nuclear Generating Station only has two units.

So one mother's fearful reaction to a simple question about another putting pink roses on her daughter's grave—that meant something. But what?

She knew better than to ask her mother or father, and Alice had already signaled that she didn't want any more discussion on that subject.

Hey, you're on vacation, girl. Give it a rest! Come on, you've got all those books to read and friends to see and God, this place is so different now. Just have a good time and don't see boogeymen under every bed.

But even with lecturing herself, the question kept playing around in her head.

One of the people she was anxious to visit was Dolan Lowe. She and the attorney had kept in touch by email and a couple phone calls, and it might be fun to have a North Dakota romance for a change. So later that week she drove over to Wahpeton to have dinner with him at the Steakhouse—a place that had been popular since she was a high school student in Northville decades ago.

They caught up on his latest cases—nothing very exciting, the normal civil stuff. He wanted to hear more about her Sammy scoop. He'd read her story and they'd had a brief discussion, but now he wanted details. And like any reporter, she loved to tell her 'war stories,' so she told him how it all began and how it cost her a boyfriend. Sammy's trial was still months away and she'd be covering that—she didn't have to tell an attorney how tedious a trial can be. Really, she confided, she needed a new story to get her juices going again.

He assured her that in a big city, the next big story couldn't be far away. Good thing, he mused, she wasn't looking for that kind of excitement around here.

"The mess in Northville was the biggest thing we've seen in these parts in years, and nobody expects a repeat performance of that kind of excitement."

They both laughed.

"You know, it seems to me that your father and Sammy have a lot in common."

The words hit like throwing mud on a wedding cake.

"What? Oh God, where do you come up with that?"

"Think about it. Both men are used to being in charge. Both were admired in their own circles. Both broke the law—one to help his son, the other to help his town. Both thought they were above the law. Only difference is, Sammy will pay for his crimes."

"So you think my father should pay something?" The words came out angry.

"No, I think your dad made a really dumb decision, but you've got to admit, the similarities are there."

"I don't see them," Joya lied. She'd never fess up that she'd had some of these same thoughts.

"A daughter's not supposed to see her father's sins."

"And a good defense attorney's not supposed to point fingers at his client."

"Got me there, kiddo. Hey, I didn't mean your dad was a Mafioso or anything. You know I like him. Not as much as I like you, so please tell me I haven't blown this whole evening."

"No, and I didn't mean to sound so snarly. You just caught me off guard."

They ordered another drink and made small talk and then Joya remembered something she wanted to tell him.

"You know, the strangest thing." She was cutting apart one of the most delicious steaks she'd ever eaten. "The mother of that girl who died of the overdose? She puts two pink roses on her daughter's grave every Wednesday. And when I asked my mom about it, she looked like the question upset her."

Joya put the tasty piece of meat in her mouth, closed her eyes and yummed at its fabulous flavor. When she opened them, Dolan Lowe was staring at her with his mouth half open.

"Really?" he gulped. She knew she'd hit some nerve.

"Oh, my God." He let the words hang there and took a long sip of his martini. He looked off, like he was seeing something else and considering the secrets of the world. "Oh. My. God."

He put down his drink and tented his hands in front of his face, resting his elbows on the table. "That's it. My God, that's it."

Joya was getting very nervous—or was it excited? A tingling of anticipation was, perversely, one of her favorite feelings.

"Dolan, what is it?"

"You know, before the prosecutor got wise, I went down to the Coroner's Office to see if they had anything else on the autopsy," he began. "They don't put everything in those reports, you know. Sometimes stuff that seems relevant is just left out."

Joya looked at him in horror and he laughed. "Hey, this is North Dakota. We're not as obsessive as you guys out in Arizona. It's not malicious or anything, but a couple cases I've had, I've found out more stuff going right to the office. So I went over and chatted with Mary—I think she's the girl you met? She thought you were really nice. Anyway, I chatted with Mary and she mentioned pink roses."

Joya stopped breathing.

"What about pink roses?"

"Well, there was plant material embedded in that guy's chest that they couldn't identify. Everybody else passed it off as grain, since he was in a silo. But Mary told me she thought it looked like tiny pieces of pink rose. We laughed about it. It made no sense that somebody put pink roses on his chest when he was shot to death during a freezing winter storm. The next day the prosecutor declared the killer was that kid who hanged himself, so the case was over. And I just forgot about it."

Joya's mind was reeling. *It couldn't be…* but she immediately knew it was.

She remembered the simple sentence in the autopsy report now—it meant nothing then. A silo has lots of plant material. She never thought to ask "what kind?" Something else jumped out at her now. Who's the only person Gertie Bach would give a pass to? Who's the only one she'd allow to sully the name of a boy she knew Amber loved—a boy she knew was innocent?

And if this two plus two equals four, what was she going to do about it?

Dolan could see the wheels turning in her eyes. "You know, if anybody needs a good defense attorney, you've got my number."

"Yes, I do."

They kissed goodnight in the parking lot after she turned down Dolan's suggestion they have a drink at his place. "Another time," she promised, but wasn't sure that would ever happen. He was nice and smart and the kiss was okay, but she hadn't felt a spark. Not like when Rob kissed her. But that spark was long gone and she had no idea she'd ever have another one.

Chapter Twenty-five

Joya's walk the following Wednesday took her out to the cemetery. There was Amber's grave, two roses now wilted, waiting for their replacements.

"Oh God, I hope it's not true." But she knew she was whistling in the graveyard.

She surveyed the grounds to find a big stone on the row above Amber's grave. She could hide there, eavesdrop there, pray for a different ending. That's where she was when Nettie made her weekly visit to Amber's grave.

"Hi, darling," she sang out, as she picked up the dead roses and gently laid down the beautiful new ones. "Here's your roses, honey. All pretty and pink. Just like you like them."

She laid down next to the grave and stroked the grass growing over Amber's casket. She told her daughter about her cousins and news from town. She spent twenty minutes talking about her new diet that had already taken off ten pounds.

Joya felt guilty, snooping on such an intimate conversation by a grieving mother, but she had no choice now but to stay hidden. As the visit continued, she became more and more convinced that there was nothing here. Nothing to worry about. Nothing to discover. She had to admit, she was greatly relieved.

And then Nettie started talking about Johnny and Crabapple.

"I'm sorry the town thinks Johnny killed him," Nettie told her daughter's grave. "I know you wouldn't like that. But it's for the best. He would have, you know. If he found him first, he would have killed him. The whole town knew that. I know that's why they kidnapped him. So Johnny couldn't find him and kill him. Isn't that something, Amber? Those men trying to protect Johnny? Doesn't that make you feel good? I know those men and they couldn't have killed him. They just wanted him to confess, so they could hand him over to the sheriff. That wasn't good enough. Not for my Amber."

Joya thought her heart stopped.

Nettie kept talking and Joya kept listening. With every word she heard, her compassion struggled with her conscience.

"Alice knew when they snatched him. They were playing cards that Thursday and she heard enough to know that was the day. She was so worried, and she let a little slip when I came in for coffee. I acted like I wasn't interested. But the next day I took the day off and watched Ralph Bonner's house all day. He met up with the others in the Legion parking lot. It wasn't hard to follow them. But then we had that storm. I couldn't get there until Sunday.

"You would have been proud of me, Amber. I know, I know, you're not a violent type, but you have to admit, he was dangerous. He had to be stopped. Well, I stopped him. Your mother took care of it for you.

"It was almost funny—he thought I had come to save him. It was so cold and he'd been left there in the storm and when I got there, he thought I was there to free him. I gave him the roses. He took them and had this perplexed look, and I said, 'These are from Amber.' And then I pulled the trigger on your dad's old shotgun and made certain he'd never hurt anyone else again. You would have been proud of me."

Joya clapped her hands over her mouth so she wouldn't scream.

"I confessed to Father John. He told me I had to turn myself in. But then, I could never come here to see you. What good does it do for me to go to prison and leave you here all alone?

Nobody's looking for me. I think some of the women suspect, but they won't say anything. No, we just have to let everyone think Johnny killed him."

Joya stood up then, revealing herself. Nettie looked at her in shock, jumping to her feet.

"What...what...who...what...?"

"Nettie, it's Joya, Ralph and Maggie's daughter."

The two women looked bewildered at one another, like they were playing a game and didn't know the rules.

Finally Joya found her tongue. "I'm so sorry about all this. You've had such a terrible loss. Amber was such a sweet girl."

Nettie took her words as condolences and lied to herself that Joya couldn't have heard everything.

"Thank you for your kind words. Yes, she was such a sweet girl. She had so much to live for. She held such promise. We were expecting a basketball scholarship...."

Joya realized Nettie would go on for an hour if she let her. "Nettie, please. I'm not here to mourn with you."

Nettie scrunched up her brow in wonder. Of course Joya was here to mourn. She refused to see any other reason.

Joya could see the shield she'd erected and took a deep breath to plunge ahead. "Nettie, honey, it's time. You can't ignore what's happened. You can't forget what you did. Please. You have to turn yourself in."

Emotions flashed across Nettie's face. Fear. Anger. Sorrow. Defiance.

"No, I don't. I do not. Nobody knows it's me. If you don't tell anybody, they'll keep thinking it's Johnny. And he's dead. He's buried over there." Nettie pointed to the back of the cemetery, but Joya wouldn't take her eyes off the woman. She fully expected her to bolt any minute.

"What good would it do?" Nettie was pleading now. "I'll never hurt another person in my entire life. I wouldn't have hurt him if he hadn't killed my Amber. I'm not a criminal. I'm a mother avenging her daughter's needless death. Can't you see that? Just walk away and forget you ever heard anything. Nobody has to know. Nobody."

Joya knew the easy thing was to buy that logic. She stood on one foot and then the other, fighting with herself. Maybe she should just turn around and continue her hike and let this grieving woman cope with her loss in her own way. Maybe someday, Nettie's conscience would get to her and she'd do the honorable thing. What did Alice say, *don't stir things up?* What did Gertie say, *let sleeping dogs lie?* She should, she should just walk away and keep her nose out of this.

On the other hand—there was that 'other hand' again—this woman was a murderer and you can't let that slide. As much as she wanted to leave it alone, her moral compass wouldn't let her.

"I can't walk away, Nettie. I know why you did it. People might say you were justified. But you murdered that boy." Joya had to stop talking because she was crying and her voice was headed toward that high shriek.

She took a deep breath and got herself under control.

"It wasn't your place. You didn't have the right."

Nettie's shoulders slumped. Her face took on its final emotion. Resignation.

"I know." She whispered.

She patted her daughter's headstone, and kissed it. She hugged her arms around the marble shrine, washing it with her tears. Joya didn't rush her. She at least could give the woman these last moments.

"I won't take you to the sheriff," she said. "I know a really good defense attorney in Wahpeton and he'll help you."

Maybe Dolan could save her. Maybe he could make a judge see she was insane with grief. Maybe a jury wouldn't convict a woman with such pain and loss. Maybe poor Nettie would be back in a few months, visiting the daughter she wouldn't let go. Maybe…maybe…maybe.

Joya clung to the maybes to salve her regrets that compassion lost out to conscience.

Nettie stood up and reached her hand out to Joya. "We'll go together?"

"Yes."

"I have to do this?"

"Yes."

"You're sure?"

"Yes."

"You couldn't just walk away?"

"No."

"No, I know." Nettie took one look back at Amber's grave. "Goodbye, honey. I love you."

Joya took her hand and they walked away.

Both women were crying.

Author's Note

I've had the title of this book rolling around in my head for almost twenty years. Ever since I read the recipe as my mother's circle was preparing a funeral dinner in the basement of St. Phillip's Catholic Church in Hankinson, North Dakota.

"Funeral Hotdish," I yelled. "What a great name for a book."

Finding the story that went with the title was harder. I knew it would be set in my home state of North Dakota, and I knew it had to be a funeral of anguish, and so the book of fiction inside these covers developed over the years.

I made up the North Dakota portion of this book from whole cloth. I've tried to fairly and honestly represent the type of people I know to be fair and honest—asking how the salt-of-the-earth types I grew up with might react if their beloved town was thrown into intolerable turmoil.

The Arizona portion is based on stories I wrote for Phoenix publications.

So many people helped me with this book, most prominently, my mother and sister, Willie and Judy Bommersbach. They created a beautiful place for me to write in the sunroom of their home in Hankinson during my summer visits in 2014 and 2015. My brothers, Duane and Gary Bommersbach, offered expertise I needed.

North Dakota classmates, neighbors, and friends were great help, including Maxine Beckstrom Atkins; Steve and Carolyn

Jacobson; Alton, Mary and Corey Theede; Brandon and Nancy Hentz; Fred Beeson; Keven Frank; Barb Pankow; and Joleen Anderson.

In Arizona, thanks to Sam Lowe, my fellow writer and North Dakotan, Rich Robertson, and Henry Escobar.

The crew at Poisoned Pen Press couldn't be more delightful to work with. Barbara Peters and Robert Rosenwald run a great house that really nurtures writers. Diane DiBiase and Tiffany White are always helpful. Beth Deveny gives my books the same care she'd give her own. And Annette Rogers is simply the best editor any writer could ever want. Thank you all.

Endnotes

These notes review the real-life incidents and situations I borrowed for this book.

Chapter One
On an Ecstasy high: Ecstasy is a street name for a drug also known as MDMA or Molly. The description of its effects is taken from the National Drug Intelligence Center and the National Institute on Drug Abuse, as well as "The Pursuit of Ecstasy" by Matthew Klam, published in the *New York Times Magazine*, January 21, 2001. It is a popular "party drug" that is still a problem. In February of 2015, as this book is being finished, twelve young adults—ten Wesleyan University students and two visitors—were hospitalized in an apparent overdose of Molly in Middletown, Connecticut. Four other students were arrested, accused of supplying the drug.

Chapter Two
On autopsies: The description is taken from the author's personal experience for a *PHOENIX Magazine* story.

On Sammy the Bull: The scene in the Tempe coffeehouse really happened, as did the police investigation and eventual imprisonment of Sammy "the Bull" Gravano. The author wrote the definitive inside story, titled "Bringing Down the Bull," for

PHOENIX Magazine on how he was taken down under the noses of the FBI. It was published in May of 2003 and was honored with a top feature award by the Arizona Press Club. It is available on the author's website: www.janabommersbach.com.

On the Arizona State University fraud case: Under the headline, "Arizona's Broken Arrow," the author exposed ASU's long exploitation of the Havasupai Tribe—misusing its blood and promising diabetes research it never conducted. The story ran in *PHOENIX Magazine* in November 2008, and is on the author's website.

On Sheriff Joe Arpaio's publicity stunt: On July 9, 1999, Phoenix newscasts led with the incredible story of how an eighteen-year-old named Jimmy Saville was apprehended as he tried to plant a bomb in Sheriff Joe Arpaio's car in the parking lot of the Roman Table restaurant on Seventh Avenue. The author eventually wrote the inside story of what really happened, and how a Maricopa County jury recoiled in horror when it discovered it had all been a publicity stunt. The jury freed Saville—who spent four years in jail awaiting trial—declaring he'd been entrapped. "This was a publicity stunt at the expense of four years of someone's life," jury forewoman Fausta Woody said. The story, "Will Sheriff Joe Stop At Nothing?" ran in *PHOENIX Magazine* in February of 2005, and won a top feature award from the Arizona Press Club. It is on the author's website. Saville sued the county, and in 2008, was awarded 1.1 million dollars in taxpayer money.

Chapter Three
On preparing the funeral: Extensive interviews with Hankinson Funeral Director Keven Frank, who also gave the author a complete tour of his facilities, resulted in the detailed account.

On Bagg Farm: This National Historical Site near Mooreton, North Dakota, is one of the last remaining Bonanza Farms—giant farms of thirty thousand acres or more that covered the wheat-growing plains of Dakota Territory from the 1870s into the early 1900s. The farms grew out of the financial collapse of the Northern Pacific Railroad—as investors took land in place of worthless rail bonds and sold it to financiers who created the largest corporate farms in the world. Bagg Farm was originally five thousand acres. Today it is a preserved and fascinating look into mega-farming and early Dakota life. It is open Fridays through Sundays, Memorial Day through Labor Day. The author's maternal grandmother, Magdalena Schlener, cooked and cleaned at the Bagg Farm when she was a girl.

On the Missoula Children's Theater: This summer theater program—built on the vision of Jim Caron and Don Collins—has been touring since the mid-1970s. Annually, its red truck full of costumes, sets, and scripts visits nearly twelve hundred communities in all fifty states, three Canadian provinces, and sixteen countries. It is funded by the Montana Arts Council and the National Endowment for the Arts.

Chapter Four
On the Don Bolles sabotage: The revelation that the Phoenix Police Department sabotaged its own investigation into the murder of *Arizona Republic* Reporter Don Bolles comes from a nine-month investigation by *Phoenix New Times*, published on the tenth anniversary of the assassination in June of 1986. The author was a member of that investigative team and co-wrote most of the thirty-six-page special report with reporter Paul Rubin and editor Mike Lacey. We discovered that while Don lay dying, someone inside the department's Organized Crime Unit was purging its files of intelligence reports on several high-profile people in Arizona, including leading politicians and some of those Bolles named as his executioners. No one ever discovered exactly who did the purging, although the intent was obvious—to protect and conceal.

Chapter Five
On Funeral Hotdish: This is the recipe from St. Phillip's Church, Hankinson, North Dakota:

Funeral Hotdish—FOR 175

3 lbs. bacon
20 lbs. lean hamburger
16 lbs. macaroni
3 bunches celery
8 medium onions
7 20-oz. bags mixed vegetables
8 cans cream of onion soup
8 cans cream of celery soup
4 big cans tomato soup
9 large cans tomato sauce
8 tall cans tomato juice

Boil water. Add macaroni and bring to a boil. Cover and let stand 5 min. Drain.

Brown hamburger. Cut bacon into small pieces and fry. Fry celery and onion in bacon grease until transparent. Drain. Add to hamburger and macaroni.

Set water to boil. Add vegetables for 3 min. Drain and add to hotdish. Mix all soups and juices. Add to hotdish. Add salt, pepper, and a little sugar. Divide mixture into electric roasters.

Bake gently at 350 degrees for 1 ½ hours.

(The recipe does not specify the amount of salt, pepper, or sugar because, as Mother says, "you just know.")

Chapter Six
On the church bell: The funeral bell used in this book is based on the bell that still rings at St. Phillip's Catholic Church in Hankinson.

On the cemetery: The author modeled the cemetery in this book on the Catholic Cemetery in Hankinson.

Chapter Eight
On Sammy the Bull: The "article" Joya is writing is based on the author's award-winning *PHOENIX Magazine* piece.

Chapter Eleven
On legend stories: The stories the town tells about itself are based on true stories that happened in Hankinson and Gwinner, North Dakota.

The blizzard tragedy is based on the true story of the heroism of thirty-one-year-old John Wolfe in the 1923 blizzard that took his life. His wife lost both her frozen hands. Both of their children came through the ordeal unscathed. The family lived just outside Hankinson. Sadly, they were just a stone's throw from her parents' home the entire time they endured the storm, which was declared the worst in North Dakota since 1887. The Hankinson Centennial Book includes a complete record of all the stories published about the Wolfe family in the *Hankinson News*.

The thwarted bank robbery is based on the true story of the August 1929 attempt to rob the Gwinner State Bank. The Bentson brothers—Ruben, Robert, Elmer, Victor, and Leonard—led the "shotgun brigade," helped by Carl and Ben Meinhardt, and many others. Ruben and Leonard Bentson received a five-hundred-dollar reward from the North Dakota Bankers Association. The Gwinner Centennial book said this: "Perhaps the most exciting thing that ever happened in the 'old days' of Gwinner happened in August of 1929…when the Gwinner State Bank was robbed…or nearly robbed…." The book included a full page of headlines from the extensive coverage of the incident in the *Fargo Forum*—perhaps more stories than the *Forum* has ever published about this small town.

On Gordon Kahl: "North Dakota's most notorious crime" is a 1983 tragedy that is still hotly debated. Patriot or fanatic. Murderous federal agents or lawmen doing their job. Two impressive books have been written about this tragedy: James Corcoran's *Bitter Harvest: Gordon Kahl and the Posse Comitatus Murder in the Heartland*, which was nominated for a Pulitzer Prize, and a self-published book by former Medina Police Chief Darrel Graf and Officer Steve Schnabel, *It's All About Power*, that raises serious questions about the handling of this case.

The author also studied versions advanced by the extreme right wing.

On Ruby Ridge: Randy Weaver was indicted for making and possessing illegal weapons. When he didn't show up for trial—he was given the wrong trial date—a bench warrant was issued. Fearing he was being set up by the government and that a conviction would seize his land and leave his family homeless, Weaver hunkered down. The Randy Weaver family was pinned down by federal agents in their home in northern Idaho from August 21 to 31, 1992. In the end, Weaver's son, Sammy, was shot and killed, as was his wife Vicki, and U.S. Marshall Bill Degan. Outrages over the showdown led to the Senate hearing and a report calling for reforms in federal law enforcement to prevent a repeat of this tragedy.

On Waco: Attempts to end a fifty-one-day siege at David Koresh's Branch Dividian compound near Waco, Texas, ended in tragedy on April 19, 1993, when the complex was attacked and firebombed by the FBI and ATF—some of the same officers, using the same tactics, as Ruby Ridge. Historians say that Ruby Ridge and Waco were the two events that greatly widened the militia movement in the United States.

Chapter Twelve
On Sammy the Bull: Sammy Gravano was arrested in February 2000, and pled guilty in 2001. He claimed that police totally

overstated his role in the ring—that he was involved only to protect his son. Police didn't buy it, nor did they think it was all bluster, as Sammy insisted, when he'd bragged that he "owned Arizona" and wanted to establish a new "Arizona Mafia." Sammy was eventually sentenced to twenty years as the ringleader. His son, Gerard, was sentenced to nine and a half years, as was Karen's boyfriend, David Seabrook. Sammy's wife and daughter got probation. And Mike Papa, the original ringleader, turned on Sammy, much as Sammy had turned on John Gotti. Papa escaped prosecution and went into the federal witness protection program.

Chapter Sixteen
On the Public Records Test: Although North Dakota has not had such a test, it has been held in several states—including Iowa, Indiana, South Carolina, and South Dakota— to test the availability of public records. Reporters pose as "ordinary citizens" trying to get records. The portrayal here is based on the history of this test—reporters in most of the states had trouble getting information from law enforcement officials.

Chapter Eighteen
On the sanctity of confession: The description of the confession being forever secret is based on the teachings and practices of the Roman Catholic Church.

Chapter Nineteen
On the Fourth of July parade: Many small towns in North Dakota hold special celebrations and parades on the Fourth of July, including the Hankinson festivities the author has often enjoyed. They're as fun as presented in this book!

Bibliography

Corcoran, James. *Bitter Harvest: Gordon Kahl and the Posse Comitatus Murder in the Heartland.* Viking Penguin, 1990.

DeCelle, Marc. *How Fargo of You—Stories from the Northern Prairie That People Who Haven't Been Here Will Never Believe.* Self-published, 2010.

Erdrich, Louise. *The Master Butchers Singing Club.* Harper Collins, 2003.

Eriksmoen, Curt. *Did you know that...47 fascinating stories about people who have lived in North Dakota.* Vol. 7. Forum Communications Printing, 2013.

Graf, Darrell and Schnabel, Steve. *It's All About Power.* Graf was Medina police chief and Schnabel was a local police officer wounded in the first attempt to arrest Gordon Kahl. Published by the authors, 1999.

Hipp, Ron. *Getting Started.* A memoir of growing up in North Dakota in the 1950s, as well as a history of Richland County. Self-published.

Hoffert, Melanie. *Prairie Silence: a rural expatriate's journey to reconcile home, love, and faith.* Beacon Press, 2013.

Lamb, Margaret. *Grasshopper Tales: Stories from North Dakota.* Privately published, 2011.

Marguart, Debra. *The Horizontal World: growing up wild in the middle of nowhere.* Counterpoint, 2006.

Norris, Kathleen. *Dakota—A Spiritual Geography.* This was the 2014 North and South Dakota One Book selection. Houghton Mifflin Company, 1993.

To receive a free catalog of Poisoned Pen Press titles, please provide your name, address, and email address in one of the following ways:

Phone: 1-800-421-3976
Facsimile: 1-480-949-1707
Email: info@poisonedpenpress.com
Website: www.poisonedpenpress.com

Poisoned Pen Press
6962 E. First Ave. Ste 103
Scottsdale, AZ 85251